Disappearances in the

MEDITERRANEAN

Stuart Gustafson

America's International Travel Expert®

Disappearances in the MEDITERRANEAN

Published by

AITEpublishing
P.O. Box 45091
Boise, ID 83711 USA

www.AITEpublishing.com

ISBN 13: 978-0-9771727-9-5

First Printing — March 2016

Books by Stuart Gustafson

Fiction:

Missing in MEXICO

Series featuring Professor Alfred Dunningham, PhD

The Math Professor, a short story introducing the professor

Murders in SYDNEY

Disappearances in the MEDITERRANEAN

Art Thefts in PARIS

Non-Fiction

Parables for Life in the 21st Century

Questions to Bring You Closer to Dad

Questions to Bring You Closer to Mom

Questions to Bring You Closer to Grandma & Grandpa

Remembering Our Parents . . . Stories and Sayings from Mom & Dad

PREFACE:

This book is a fictional mystery story. Most of the events in the story are not real, although some of the locations and local items are ones I've experienced in my travels on cruise ships and in various ports and countries. I've been on more than a dozen cruises, have sailed on various cruise lines, and I've visited over forty countries (so far) while on a ship. Those forty countries overlap the total of fifty-five countries and more than one hundred twenty cruise ports that I've been to in my worldwide travels as *America's International Travel Expert®*. One of the many great experiences I've enjoyed on a cruise ship has been the opportunity to give enriching, entertaining, and informative presentations to the other guests on board. These presentations typically are about the arts, history, and culture of the areas we're visiting. Other talks I've given are called Port Lectures, where the guests are given current logistical information about the next port of call. **Of course, after this book hits the shelves, I might not be invited back to speak on cruise ships!**

While the reporting of a missing passenger, typically one who's gone overboard, receives a lot of press, it is actually quite an uncommon occurrence. Various statistics show that there have only been about 200 passengers who've gone overboard during a cruise since 2000, and a good percentage of them were rescued alive. Given that there about sixteen million cruise passengers per year, the number of overboard passengers is an extremely small percentage, roughly 0.00012%. That's not an alarming number, but when it happens, it makes headlines. I don't mean to trivialize the events; however, the majority of them are self-induced: either suicide, or caused by drunkenness or foolish activities (walking on railings, attempting to jump from one balcony to another, etc.). I consider cruising on a ship to be very safe, just as I also consider flying to be very safe (I have Million-Mile Flier status on a major international airline).

You might be asking yourself then, "Why is he sensationalizing this?" That's not my intent. Keep in mind that this is purely a fictional story. None of the events in the story have actually happened on any cruise I've been on, nor do I have any factual information on them. I do know a fair amount about cruising, and I know that sixteen million cruise passengers each year also like cruising; so there has to be something good about it. And there is. One popular advertisement says, "Cruising is FUN!" Yes, indeed. Cruising is fun; it's a great way to visit many locations; unpack your suitcase just one time; enjoy great food and entertainment, and it's all available at a decent price.

Perhaps we'll meet on a cruise someday. Until then . . . *Bon Voyage!*

Stuart Gustafson
Boise, Idaho
March 2016

Main Characters

Becky Anderson. Cruise Director. Single (married once), age 34; from Harwich, U.K. When not cruising, she likes to paint seascapes and write poetry. Her favorite seafood is white fish and she really likes sushi.

Konstantinos Christopolous. Ship's Captain (Master of the Vessel). Married, age 57; from Mykonos, Greece. Is a student of classic literature and likes to collect rare editions. To get away from it all, he and his wife go to the big cities where they are just two among many.

Alfred Dunningham, PhD. Mathematics Professor. Married, age 64; from Napa, California. Grows Shiraz grapes; loves red wine and art. Conducts seminars such as, "Making Detective Work Easier Through Mathematics," and helps police departments around the world.

Antoine Moreau. Interpol Agent. Married, age 55; from Lyon, France. Trained as a classical pianist, he moonlights as a nightclub pianist and a ventriloquist. He is one of the rare Francophiles who doesn't really like wine; perhaps that's because of his line of work.

Clive Stewart. Head of Ship's Security. Single; age 54; from Toronto, Ontario, Canada. An amateur sleuth, he likes to create mystery settings for friends and dinner groups. His parents were born in Jamaica, but he's never been there. He's a big fan of Ballroom dancing.

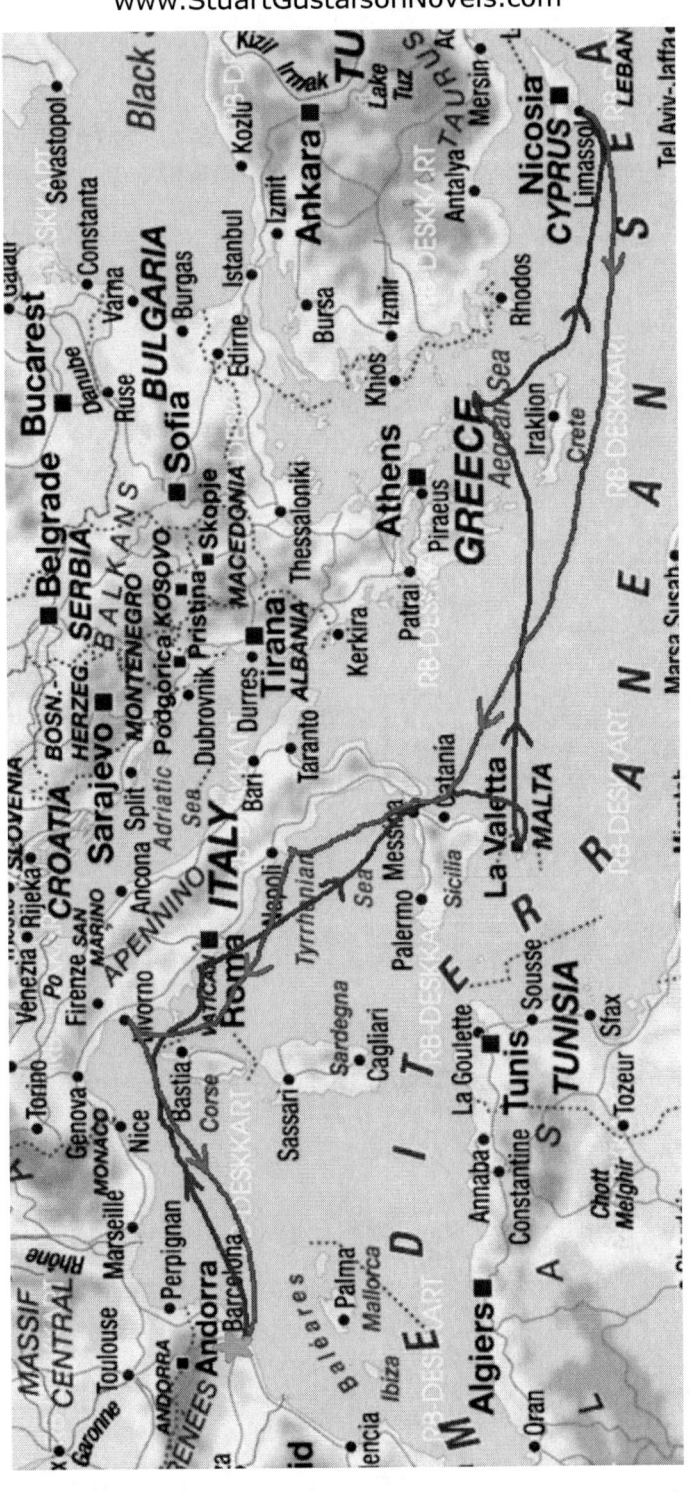

Advertisement for

"Mediterranean Delights" Cruise

Come savor the warmth of the Mediterranean Sea on this 15-day cruise on the magnificent *Royal Holiday*. With only 564 cabins and suites, you and your fellow passengers will enjoy an intimate balance of enchanting ports plus plenty of time at sea to bask in the sun, participate in the wonderful ship-board activities, and there will still be plenty of time for reading and relaxing. All this is yours, along with the gastronomic delights from our Executive Chef and his talented team.

Just look at the exciting itinerary and the fantastic Mediterranean ports of call — what are you waiting for? Reserve your cabin or suite on the *Royal Holiday* now!

Date	Port/City	Activity	Arrival	Departure
Friday July 12	Barcelona, Spain			4:00 PM
Saturday July 13	At Sea			
Sunday July 14	Civitavecchia (Rome), Italy	Docked	8:00 AM	6:00 PM
Monday July 15	Messina, Sicily, Italy	Docked	9:00 AM	9:00 PM
Tuesday July 16	Valletta, Malta	Docked	8:00 AM	5:00 PM
Wednesday July 17	At Sea			
Thursday July 18	Santorini, Greece	Tender	9:00 AM	9:00 PM
Friday July 19	At Sea			
Saturday July 20	Limassol, Cyprus	Docked	8:00 AM	6:00 PM
Sunday July 21	At Sea			
Monday July 22	At Sea			
Tuesday July 23	Amalfi (Capri), Italy	Tender	9:00 AM	5:00 PM
Wednesday July 24	Livorno (Florence, Pisa), Italy	Docked	9:00 AM	6:00 PM
Thursday July 25	At Sea			
Friday July 26	Barcelona, Spain		5:00 AM	

1

Sunday, July 14

5:45 PM

"Ladies and gentlemen, may I have your attention, please," the voice over the ship's Public Address system announced in a stern, yet professional voice. Happy Hour was still underway in most of the ship's bars and there was considerable chatter going on. The main dining room had not yet opened, although there was a line beginning to form at its Deck Four entrance. Most passengers had gone ashore on an excursion in Civitavecchia or spent some time in the small port town so they had worked up an appetite. The railway station, a fifteen-minute walk from port, was a jumping off point for some seasoned cruisers who had destinations other than Civitavecchia in mind for the day.

All-aboard time for the passengers was at 5:30, so everyone was back on board the *Royal Holiday* when she was ready to set sail for her next port of call in Messina, on the isle of Sicily. At least, everyone was supposed to be on board by now.

"Once again, ladies and gentlemen, may I have your attention please," the PA voice said. "Will Mr. Tyler Jacobs in stateroom 7043 please contact Guest Relations on Deck Three immediately." The grammar was technically that of a question, but it was understood as a command. "Again, Mr. Tyler Jacobs in stateroom 7043, please contact Guest Relations on Deck Three immediately."

A first-time cruiser in the Martini Lounge turned to her husband and asked in a slightly slurred voice, "Why are they paging him? Why don't they just go to his cabin?"

"It probably means that his room key didn't register properly when he came back on board. They're required to account for every passenger who leaves the ship, and so they have to make sure they also come back on board."

"Oh," she said as she took another sip of her pink lady cocktail and then smiled at the bartender. "I think I found a new favorite drink, honey. What time's dinner?"

2

Friday, July 12

9:15 AM

"You'll like it, I promise," Patricia Stevens said to her husband Robert as they savored the delightful flavors of their last breakfast in Barcelona. After their nonstop flight from Newark's Liberty Airport, they'd spent four days walking around the city, the capital of the Catalan people, and taking a tour of the sites at the former Olympic Village. A retired stock broker who'd also done quite well in real estate, Robert was tired of the walking and was eager to board the ship for their 15-day cruise.

"So, what's this place you want to go to?" he asked, knowing that giving into her wishes would make the whole day go a lot better. Sightseeing wasn't high on his list of things to do, unless it included art galleries and museums.

"It's called the Güell Palace; it's one of Gaudí's finest works," Patricia replied. "It's only a couple blocks from here, right off La Rambla. Come on; it's the last thing I'll drag you to."

"I didn't know there was a palace right here in the city," Robert said in a facetious retort. "And I thought Gaudí was a painter."

Sensing her husband's sarcasm, Patricia decided to take another approach. "I'm going whether you are or not. And since it sounds like you're not going, you're going to listen to my little lecture because I've read up on this. Antoni Gaudí was probably the most famous architect in this area of Spain, and his projects reflect an enormity of scale and detail that haven't been replicated. He used his creativity, along with his novel uses of ceramics and glass, to manifest beauty in everything he touched. You know that large church we saw?" Patricia paused to see if Robert was actually listening—he was. "That magnificent church is called Sagrada Familia, and it was actually begun in 1882, and it's still another ten or fifteen years from being completed. Seven of his projects are UNESCO World Heritage Sites. The Palace Güell is not really a palace as we think about it, but it was a palatial estate for a very wealthy family. Locally, it's called Palau Güell, as Palau means Palace in Catalonian."

"Is there artwork to view in there?" Robert asked.

"Some, but it's not like the Metropolitan Museum. The entire building is a grand piece of art," Patricia replied, seeing that she'd grabbed his attention. "There's even a pipe organ in the music chamber," she added, knowing that would seal it for Robert; he loved pipe organs almost as much as he liked collecting fine art.

"Okay," Robert said as he put down his fork, wiped the linen napkin across his mouth, set the napkin on the plate, and said, "Let me pay and we'll go check out of the hotel. They've got a place to store our luggage, so we can come back for it as we head to the ship." Robert saw the upturned corners of his wife's lips; she was happy. She would have gone on her own, but she really preferred doing things with him, or with some of her socialite lady friends. "*Señor*, the bill, please," Robert said as the waiter passed by their table. For all his travels, Robert was not adept at foreign language. He was polite; he was a generous tipper; he just wasn't good at learning more than a few basic words in other languages.

After brushing their teeth and doing the last bit of packing, Robert and Patricia rolled their luggage down the narrow, but brightly lit, hallway to the front desk. "Oh, you're leaving us so soon?" the attendant feigned sadness as he saw them approach.

"Yes, I'm afraid so," Robert replied. "May we keep our bags here for a few hours before we ahead off to the ship?"

"Most certainly," responded José. "If you know what time you'll be back, I'll have a taxi waiting for you. And how did you enjoy your stay here in Barcelona? Here's our card that will give you a discount the next time you visit."

"Thank you," Patricia said accepting the card while she was opening the boarding papers for their cruise. "We're supposed to check in at 2:30."

"The taxi ride is only fifteen minutes, even on a busy day. I will have the taxi here at ten minutes past two and you will be fine with your check-in time. Do you need a suggestion on what to go see in your last few hours here?" José asked.

"No, thanks," Patricia answered. "We're walking over to Palau Güell, and then maybe one more stroll along La Rambla."

"*Excellente*," the attendant said. "You are going to the Palau at a good time; you won't have any lines to worry about. Your bill was pre-paid, so there's nothing else to do to check out. I'll see you in a few hours. Enjoy!"

"Thanks," the Stevens said in unison as they turned toward the hotel entrance and headed out into the bright sunshine. As they stepped across the narrow traffic lane onto the pedestrian area, wavy lines along La Rambla seemed to float in the warmth and the humidity of the summer's day. They turned left to head downhill toward the harbor. Robert stopped as they approached the Miró mosaic that had been in the walkway for forty years.

"Isn't this amazing," Robert began. "Most people would love to have an original piece of art by Joan Miró, and here's one that thousands of people walk on every day without paying any attention to it. Wow." Robert stared down at the pavement mosaic and shook his head sideways in disbelief. "So where's this palace?"

"The next street down there on the right, Nou Rambla," Patricia replied as she led the way.

3

Friday, July 12

10:30 AM

Sipping on a mint and pineapple smoothie as he left Barcelona's famous open-air market La Boquería, Gary Marsing turned right on La Rambla and then an immediate left just past the Miró. His map showed him that this would be the shortest way to the Picasso museum. An avid Picasso fan, Gary had visited many museums and exhibitions just to see as much Picasso as he could. He even took the train once from Chicago to New York City to see the complete Picasso viewing at the Metropolitan Museum of Art, the only time they'd ever brought out every Picasso item in their vast collection. He really liked Musée Picasso in Paris, but he was sure that this one, the artist's largest collection in Spain, would soon move to the top of his list. Someday perhaps, he would own his own piece of Picasso art. *Someday*, he thought.

The names of the roads, some would consider them as alleyways rather than actual roads, kept changing every few hundred meters. He started on Boquería (that made sense), but then it was a slight left turn onto Ferran. That lasted through the intersection of two little plazas until the road became Princesa, and then his map showed that he should take a quick right jog down a really narrow lane called Barra de Ferro. A couple minutes later and he was right at the entrance: **Museu Picasso**, the sign said. Gary smiled as he envisioned all the works he would soon be seeing. Picasso had spent his formative years in Barcelona, from about age fourteen to twenty-one, and so this museum had the most and the best examples from that period of his life.

Gary pulled the Articket Card from his wallet and went to the front of the winding line. As a frequent traveler, he knew how to check for the tricks to avoid standing in lines and wasting time with the crowds. He had already purchased his guide book, so he headed to the right once he entered and went straight for the stairs leading up to the gallery floor. He knew that the ceramics were a must-see, but he also wanted to go room by room in order as that presented the best growth of Picasso's artistic development. He looked at his watch and realized he'd have to pace himself through the rooms so he'd still have time for lunch before heading to the ship.

His stomach started growling, telling Gary it was time to eat as he finally got to room 15, the first of the two ceramics rooms. Fortunately, they were the last two rooms on the floor; unfortunately, there were only forty-one pieces on exhibit. One of the exciting things about Picasso ceramics was that there were so many individual pieces that were still rather easily obtainable, for a price of course. He wanted to study each of the pieces in the museum to help him determine the type of piece that he would set his sights on someday owning. There's that *someday* again. As he looked at all of the ceramics, each one a gift from Picasso's widow Jacqueline after his death, he envisioned what it would look like in his display case at home. Would a pitcher look just right on the illuminated glass shelving? Would a long plate capture the focus and be the center of attention for most viewers? After much thought, he knew the type he wanted and he headed downstairs to the gift shop to buy postcards of the round plates, the choice for his *someday* purchase.

Walking with a much lighter step, as if he'd been drawn closer to the heavens from enjoying each and every piece that was displayed, Gary walked out of the museum and decided to let his senses pick a place to eat. He normally would look at the menu; see what others were eating; try to determine if it was a good café based on how many locals were there. Not now. His mind was still absorbed with the artistry of Picasso and he didn't want his gastronomic decision to be guided by rational thoughts. He wanted to just let it happen.

He left his map in the backpack; he knew the basic direction he had to go to get back to the hotel for his suitcase. Besides, he hadn't seen anything that struck his fancy on his way to the museum, but his focus hadn't been on food then. Now he wanted art to be the decider in finding him just the right place for his last meal in Barcelona. As he strolled along the lanes, oblivious to those around him, he thought again of the round ceramic plates.

Did anyone ever use them for eating? That wasn't their intention, but maybe there was an eccentric who placed them on the dinner table for show. *Utter blasphemy*, he thought. To use such a cerebral object in such a banal fashion was just out of the question. *Art is to be enjoyed, not consumed.* Once one begins to consume the artistry, what is really left of it? Gary's philosophical mind had taken over the mental conversation, when what he wanted was for his artistic mind to find him a place to eat.

Hearing some excited yet not overbearing chatting coming from the little sidewalk café at the next corner, his mind said that was where he was to have lunch. The inside design was a cross between art nouveau and art deco; the menu itself was like small paintings bound together to create a story-telling experience. The waiter appeared quickly, bringing both a carafe of water and a carafe of white wine; after all, it was still early in the day and red wine wouldn't be automatically served until the evening hours. Yes; this was the right place to conclude his Catalonian experience.

"Do you speak English?" Gary asked the waiter.

"I do, but not very well," the polite man answered.

"That's okay; please bring me what you think would help me remember this day forever. I've just been to the Picasso Museum, and I'd prefer not to make any decisions. I just want to enjoy good food and drink. Okay?"

"Of course, it's okay, *señor*. The chef has just the right items for you that will let you remember this day and Barcelona forever. Whenever your mind experiences the smells you're about to enjoy, you will be brought back to this place and it will feel as if you've never left here. I hope you enjoy the wine. Your food will be right out."

The waiter's command of the English language was surpassed only by the eloquence in which he was able to describe the sensory exploration upon which Gary was about to embark. *The waiter must be a poet or an artist of another realm. This should be pure enjoyment.*

And it was.

The waiter was right. The smells and the blends of various aromas made indelible impressions in Gary's mind. These would be foods he would be able to recall just from a hint of aroma that he would capture as he breathed in. *Oh, why does the ship have to leave this afternoon; couldn't it stay in port just one more day?*

4

Friday, July 12

12:15 PM

"Every one of the ports sounds exciting," Margaret Abrahms said to Tricia Long as the two ladies and their husbands began their walk down La Rambla in search of one more café experience before they left Barcelona. "How did you manage to pick your excursions already?" Margaret continued as the two couples meandered down the wavy walkway that was where effluent used to flow from the outskirts of the ancient city down to the Mediterranean Sea.

"I looked on Cruise Critic to see what others were saying about the port excursions from previous cruises," Tricia replied. "And it's not as if any particular one was that much better than all the others; for some ports, it was just a matter of picking one from several great possibilities. Oh, look at the birds," Tricia said as they approached a stand that sold all sorts of small animals that could be kept in apartments: birds, turtles and fish.

"I thought I heard some birds chirping last night when I opened the bedroom window," Tricia's husband, Maxwell, said. "I guess it wouldn't be too convenient to cart all of them somewhere else at night. You know," he continued, "it seems like a strange business to have here, but I read that this setup has been here for decades."

"Really?" Peter Abrahms asked in disbelief.

"Right," Maxwell answered. "I guess the tradition was that families would stroll leisurely down La Rambla after Mass on Sunday. As they approached this area, the children would drag their parents over here and beg them to buy a small pet. Those living in an apartment couldn't really have a dog or a cat, so one of these small animals would be fine. They don't require a lot of attention and they're fairly quiet. I imagine that the very first person here had only a few of them. But as the tradition grew and word spread about the man selling apartment-sized pets, it was almost a status symbol to say that your bird or fish or whatever came from La Rambla."

"That's quite interesting," Peter said. "Hey, everyone check your watch. See that clock over there," he said as he turned away from the birds to point to a building on the opposite side. That's the Academy of Science and its clock marks official Barcelona time." Peter paused and looked at his atomic watch and noticed that it was one minute ahead of the Academy of Science time. "Hmm," he mused. "It seems that the official Barcelona time is one minute behind the rest of the world."

"Just so long as that doesn't make us late for the ship," Margaret quipped.

"Not to worry, my dear," Peter replied. "You fair ladies are in the company of two gentlemen whose duty it is to get you to the ship on time. Do you agree, my good friend?" he gesticulated as he bent his body to turn toward Maxwell.

"But, of course," Maxwell answered in a pitiful imitation of a British accent. The two women looked at each other and could do nothing but just shake their heads.

"Okay, Sir Galahad," Margaret said, "where are you knights planning to take these two fair damsels before we die of starvation?"

Tricia couldn't help herself; she had to laugh. "The comedy's begun and we haven't even left shore. This could be a long cruise."

"Let's take one of these side roads rather than eating here among the masses. We'll have enough of that on the ship. Here, let's turn at the church," Peter said as they approached a huge Baroque church that really looked out of place alongside the peaceful pedestrian way.

As they made a couple quick right turns around the church, they came upon a delightful little shop with a small sign hanging over the doorway: **Café Ganja Viader, desde 1870**. The exquisite pastries in the window served their purpose well; the two couples couldn't resist. They saw an open table for four and they went inside.

"Heaven on earth, I'd say," Maxwell remarked as they reluctantly got up from their table to return to the hotel. They hadn't understood a single word the proprietor said as he described in detail the tasty morsels that they pointed to in his showcase. They knew the word for wine, *vino*, and the slightly chilled semi-dry white wine proved to be fantastic accompaniment to their snacks. They'd originally headed out to have lunch, but their stomachs won the argument when it came to picking what to eat.

"Undoubtedly," Margaret replied as she was mentally filing away the delicious combination of flavors, textures, and smells of this assortment of pastries and baked goods. "I've always had marvelous pastries in Paris, but these certainly would give them a good run for first prize. What do you think, Trish?"

"Fantastic," Tricia responded. "As great as this place was, I'm glad we didn't discover it right away or I'd never fit into any of the clothes I brought."

"You can always buy more clothes, Trish, but you can't always find great food," Margaret said, and then the two women chuckled. Whether it was the comment or the *vino* that made them giddy was irrelevant; the two women were having a good time. No; they were having a great time. "Oh, Sir Galahad," Margaret mocked, "did you forget our chariot?"

The women laughed again as the two couples, hand in hand, began to walk back to the hotel to retrieve their luggage for the taxi ride to the *Royal Holiday*.

5

Friday, July 12
2:30 PM

"That was pretty easy," Tricia Long remarked as she handed the passports and room keycard holders to her husband. "I'd read some horrendous stories on Cruise Critic about passengers standing in two-hour lines."

"I can imagine that's fairly normal for those larger ships with three thousand or more people on board," her husband said. "What did they say the capacity was on this ship, around eleven hundred?" he continued as he placed the key holders and passports inside his coat pocket as they stepped away from the check-in counter inside Barcelona's Moll D'Adossat Cruise Terminal.

They were soon greeted by a white-gloved crew member. "Good afternoon and welcome aboard the *Royal Holiday* Please let me take those for you," he said as he reached for the carry-on bags that Maxwell and Tricia were pulling.

"Thank you," Maxwell said.

"Cabin number, please?" the crew member asked as he started to lead the Longs toward the red-carpeted gangway.

"7048," Maxwell replied.

"That's a beautiful location," the helpful crew member responded. "When people have asked me, I've always told them that a cabin in the mid-ship's area is the best place."

"Why's that?" Tricia asked as they reached the slightly inclining gangway steps.

"It's just my personal preference," the reply began, "but you're never far from anything, plus you won't feel the rocking as much when we encounter a few waves."

"I guess we owe our travel agent a big 'Thank you' as she's the one who arranged everything for us," Tricia said.

"You'll need your room keys and your passports for the security officer when we get aboard. He's going to take your picture, and then I'll show you where your cabin is." The crew member let the Longs walk up the shallow steps first.

Sixty-four. That's how many steps Maxwell counted as they stepped onto the red mats in the ship's spacious lobby area.

"Passport, please," the security officer said in a polite voice.

"Go ahead, dear," Maxwell said as he handed Tricia's passport to the officer.

The officer opened the passport and looked at the picture then at Tricia. "Welcome aboard, Ms. Tricia Long. Please put your room key in the slot with the arrow facing me and then smile for the camera." The camera flashed and the machine beeped. "You're all checked in, thank you. You may take your room key and here's your passport. I suggest keeping it in your room safe until it's needed, which won't be for several days."

The process was repeated for Maxwell Long. The crew member playing their personal guide walked alongside them. "Help yourself to some champagne or a mimosa if you'd like before we take these bags to your cabin. You're certainly welcome to come back down here for more, plus there's plenty topside on the pool deck."

"Sure; why not?" Maxwell said as he took a glass from the tray being held out for them by a smiling waiter.

"This is the Central Lobby, and we're on Deck Three," their guide said once both the Longs had a glass. "This is where you'll get off the ship in most ports. Also, Guest Relations is over there," he continued as he pointed toward a counter where there was a short line of people. "They're open twenty-four hours a day, and they're your primary resource for almost anything you'll need. Shore Excursions is on the opposite side. They'll take care of all your tours. The main dining room is up one deck and straight back, and the ship's theater is also up one deck and all the way forward. Shops all along your way. The main elevators are over here behind the Grand Staircase," he paused as he pulled the bags leading the way around the glass stairs.

As the three of them stepped out of the elevator, Maxwell turned left when he should have turned right. "I got turned around," he said as he made a one-eighty and headed toward the starboard side of the ship. He followed the others to their cabin, which was just three doors down the hall. Maxwell slid his room key into the electronic lock which beeped and flashed green. They stepped into a cabin flooded with sunlight.

"It's beautiful," Tricia exclaimed as she stepped inside and headed straight for the sliding door to a verandah.

Their guide followed Maxwell inside and placed the rolling bags near a small oval table. "Did you have just two checked bags, sir?"

"Yes, that's them," Maxwell replied as he pulled a ten euro note out of his right pocket and handed the tip over.

"Thank you, Mr. Long, but we have a no tipping policy on the ship. We're here to help you, and it's our pleasure to do so. You can reach your cabin steward at any time by just dialing 2222 on your phone. Is there anything else I can help you with?"

"Do you know if lunch is still being served?" Maxwell asked, now wishing he'd had little more than just pastries at that sinful café.

"They're serving a buffet lunch in Oceans Café; that's on Deck Eleven. Also the Pool Grille has hamburgers and hot dogs; it's also on eleven."

"Great; thanks," Long replied. "Thanks again for your help," he added as he opened the cabin door.

"You're welcome; I'm sure I'll see you around the ship," the crew member said as he walked toward the stairs to assist more passengers.

The check-in counters inside the port terminal were idle as most of the passengers had already checked in. A forties-something bald man approached the counter that had the **M-P** sign hanging overhead. James Phillips handed his passport and Express Check-in paperwork to the clerk who returned his friendly smile. "Here you are, sir. You won't need this paperwork anymore, but security will need your passport and room key once you board the ship. Enjoy your cruise," she said as she handed James Phillips his paperwork, his passport, and a leather room key holder that held his key to cabin 7053.

"Thank you," said Mr. Phillips as he turned toward the ship.

"Oh, Mr. Phillips," the counter agent called out. "I see that John Phillips, your brother I presume, hasn't checked in yet. Is he on his way?"

Pausing ever so slightly, James Phillips smiled at the agent again. "He's always late," he said in that convincing manner.

"I know the type," the agent replied as James turned away again and headed out to the carpeted area.

"Good afternoon, sir," was the friendly approach from one of the gloved crew members who were now lined up waiting for more passengers. "May I assist you on board, sir?" the eager guide asked.

"Thanks, but I've been on this ship before, so I've got it pretty well figured out. But thanks any way," Phillips said in a polite but firm manner as he continued walking toward the gangway. He stole a quick glance behind him before he swiftly walked up the sixty-four steps to the Central Lobby check-in. Knowing what to do, he handed his passport to the security officer.

"Good afternoon, Mr. James Phillips," the officer said. "Will you please insert your room key into the slot with the arrow facing me and then smile for the camera?" James did as asked, the camera flashed, the machine beeped. James Phillips was now checked onboard the *Royal Holiday*.

Instead of heading directly into the Central Lobby, James immediately turned around and ran down the vacant gangway.

"Sir, you can't do that," the security officer yelled in vain as James was already nearing the bottom step. "You must use your room key to check off the ship."

"My camera bag," James hollered as he turned back toward the ship, not slowing down at all as he reached the terminal building. Once at the door, he slowed to a calm walk and gently strolled through the building to the exit on the other side, even though he was slightly out of breath.

6

Friday, July 12

3:45 PM

"Good afternoon, ladies and gentlemen. It's a pleasure to welcome all of you aboard the beautiful *Royal Holiday* as we get ready to embark on this fifteen-day Mediterranean Delights cruise. My name is Becky Anderson, your cruise director aboard the *Royal Holiday*, and I look forward to meeting every one of you at some point during the cruise. Right now, however, I have a very important announcement to make. In thirty minutes from now, we will be conducting a mandatory emergency evacuation drill in accordance with maritime safety standards and the safety policies of Holiday Cruise Lines.

"It's an absolute requirement that every guest on board the *Royal Holiday* participate in the emergency evacuation drill, whether this is your first cruise, your one hundredth cruise, or even if you're continuing on with us from our previous cruise. The drill consists of a signal on the ship's whistle followed by your going to your designated emergency station. The signal that you will hear is seven short blasts followed by one long blast on the ship's whistle. As soon as you hear that signal, you are to take the life jacket that's in your cabin and go to your assigned emergency station. The designation and the location of your emergency station are listed on the back of your cabin door, and the location code is also printed in bold letters on your room key. You don't have to wear your life jacket, but you must bring it with you to your station so our trained staff can show you the proper way to put it on in the very unlikely event that it's needed.

"Once again, this is a mandatory emergency evacuation drill; attendance will be taken and it will begin in twenty-five minutes. Remember, you must bring your life jacket and your room key with you to your emergency station. Crew members will be standing by to help guide you to your station when the emergency signal is sounded. I'll be making another announcement in fifteen minutes, at which time all ship's food and beverage activities are required to cease operation. Thank you for your attention and your cooperation."

7

Sunday, July 14

Afternoon

The tour of the countryside area away from the Italian port of Civitavecchia, and the enormous castle on the hill were quite interesting, but it was a warm day and it was time for lunch. The restaurant was an excellent choice and the outside tables were on a charming deck that reached out over the lake's edge. John Saxton waited until Gary, Robert, and James selected a table before he guided Mary to the opposite side of the area reserved for their tour. Gary was oblivious to the actions John was taking; he was enjoying listening to the stories the other guys were telling about living in the Big Apple.

"House wine and beer are included with your lunch," the tour guide said as she walked from table to table to explain the menu, printed in Italian. "If you want a premium wine or beer, you have to pay cash for that, but the *vino di casa* is really good."

"I think we got lucky with the tour escort," Gary said as he considered the choices deciding on the baked lasagna.

"She's cute; that's for sure," Robert replied. "How could someone that good looking stand to be cooped up on a ship for six or eight months?"

"Maybe her boyfriend is also on here," James offered. "Besides, I hear they make pretty good money, and there's always the possibility of a talent agent seeing them and signing them to something bigger."

"Cheers," Gary said as he raised a glass of red wine. The tour guide was right; the house wine was really good. And the smells wafting from inside the restaurant foretold of some very tasty food that was about to be brought out to them.

Delicioso; was the only word that could adequately describe the food. And then they brought out the dessert trays; each tray held six desserts and there were only the three of them at their table. The math was appreciated.

"I could die right now and be happy," Gary said as he washed down the last bite of cannoli with a mouthful of the red wine.

"Well, that would be one way to get the attention of our dancer escort," James said.

"I hope you all enjoyed your lunch," the tour guide said loud enough for all to hear. All the members of bus number two applauded in appreciation of the wonderful food and service. "If you feel like leaving a little extra tip for the servers, I'm sure they'd greatly appreciate it. We need to be back on the bus in," and she paused as she looked at her watch, "on the bus in twenty minutes. We then head to the winery where there's more food and lots of great wine just waiting for your enjoyment. Twenty minutes, bus number two."

"You guys want to go check out the lake? I saw some neat trails just down the road." Gary looked at Robert and James, who weren't the adventuresome type. "Okay, well, I'll see you guys a little later," Gary said as he got up from the table and headed through the restaurant to the street area.

"Where are you going?" Mary Saxton asked as her husband got up from the table.

"Oh, I'd better go to the restroom before we get back on the bus," John said as he headed toward the restaurant.

"I'm going to walk back to the bus so we don't have to hurry later," Mary said as John was walking away from her. He didn't hear a thing; his mind was focused elsewhere, and it wasn't about getting back on the bus.

The twenty minutes went by quickly. Some had another glass of wine, while others enjoyed the peaceful nature of the lake. Most were already back in their seats and a few of the stragglers were walking briskly to the bus. John and Mary were settled in when Mary asked, "What happened to your shirt? Did you fall or something?"

"That's it," John responded. "I, uh, went to the edge of the lake near that patio area and I slipped on a loose rock."

"You okay?"

"I'm fine," John answered. "I'm fine."

Outside the bus, the tour guide scanned the area, not seeing anyone heading toward the bus, "Count?" she asked.

The tour escort stepped inside and started counting by twos. Everyone was paired with someone else, but there was an empty set of seats next to Robert and James. "Where's your buddy?" the escort asked.

"He said he was going to check out some of those trails by the lake," Robert answered. "He knew what time it was and when we had to leave. Do you want me to go look for him?"

"No," the escort replied. "He's not your responsibility. Thanks." She went outside and told the tour guide about Gary.

"We have to leave here in no more than five minutes or we won't have enough time at the winery to get back to the ship on time," the tour guide said. "I'm not supposed to leave anyone, but I also don't want to ruin the tour for everyone else."

"I'll go look for him," the escort said.

"Okay, but just to the restaurant area," the guide said.

Her dancing and training came into use as she jogged back to the restaurant and asked if anyone there had seen their missing person.

No, was the only reply. She went out to the street and looked up and down to see if he was at any of the souvenir shops. Nothing; there was no sign of Gary Marsing. A ship employee, she also knew that as a tour escort she wasn't to leave any passenger behind. But what was she supposed to do? If someone essentially disappeared, what could she do about it?

Back on the bus, the rest of the passengers were getting impatient. It was warm inside even with the air conditioning running and they wanted to get to the winery. "Let's go, already," one restless passenger hollered, which started others mumbling.

Mary Saxton looked over at her husband.

The escort jogged back to the bus, shaking her head sideways as she approached the guide. The guide muttered something in Italian and then said in English, "I have to call my company and report this right away. Why don't you tell them inside that we'll be leaving for the winery in just a couple minutes? Right after I make my call."

Bus number two left for LRV Winery, minus one passenger. John Saxton smiled as the bus got underway.

8

Friday, July 12

4:45 PM

"Hello again, everyone. This is Becky, your cruise director, and it's such a pleasure to have all of you here on the *Royal Holiday* for our magnificent Mediterranean cruise under the guidance of our captain, Konstantinos Christopolous. The captain's informed me that we're only about fifteen minutes from pushing off from our port here in Barcelona, and I want to tell you about all the activities we have going on around the ship. First, however, I want to tell you about what announcements are made over the public address system, when they're made, and where you'll be able to hear them.

"First off, we know that you're here to enjoy a nice relaxing vacation and you don't want us constantly breaking into that vacation time; so we'll keep our announcements to a minimum. Obviously, if there's a need to make an emergency announcement, the captain or someone on his staff will broadcast that, and it will be announced throughout the entire ship, including your cabins and suites. On the other hand, other announcements will be broadcast only in the public areas so as not to disturb you when you're looking for some peace and quiet."

Sitting on their verandah, Robert and Patricia Stevens were enjoying the view and a glass of chilled Chardonnay that he'd pre-ordered to be delivered right before they set sail from Barcelona. They were seasoned travelers, yet they always enjoyed going to new places, meeting new people, and enjoying the sights, sounds, and smells of the local areas.

Patricia enjoyed doing all the planning and Robert was more than happy to let her do all the work. She'd arranged most of their port tours through Cruise Critic; two of them were private, but the others were with friends she'd met online. Becky's announcement was coming into their stateroom, but they pretty much knew what else she was going to say. They'd probably go to one of the upper decks when it was time to pull out, but they weren't really into the party atmosphere that came with most of the Sail Away activities. They'd have another glass of wine on their verandah, then they might go to the upper decks while the festivities took place as the ship pulled out. But they wouldn't be on the Pool Deck dancing to the party band.

The light breeze on the verandah, combined with the chilled Chardonnay, helped offset the warmth of the late afternoon's sun as it focused its energies on the painted white sides of the ship. The few days in Barcelona were enjoyable, but the solitude here in their own private area brought peace to Robert and Patricia. They liked socializing, but they also liked to have some time and space of their own; this was that time and this was that space. Even though there were almost one thousand seven hundred other people on the ship, this peaceful respite was a heavenly gift. It was Nirvana.

Three blasts on the ship's whistle rudely interrupted their sanctuary. The ship was backing up, beginning its journey out of Barcelona. Robert sighed; he was enjoying the peace and tranquility of just sitting. He'd reluctantly admitted liking the Güell Palace, but he'd done enough walking and he now wanted to just sit.

As he poured the last bit of wine into Patricia's glass, he asked, "You want to go topside, or do you just want to stay here until dinner?" The tone of his voice gave away his preference.

"Let's just stay here for a while," she responded.

"Sure, that's fine with me," Robert said as his body relaxed and molded itself to the slatted deck chair.

The noise from the upper decks was audible but Robert and Patricia didn't hear it at all. They'd come on this cruise to disappear from the world for fifteen days, and it was time for that disappearing act to begin.

9

Friday, July 12
That Evening

The line from the Grand Dining Room entrance back into the Masthead Bar was growing longer. Those in line were moving from fidgety to restless to impatient. The comments and the questions they were exchanging held a common theme: We signed up for fixed seating; We have our table number, why can't we just go in?; What's the hold up?

All the comments and questions were the result of a computer malfunction at the hostess stand. Adriana, the charming hostess, was trying to check people in for dinner, but the system wanted to reassign everyone to different tables. Finally the Maître D', sensing her frustration, came to her side.

"Ladies and gentlemen," the Maître D' said in a booming voice to the impatient gathering. The English accent added authority and captured everyone's attention. "It seems that our computer is playing horrible games with your reservations. If you know your assigned table number, then please allow us to escort you there. If you don't know it, and your friends are already inside, feel free to look for them, or just go inside and find a table that suits you. Please accept my apologies and inform your waiter that I want to buy your first glass of wine tonight." The offer of a glass of wine had a settling effect on the restless line as couples began to make their way toward tables.

The hostess had discreetly slipped past the line and went through the side door leading into the servers' area. She had finally worked her way up to lead hostess, and then this happened on her first night in the Grand Dining Room. The head waiter took over welcoming guests as the Maître D' went to console Adriana. She was nowhere to be found—it was as if she had completely disappeared from sight, something that was hard to do even on a ship the size of the *Royal Holiday*.

The wine worked its magic; the guests were chatting away and there was no mention of the computer glitch that slowed down their first entry for the epicurean delights that they were certain to enjoy on the cruise. The wine sommeliers were extra busy as most of the diners were ordering more wine than usual. And with the automatic fifteen percent gratuity added on to the tab, the sommeliers were making some nice tips. They were smiling as they hustled from one table to the next, making sure that everyone was happy.

Names and cabin numbers were being exchanged by some passengers seated at larger tables. Previous strangers were now on their way to becoming good friends. There was the occasional surprise when one diner would find out that his tablemate was from the same hometown.

The public address system chime rang throughout the ship, which only barely lowered the noise level in the Grand Dining Room. "Good evening, ladies and gentlemen. This is your captain, Konstantinos Christopolous; speaking to you from the Navigational Bridge." The captain's thick Greek accent actually forced the diners to cease their conversations and listen more intently to be able to understand. "I want to offer my welcome to you aboard the beautiful *Royal Holiday* on this exciting fifteen-day voyage around the Mediterranean Sea. My crew is here to provide you with outstanding service to make your vacation with us the most enjoyable trip you've ever had. In a couple of days we'll be passing by my home town of

Mykonos, Greece; but you don't need to worry that we will get too close to shore."

The captain's dry sense of humor wasn't lost on the passengers who recalled the horrific incident off the coast of Italy where a ship got too close to the coastline and capsized after running into the rocks. While the news of that ship wasn't good for the cruise industry, most rational travelers knew that it was an isolated incident caused by human error. It did seem strange, however, for the captain of another ship to mention it, but it did let them know that their captain was going to make sure that nothing happened to them.

"So, ladies and gentlemen," the captain continued, "if there's anything that we're not doing to make this your most pleasurable vacation, you will do me a big favor by telling one of my officers what you'd like us to do. Thank you very much for your attention, ladies and gentlemen, and now I'd like to turn the microphone over to the cruise director."

"Thank you very much, Captain Christopolous, for that warm welcome. And while I know that all our guests would love to see your home town, I also know they're quite grateful that you'd rather keep the beautiful *Royal Holiday* well away from those rocky shoals. Ladies and gentlemen, this is Becky, wanting to once again give you a warm welcome aboard and to give you just a quick snapshot of the activities that are taking place around the ship on our very first night at sea." Becky's voice was charming, but the conversation levels picked back up as diners resumed eating and drinking and chatting away.

10

Friday, July 12

Later That Evening

"Good evening and welcome to *Spotlight on Broadway*," the tuxedoed and white-gloved waiters said as they greeted each guest entering the ship's Royal Theatre. Balanced on their left hand was a silver tray with glasses of champagne and wine. Napkins were deftly held in the right hand and offered to each guest as they selected a glass.

"Our second free glass of wine tonight," Gary Marsing turned and said to the couple behind him. "I hope this trend continues," he added. Noticing that the couple didn't seem to be interested in casual conversation with him, Gary said, "Have a good evening," with a sarcastic smile as he turned back around and walked down the aisle to find a seat near friendlier people. He'd chosen a champagne flute and as he entered a row and sat down next to a couple who were laughing, he noticed that they had also selected the champagne.

"Cheers," Gary said as he looked at them and raised his glass. "My name's Gary."

"Cheers to you, too. We're John and Mary," the woman replied. Gary had sat down in the seat next to her, so she felt that she needed to respond to him.

"Nice touch with the free booze, right?" Gary asked as he smiled at Mary but looked past her to John.

"Yes, indeed," John Saxton said. "Mary and I were just commenting on how the other cruises we've been on didn't do this. I don't know if that free glass of wine with dinner was truly because of the computer foul up or if that was just a convenient reason to get us started so we'd order more. But, hey; who cares? Right?"

"I agree," Gary replied. Gary looked at Mary and said, "Those are really nice earrings. Are they—" he was cut off mid-sentence.

"Ladies and gentlemen; welcome to the Royal Theatre, certainly one of the most glamorous theaters afloat. Don't you agree?"

Whistles, cheers and clinking glasses accompanied the clapping from those who weren't holding a glass at the time Becky asked the leading question. Give the crowd free wine and champagne and they'll agree to just about anything.

"I've met a few of you already, but for the rest of you, I'm Becky, your cruise director here on the fabulous *Royal Holiday*. I hope you all had a great evening meal, and so before you settle in too comfortably in those great theater seats, I'd like you to all get friendly with those around you and move in toward the center of each row." As she said this, Becky put her arms out in front of her, and then brought her hands toward each other to indicate what she wanted the passengers to do. "This way, we can make sure that everyone can come in and enjoy our first show of the cruise, *Spotlight on Broadway*, starring our own singers and dancers. The show starts in just five minutes. I'll be back at the end of the show to talk about other activities going on around the ship later tonight and what we've got in store for tomorrow. Enjoy the show," Becky concluded as she exited stage right to a warm round of applause.

As many in the theater stood to move toward the center of the row, Gary took the opportunity to scan the area. He was looking for someone, or something. His happy demeanor changed as he looked over to the far right. His eyes squinted as he stared. *What is it? Who is it?* He shook his head a couple times, and looked back to his left to see that John and Mary had shifted a couple seats to the left. He caught her glance, smiled, and moved over two seats. "Hi," he said to her as he sat down.

"Any plans for when we get to Civitavecchia?" Mary asked.

Gary's focus was elsewhere. He heard Mary's words, but they weren't where his attention was focused. "I'm sorry," he said. "My mind was somewhere else. What was that?"

"Any plans for our stop in Civitavecchia?" Mary repeated.

"Something about going out into the country and then wine tasting. It just sounded like fun and who doesn't like wine tasting?" Gary had reengaged with his neighbor.

"I think that's the one we're going on; right John?" she remarked as she also looked over at her husband who seemed distracted.

"I think so," John said.

Mary turned back to Gary and smiled. "I think that's it. Maybe we'll be on the same bus together," she said as she put her right palm on his left shoulder for a quick tap.

John's eyes quickly glanced to his right; he didn't like what he just saw.

Becky's voice once again was heard, although she wasn't seen as the theater lights had dimmed and a low fog covered the stage area. "Ladies and gentlemen; sit back and relax as the *Royal Holiday* singers and dancers delight you with this evening's show *Spotlight on Broadway*."

The greeting applause was mixed, with the most enthusiastic response coming from the first few rows in the center section of the theater. Some people were clapping a ring against their glasses.

The curtains opened and a beautiful blonde singer in a brilliant red outfit began her melodic rendition of Barbra Streisand's *Memories*. The audience was drawn in not only by her appearance, but also by her Streisandesque voice and animations.

"She could be on Broadway," Gary leaned to his left and whispered to Mary.

Mesmerized, Mary kept her focus on the stage and nodded.

John's face tightened as his eyebrows dropped down closer to his piercing eyes.

11

Saturday, July 13

8:00 AM

"Good morning, ladies and gentlemen," the announcement began in the ship's public areas. "This is Becky, your cruise director, and I hope you had a fantastic evening last night whatever you did here on the *Royal Holiday*. Well, today is our first full day at sea and I guarantee that we have something for everyone."

Not everyone was hearing Becky's cheerful voice as the announcement was only going to the public areas. There were quite a few people who'd partied the night away in the Sky View Lounge and most of them were still sleeping it off in their suites and cabins. Fortunately, the water was calm in this section of the Mediterranean Sea. The ship was following the contour of the French coastline while staying about forty miles out to sea.

One of those who'd actually done too much partying—but who also knew better—was Scott Eaton, stage manager for the Royal Theatre. He'd been on the *Royal Holiday* for seven months and this was his last cruise before he left the ship for a ten-week holiday. Scott was a player and he knew that he had to always be on guard. But this was his last cruise so he would be afforded a little leeway, just so long as he didn't overdo it. He did overdo it last night as far as drinks were concerned. His self-imposed maximum of four cocktails was quickly blown away as he got into the groove of the party band playing in the Sky View Lounge. He thought he made a pass at a couple of the married women, but his throbbing head clouded away those memories.

Becky's announcement continued, "We have Zumba starting in the theater at nine o'clock. Now, in case you've never heard of Zumba or have never experienced this amazing way to stay fit, come down to the theater and see what it's about. You will be hooked on it once you try it for the first time. Then at ten thirty, right there in the theater, our enrichment speaker, Fernando Moretti, will be giving his first talk entitled *Coastal Life in the Mediterranean.* You won't want to miss this amazing presentation, and single ladies, you'll want a seat up close. So get there early."

Fernando Moretti was having breakfast in Oceans Café when he heard Becky's announcement. What was she doing? Putting him out there as bait for the single women? He slowly scanned the room and he was thankful that no one was intently staring at him; he was still an unknown. *Whew.*

"Following lunch, there's plenty of time for sunbathing or just relaxing by the pool as the Party Band plays your favorite oldies. Then there's Bingo at 2:45 in the theater, followed by Fernando Moretti again in the theater at four o'clock to give you the highlights of tomorrow's port, Civitavecchia, Italy." Becky's enchanting voice made every activity sound as if it were the most important one of all.

"Just two more items and then I'll let you get about your day. Tonight is our first formal night, and our ship's photographers will be roaming the decks, inside and out, to snap those fantastic shots that you'll want to take home as part of your special memories of this voyage. And then after dinner, at nine o'clock in the Royal Theatre, get there early for world famous hypnotist Olivia Cromwell. Her show is every bit of amazing and fun to experience. Since it's a formal night, you'll be offered a glass of wine or champagne as you enter the theater. But be careful, you might end up doing things that you wouldn't ordinarily do, and you might be left to wonder—was it the wine or the hypnotist?" Becky cut it off at that; after all, it was only eight in the morning.

12

Saturday, July 13

10:30 AM

The music was blaring away as Fernando Moretti entered the Royal Theatre on Deck Four. Zumba was still going on as people in all sorts of exercise outfits were moving and dancing while trying to do what the leader was doing on the stage. There were about fifty people there, with dozens more in the aisles. Fernando saw that there wasn't an open way for him to get to the stage, so he just sat down in an aisle seat in the last row.

He looked at his watch; two minutes past ten, so the Zumba class should have already ended. He noticed that the pace of the music and the corresponding exercise movements were beginning to slow down. That was a good sign; it meant that the energetic leader was nearing the end of her session. From previous cruises, Fernando knew that the music was choreographed and timed to last about fifty minutes, so the session must have been a little late in getting started. He hoped it wouldn't happen again; he liked to be set up and able to chat with the guests for at least fifteen minutes ahead of his scheduled starting time.

"Thank you so much, ladies and gentlemen; you were awesome," the lithesome Zumba instructor cheered on her class as the music stopped.

Fernando was working his way down the aisle toward the stage. "Good morning," he said with that charming smile of his as he passed all the women and a few men who were working their way up the aisle. He didn't expect many of them to stay for his talk. Some would, but experience told him that most would go back to their cabins for a shower that had been well-earned.

"I'm sorry I can't stay for your lecture," an attractive forty-something lady said as she smiled at Fernando.

"I understand," he responded. "Fortunately, you can catch a replay of it on channel nine in your room starting at eleven thirty this morning."

"Oh, really?" one of the men asked. "Is it only on at eleven thirty?"

"No," Fernando answered. "It plays continuously until my next talk is recorded and played. So you can watch it at any time."

"What channel was that?" asked someone else.

"Just a moment," Fernando said as he headed over to the Zumba instructor who'd just removed her microphone headset. "May I use that for a quick announcement?" he asked her as he pointed to her microphone.

"Sure," she replied handing it to him. "Sorry about running late this morning; I had to do my own set up since the stage manager didn't show up to help me."

"That's okay," Fernando offered as he held the microphone up to his mouth. "For you folks who can't stay this morning, my talk on *Coastal Life in the Mediterranean* will be replayed on channel nine in your cabins starting in a little over an hour, and it will play continuously until my next talk. You're all welcome to stay if you wish, but don't forget to look at channel nine. And what about your Zumba instructor; isn't she amazing?"

Most of the departing exercisers gave her a modest ovation as Fernando handed the microphone back to her. "Thanks," he said.

Knowing where the podium was kept offstage, Fernando stepped behind the curtain to get it. For obvious reasons, the podium didn't have wheels, so he had to gently maneuver it out to the stage to avoid marring the floor. He had just placed it on the four L-shaped taped areas when a few people started filing into the theater. "Hi; good morning," Fernando said as he looked up to acknowledge them.

One person kept walking toward the stage; Fernando noticed that he had a ship's nametag on his shirt. As the fellow got closer, Fernando looked up again and was able to read the tag: Scott Eaton, Stage Manager. "Mr. Moretti. Hi, I'm Scott Eaton, your stage manager. Sorry I'm a bit late this morning; too much party band last night. You've been on here before, haven't you?"

"Hi, Scott. Yes, I was here with you about six months ago," Fernando answered as he extended his hand to shake Scott's. The bloodshot eyes confirmed Scott's own admission.

"I thought I recognized you, although my eyes aren't functioning too well right now. I'll go back to the booth to get the screen set up for you and to test your sound. Are you okay with the wires and the plugs?"

"I've got it covered, Scott. Let me just open my file and get into presentation mode and we'll be ready for the audio and the video checks."

"Gotcha," Scott replied as he wandered back up the aisle.

Fernando Moretti had his doubts whether or not this talk would actually get recorded today. *Oh, well. That will be the cruise director's problem, not mine.*

Everything checked out fine; Fernando was pleased to see people coming into the theater and almost filling it to capacity. His talks were typically standing room only affairs, except for the first one on each cruise. But once people saw and heard him, whether in the theater or on channel nine, they would then show up anywhere from fifteen to thirty minutes early to sit up front as he gave another informative, entertaining and educational presentation. He was good.

He looked at his watch; ten twenty-eight. Just then he saw Becky. Heads turned to follow her as she made her way to the front; she was definitely attractive. Fernando switched off his microphone as he stepped away from the podium. "Good morning, Becky."

"You ready to do this again, Fernando?" she replied as she smiled and shook his hand.

"Let's get it going," he replied.

The cruise director brought the hand-held microphone up to her mouth. She scanned the almost-full theater, then began, "I can see that some of you have already heard how fantastic his talks are, and here on the *Royal Holiday*, we are so pleased to have Mr. Fernando Moretti back with us again. So please give a very warm welcome to the gentleman who'll be up here on stage quite often with presentations that you will not want to miss. Born in Italy, he knows the Mediterranean region so well; he is Mr. Fernando Moretti."

13

Saturday, July 13

Just Past Noon

The beautiful weather and calm sea were a magnetic combination. Every lounge chair around the pool was occupied and not just with an empty towel. An impromptu volleyball game was underway in the shallow pool. One person was swimming laps in the "No Games Allowed" pool. There were going to be plenty of sun burns today as the rays of the sun were coming down in full force and more sun bathers were applying tanning oil rather than sun block.

Even though the Grand Dining Room was open for lunch, as it was on every sea day, only a few people were down there on Deck Four. Oceans Café was quite busy as was the Pool Bar and Grille. The Grille's specialty was an Angus beef hamburger with all the trimmings; there were also salads, veggie burgers and cold cuts for those who wanted to create their own sandwich. It was a perfect day for having beer with an outdoor lunch. The waiters were filling drink orders as quickly as they could.

One particular couple was drinking sparkling water as they sat at a small table next to a crystal clear floor-to-ceiling window. She was eating a salad as he enjoyed the delicious hamburger, minus the bun. "What are your plans for the afternoon, dear?" he asked.

"I'll probably go play Bingo," she replied. "And you?"

"I haven't had an opportunity to visit the library yet, so I think I'll check out their selection." He was a maritime buff and he liked reading about old sailing fleets, especially the tall-masted schooners. "Are you having your hair done for tonight?"

"Yes; I was lucky to get their last appointment at four o'clock, so I hope Bingo doesn't run late."

"You can leave early; the jackpots aren't that big anyway."

"Yes, dear," she said.

"Bingo at two thirty in the theater. Get there a little early to buy your cards," a voice announced just as the band stopped playing. "Bingo at two thirty in the theater," came the repeat announcement. It was Larry Allen, the assistant cruise director who was outfitted in crisp white pants and a navy blue polo shirt.

"How much are the cards," a lady asked as Larry was walking by.

"Two for ten dollars; five for twenty," Larry replied. "Will we see you two there?"

"Just me," she said. "Will it be very crowded?"

"We typically have about forty players, but today is such a beautiful day that we'll be lucky to have half that many." The patient young man smiled as he waited to see if she had any other questions.

"Thanks," she said as she turned her head back to look at her husband.

"Bingo at two thirty in the theater. Get there a little early to buy your cards," Larry called out as he left their table and continued through the Grille area.

14

That Afternoon

2:30 PM

Larry was wrong. Instead of forty players, or twenty, there were about seventy people inside the theater. Most of them were buying cards; a few men were there just because they always went where the wives went. "We're starting in five minutes, so get your cards now," Larry said, the sound echoing throughout the theater. He looked back to the sound booth and pointed to his ear piece.

"Try it now," said the person in the booth, his voice was crisp and clear through the speakers.

"Testing, testing," Larry said. "Is this sounding better?"

"Yes," was the reply from many of the Bingo players.

Larry gave a thumbs-up signal back to the sound technician. The computer screen came to life and it was relayed to the theater's screen for all to see. The computerized game was easier for the staff, plus they didn't have to worry about losing any Bingo balls.

15

Later That Afternoon
4:00 PM

First it was Zumba; now it was Bingo that was running late. Fernando Moretti had spoken on many cruise ships with several different lines; it seemed the activities before his presentations always ran late. He was punctual and was done and out of the theater in his allotted hour, but he knew there was nothing he could say when it was a crew member whose activity encroached on his time.

The theater was always a busy place. In addition to the presentations, exercise classes, Bingo games and other demands on the valuable property, there had to be time for closed-door rehearsals for the shows and musical performances. Most of the Bingo players were in the center section, and, unlike the Zumba class, no one was in the aisle. Fernando calmly walked down the stage right aisle and sat in a front-row seat next to one of the crew members who was assisting Larry. "Hi," he whispered to her as she smiled at him.

"He's always late," she said. "He likes to see the old ladies win, so he keeps going as long as he can."

Fernando turned around to look at the crowd; he wouldn't call them 'old ladies' but he wasn't seeing them from the vantage of a twenty-something. He pulled up his left sleeve to look at his watch; three forty.

"Okay, folks. We're running a little late today," the Bingo caller announced, "so we're going to draw seven more numbers and hopefully one of you lucky people will have completed both diagonals." It took only three more numbers when

"Bingo" was hollered by a man who was looking at his wife's card.

"Yea," Fernando said quietly to himself as the young assistant went to check out the winning card. The numbers matched so the lucky couple left with a seventy-five dollar certificate good in any of the shops on board.

Larry shut down the game and began to disconnect the laptop from the podium cables. Fernando took that as his signal to begin his process of getting ready. About two dozen people had already entered the theater to hear his lecture on the next day's port in Civitavecchia, Italy. Only one Bingo couple stayed; that was typical.

"What channel did you say your talks are on?" asked one man.

"The one from this morning, a destination presentation, is on channel nine. It will play continuously until my next one, which is on our next sea day. This afternoon's talk is called a port lecture, and it will be on channel ten."

"What's the difference?" another man asked.

"Were you here for this morning's talk?" Fernando asked. "It was about the arts, history and culture of the general area. Thus, my talk this morning was called, *Coastal Life in the Mediterranean,* and it was about the general area. This afternoon's talk is about the specific port we're going to tomorrow. It's about Civitavecchia, the port layout, where the good shops are, how to get around town, et cetera. I'll explain a little more when I get started. Okay?"

Fernando returned his attention to the computer, opening the Port-1-Civitavecchia file and selecting presentation mode. The cover slide was now showing on the theater screen. "Hi," he said to a couple in the front row of the center section. They'd sat in the same seats during the morning talk and an open notebook indicated they were serious travelers who were going to take notes from the expert speaker.

Fernando scanned the room; it was roughly eighty to eighty-five percent full. It would be full come the four o'clock starting time. Five minutes later, and with only five minutes to go, he saw Becky chatting with a couple as she was heading down the aisle to the stage. He greeted a few more couples before she reached the stage.

"Plans for tomorrow?" she asked.

"I'll probably take the train up to Pisa," he answered. "A colleague is doing some research there; we're going to get together for lunch." He didn't ask if she had any plans; it was just another work day for the crew.

The stage lights flashed. Becky flipped on the microphone and stepped to the front of the stage. "You're in for a real treat this afternoon, ladies and gentlemen. Mr. Fernando Moretti will be giving you all the details about tomorrow's port, and he will be giving a similar talk about each of our ports on the day before we arrive. Once again, here is Mr. Fernando Moretti." Becky smiled at him as she walked back up the aisle. It was hard to tell how much of the applause was for him and how much of it was for her. He was a professional so he didn't gauge his success by accolades or standing ovations. He was here to do a job, and he always did it very well.

"Thank you all very much. And let's hear it for the best cruise director at sea, Miss Becky Anderson." The applause was polite, but it could have been louder. Becky turned around and threw Fernando a kiss; he smiled.

"It's great to see all of you here in the Royal Theatre for the first of my port lectures. How many of you have been to Civitavecchia before?"

Over half the audience raised their hands, which wasn't too surprising. Civitavecchia was one the standard ports on most Mediterranean cruises. "Now," Fernando continued, "how many of you actually thought that we'd be docking in Rome just because the itinerary says Rome?"

Laughter was a solid response, although there were a few people who sheepishly raised their hands. "The Tiber River used to be a navigable route in from the Tyrrhenian Sea to Rome, but over the centuries it kept getting clogged by sediment flowing down from the mountains. There are trains to Rome, and that's just one of the details I'll be giving you in the next forty-five minutes. And don't worry if you didn't bring pen and paper with you.

"Civitavecchia is an easy town to get around, whether you're taking a train or just out for a stroll. You can't miss the train tracks as you head out from the ship, and you'll want to turn right before you cross them. The marked walkway will take you to the train station in about fifteen minutes. You'll pass plenty of little cafés on your way as well as some souvenir shops. It's a safe town, but always be mindful of your possessions and especially if someone is getting too friendly with you; that could be a setup for pick pockets or scam artists."

Fernando clicked through the slides and told the audience where they could find free wi-fi, where the best shops were for good bargains, and how to find his favorite espresso stand. The time went by quickly; he had enough material that he could have continued talking for another thirty minutes.

"Remember that all-aboard time tomorrow is at five thirty and you don't want to be late. The last I checked, the trains weren't running between here and Sicily. Thanks for your attention, and have a wonderful evening tonight and a great day tomorrow in Civitavecchia." Fernando began shutting down his computer even as the full theater gave him a very warm round of applause. He was a seasoned veteran speaker, but giving two talks in a day did take a lot out of him, and he wanted to get some rest before tonight's formal evening.

"Would you recommend taking the train to Rome and then walking around on our own?" a young couple asked as they came up to the stage.

"I wouldn't recommend it," Fernando replied, "unless you've been to Rome before. Roma Centrale is a big station; it can be very confusing if you're not used to it."

"We've got our guide book with us; I think we'll be okay," the young man said.

"Have a good time," Fernando said as he thought to himself, *Then why did you ask me?*

A crowd of people waited for Fernando at the top of aisle. So much for that rest that he was wanting.

16

Saturday, July 13

6:30 PM

Not everyone was a fan of formal night. While not full, Oceans Café had a fair amount of customers for tonight's dinner. The sushi was popular as was the carved roast beef and horseradish sauce. But in keeping with the evening's theme, all the servers in the café were in formal outfits, even though many of the guests were in casual pants and tops.

Many of the seasoned travelers brought their own formal wear or had arranged to rent it on the ship. With many men dressed in classy tuxedos and women in formal gowns and jewelry; it was a perfect combination for professional photographs. Photographers were set up in strategic locations: the main staircase, in the photo lounge itself, and, of course, in the Grand Dining Room. Some of the first-time cruisers definitely wanted their picture taken, while an equal number didn't. But those who'd been on several cruises realized it was easier to just let them take the pictures; they knew they didn't have to buy them.

Wine was flowing again tonight, even though the first glass wasn't free. It was a festive evening with the occasional champagne cork popping to add an exclamation mark to the good times that were being enjoyed. The choices on the menu were all delicious; the hard part was choosing which delectable item to have.

No one wanted to leave; the entire dining experience had been magnificent, but it had taken two hours and most wanted to go to the show that was starting at nine.

"What a perfect evening," one diner said.

"And an absolutely perfect cruise," replied another.

17

Friday, July 12

9:00 PM

As promised, the tuxedoed waiters were once again serving chilled wine and champagne as the well-dressed guests entered the theater. Those who opted to stay casual were denied entrance to the theater as well as the other public areas, except for Oceans Café where they were welcome to eat and drink. But tonight's attire was formal and in keeping with the rich tradition of ocean cruising, formal attire (or at least quite dressy) was required around the ship to maintain the atmosphere.

Those who thought they could arrive a few minutes early and find a seat were wrong; every seat was occupied by ten minutes to nine. Becky was handed a full champagne glass as she entered the theater. A couple who couldn't find a seat stopped her. "There are no more seats; what are we supposed to do?" As if it were Becky's fault that they didn't get there early enough.

"Just wait around; I'm sure someone will leave. Not everyone is a hypnotist fan," Becky said politely and then continued down to the stage.

"Well," the woman huffed as she gulped down champagne.

Becky mingled with friendlier folks near the stage area. She recognized one couple from a previous cruise and she went to chat with them. The stage lights flashed off and on signaling Becky that it was time to start. She stepped up on the stage, held up her still-full champagne glass and spoke into the microphone. "Good evening!" she exclaimed.

"Good evening, Becky," was the reply.

"Well, I hope you had a great meal tonight, right?"

The crowd responded again, just as they'd been led.

"For those who still have a bit of champagne or wine left, or even just an empty glass; raise them up and we'll all say *Salud* together. Ready? One, two, three."

"Salud!" was the synchronous response.

Becky raised the glass to her lips and took a small sip. "I can see you're ready for another great show. Did you enjoy last night's *Spotlight on Broadway*? Weren't those singers and dancers simply awesome? Well, you'll have a chance to see them again in a few more nights. But tonight…"

A backstage drumroll began.

"As I was saying," Becky tried again. "Tonight…"

The drumroll again cut her off; the audience thought it was funny. It was all a planned act, of course.

She raised the microphone to her mouth and silently lipped the word, "Tonight." No drumroll. She smiled.

"From standing room only crowds in London, including an audience with the Queen, the hypnotist who's wowed them all around the world; let's hear it for Olivia Cromwell."

The curtain opened as Olivia walked out on stage, curtsied to Becky and grabbed the champagne glass from her. Laughter ensued. Olivia then tipped the glass up and downed it completely. A shocked look came across her face. "Sparkling apple juice?" More laughter.

"I told you I don't drink anything stronger than soda," Becky replied.

The crowd laughed as Becky strolled up the aisle to exit the theater. The stage now belonged to Olivia Cromwell and to those fateful souls that would come under her spell. Actually, they didn't even have to come on stage for Olivia to hypnotize them; she usually reserved that "special treat" for the hecklers or naysayers who stayed put in their seats.

She had people doing all sorts of crazy things, from crowing like a chicken to singing opera. She had one man singing Frank Sinatra and making over a woman, but she had to quickly pull him out as his actions were moving beyond the edgy to the risqué. The man was shocked when he was brought out of the trance; he'd never seen that woman before and he looked around for his wife. She was laughing along with the rest of the audience.

"Not a bad Frank Sinatra imitation; what do you think?" Olivia asked the crowd. They agreed with her.

The hour went by quickly as Olivia was as adept at her craft as she was on managing the performance and keeping everyone entertained. Everyone except that cranky couple who never found an empty seat. That's show business.

18

Sunday, July 14

8:00 AM

"Good morning, ladies and gentlemen," began the cruise director's cheerful voice. Welcome to our first port of call: Civitavecchia, Italy. Even though we're in port, there are plenty of activities taking place both on and off the ship, so you're encouraged to read your daily paper and carry it with you at all times. The captain has informed me that we're securely tied up at the pier and that we've been cleared for entry by the local authorities.

"If you are going ashore today, you won't need your passport, so you can leave it securely in your room safe. Today is Sunday, which means that some of the shops won't be open until a little later in the day. For those of you with tickets for a ship excursion, look at the ticket for the time you are to be at the Royal Theatre for further instructions. You will need to get a sticker before you go ashore. And that's the same whether you're on a coach excursion or a walking tour. The Shore Excursion staff in the theater will be able to answer any questions you have.

"For those going ashore on your own, proceed to the Central Lobby on Deck Three with your room key along with a map or other papers you want to take with you. Make sure to grab a bottle of water near the check-out area there on Deck Three. The water's free and we want you to stay hydrated today as it's expected to get quite warm. All-aboard time is five thirty. That means that if you're not checked back in by that time, you're on your own to get to our next stop, which is

Messina in Sicily. It's been a long time since we've lost anyone and the captain really doesn't like all that paperwork he has to fill out. So try to make it back here on time. Okay?"

Oceans Café was extremely busy this morning even though the Grand Dining Room was open for a Sunday buffet. The passengers with early excursions wouldn't have enough time to thoroughly enjoy the fancy spread down on Deck Four. There were a few open tables but all the ones next to the windows were taken.

19

Sunday, July 14

8:30 AM

People were leaving Oceans Café and standing at the aft bank of elevators. The electric lifts were running slower this morning, or more accurately, more people were using them to go to the theater or to Deck Three to leave the ship. "Let's just take the stairs," a few passengers said after realizing it was going to be a long wait for the elevator.

Once on Deck Four, passengers who'd come down the aft stairs or elevators had to walk through the shops to get to the theater. Many a husband was heard facetiously saying, "Too bad the shops are closed, dear." The seasoned travelers knew that the tax- and duty-free shops were required to be closed when a ship was in port.

"Only one person needs to take all the tickets down to the stage to get your stickers." The assistant cruise director was standing at the entrance to the Royal Theatre and repeating his instructions as more groups arrived. "Make sure you take all the tickets for your entire group or you might not end up on the same bus. It's early in the cruise, so you're probably all still friends."

"A couple of reminders," the excursion staff member continued. "You must have your room key to leave the ship and we strongly recommend that you stay here in the theater once you get your sticker because the tour might leave without you if you've left the area."

20

Sunday, July 14

9:15 AM

As the last of group one left the theater, the excursion manager announced, "Now it's time for bus number two, and here's your escort for today. She's one of the ships dancers, so you're going to have to walk fast to keep pace with her." As the dancer walked up the aisle with her escort paddle in the air, more heads turned than just the guests on that tour. As members of that tour got up, John and Mary Saxton got in line.

"I guess we missed her in the show the other night," Robert Arnold, in line right behind the Saxtons, said to James Burton.

"We were at that private party instead of going to the show," James said. "We'll have to find out when they're dancing again," he continued.

"No doubt," Robert replied.

John Saxton smiled; he was glad he wasn't that young any more. She was cute though, not that he was really paying any attention.

As they reached the Central Lobby, the dancer stopped and waited for everyone in her tour to be able to hear her. "Everyone grab a bottle of water; it's going to be warm today, and I don't want you to be dehydrated by the time we get to the winery, or it will really hit you hard. Each one of you has to have your own room key out for security, so husbands go ahead and give your wife her key. I'm sure she won't lose it."

The women in the group laughed as did Robert and James. Most of the men didn't find it funny, but it wasn't meant to be funny. Yes it was.

"Is this group two?" a panting Gary Marsing asked as he reached the group. He'd forgotten his room key and just ran back from his cabin with it.

John Saxton turned around and sneered at seeing Gary again.

Robert looked at Gary and said, "You're cool, man. This is it, the 'Countryside Tour and Wine Tasting' group. You okay?"

"I think so; I forgot my room key, and then I couldn't find it in the room. I was sure I was going to miss the tour. My name's Gary," he said as he extended his hand.

"Robert, and this is James."

"Nice to meet you guys. Where do you live?"

"New York City; and you?"

"Las Vegas," Gary replied.

"Room key, please," the security officer said as Gary approached the exit.

21

Sunday, July 14

Afternoon

The tour of the countryside area away from the Italian port of Civitavecchia, and the enormous castle on the hill were quite interesting, but it was a warm day and it was time for lunch. Overlooking the lake's edge, John Saxton waited until Gary, Robert, and James selected a table before he guided Mary to the opposite side of the area reserved for their tour. Gary was oblivious to the actions John was taking; he was enjoying listening to the stories the other guys were telling about living in the Big Apple.

After lunch, which included free beer and house wine, the tour group was to meet at the bus. Outside the bus, the tour guide scanned the area, but didn't see anyone else who was heading toward the bus. "Count?" she asked.

It was soon determined that Gary was missing. "I'll go look for him," the escort said.

"Okay, but just to the restaurant area," the guide said.

The passengers waited impatiently until their dancer escort came back alone. After some phone calls made at the front of the bus, they started off toward LRV Winery, short one man.

22

Sunday, July 14

5:10 PM

Bus tour number two returned to the dock with a bus full of very happy passengers. The wine tasting at LRV Winery turned out to be more drinking than tasting as there was an unlimited amount available to each guest. The food was pretty good too, although most were still quite full from the great lunch. The Shore Excursion manager was there to meet the bus as it arrived, and both the tour guide and escort gave their reports on how Gary Marsing just disappeared while at lunch. A few of the passengers needed help climbing the gangway's sixty-four steps up to the Central Lobby where they presented their room key to check back aboard the ship. Taking a nap seemed like a good idea for most of them. Thoughts of the missing man had left their minds.

A taxi pulled up to the dock and a disheveled passenger got out of the back seat. He paid the driver and then headed toward the ship. His right shirt sleeve was torn; his hair looked like he'd applied super gel and then ran a mixer through it; his hands were scraped and he had scratches on his face. The taxi driver had been kind enough to stop at a pharmacy shop and got some bandages for him. Gary Marsing looked as if he'd picked the wrong pack of wild animals to get rough with.

A port security guard, thinking that Gary was a panhandler, blocked him as he started to walk up the gangway. "I'm a passenger on this ship," Gary managed to say as he reached for his room key in his front left pocket.

"Let me help you, sir," the guard said as he saw the room key.

The walk to the top of the gangway was difficult for Gary, and he'd not even been to the winery to enjoy all the free wine as had the rest of his tour group. He handed his key to the security officer who inserted it into the machine and a loud audible tone sounded. "He's the one who was reported missing from the tour," one of the security officers said. "Sir, let me take you to Guest Relations right away."

"Why?" Gary asked. "I didn't do anything wrong," he insisted.

John and Mary Saxon were walking across the Central Lobby when Gary was taken past them. "That's the fellow who was missing from our tour. Looks like he got into quite a fight," Mary said.

"It sure does," replied her husband as they kept walking.

23

Sunday, July 14

5:45 PM

"Ladies and gentlemen, may I have your attention, please," the voice over the Public Address system announced in a stern, yet professional, voice. Happy Hour was still underway in most of the ship's bars, and there was considerable chatter going on. The main Dining Room had not yet opened, although there was a line beginning to form at its Deck Four entrance. Most passengers had gone ashore on an excursion in Civitavecchia, or spent some time in the small port town. The railway station, a fifteen-minute walk from port, was a jumping off point for some seasoned cruisers who had other destinations in mind for the day.

All-aboard time for the passengers was at 5:30, and so everyone was back on board the *Royal Holiday* as it was ready to set sail for its next port of call in Messina, on the isle of Sicily. At least, everyone was supposed to be on board by now.

"Once again, ladies and gentlemen, may I have your attention please," the PA voice said. "Will Mr. Tyler Jacobs in stateroom 7043 please contact Guest Relations on Deck Three immediately." The grammar was technically that of a question, but it was really more of a command. "Again, Mr. Tyler Jacobs in stateroom 7043, please contact Guest Relations on Deck Three immediately."

A first-time cruiser in the Martini Lounge turned to her husband, and asked in her slightly slurred voice, "Why are they paging him? Why don't they just go to his cabin?"

"It probably means that his room key didn't register properly when he came back on board. They're required to account for every passenger who leaves the ship, and so they have to make sure they also come back on board."

"Oh," she said as she took another sip of her pink lady cocktail and then smiled at the bartender. "I think I found a new favorite drink, honey. What time's dinner?"

24

Sunday, July 14

6:15 PM

The ship had been pushed away from the dock and was maneuvering out to sea. Many passengers were on the top decks enjoying their last view of Civitavecchia. Gary Marsing was in the infirmary being checked out by the medical staff; he had some physical injuries, but those didn't explain everything.

Chimes sounded to indicate an announcement over the PA system. "Ladies and gentlemen," it began. "This is your captain, Konstantinos Christopolous, speaking to you from the Navigational Bridge. I hope that you enjoyed your stay in the lovely port of Civitavecchia, Italy. Tonight we will sail slowly across the Tyrrhenian Sea to the port of Messina on the island of Sicily. Sicily is home to the famous Mt. Aetna volcano as well as many other delightful sights. We should be alongside the dock at nine o'clock in the morning and you should be able to go ashore by nine fifteen. I hope that you're enjoying your cruise on the beautiful *Royal Holiday*, and now I'd like to turn it over to your cruise director, Becky."

"Well, thank you very much Captain Christopolous. Ladies and gentlemen, the captain has told me we should have very smooth sailing tonight as the seas are calm and the winds are very light. As always, we have great entertainment all around the ship tonight." At that point, most people stopped listening as they knew that she was going to mention the show in the theater and the late night entertainment in the Sky View Lounge.

The starboard side of the ship's upper decks was filled as people were watching the sun sink toward the edge of the Mediterranean Sea. It was as if the sun were doing a disappearing act; it would go into hiding in the west and then resurface twelve hours later in the east. A few people looked at their watches and realized it was time to head to the dining room.

"One thing about these cruises," one lady commented, "is that you're never going to go hungry."

"Not unless you disappear for a week at a time," another replied. The two ladies enjoyed a laugh as they headed toward the elevators.

25

Sunday, July 14

6:45 PM

"I'm sorry, Miss Cromwell, but I don't have any available spots in that area of the dining room." Lead hostess Adriana was trying to accommodate Olivia Cromwell, but her requests were outrageous.

"Do you know who I am?" the hypnotist asked in an unbecomingly loud voice.

"Yes, ma'am, I do, and I will do whatever I can for you even if you weren't one of our entertainers. But I just can't tell passengers that they have to move to a different table." The cruise had not gotten off to a great start for Adriana. She suffered through the first-night chaos of the computer system reassigning people to different tables. And now she had this demanding entertainer. "Let me call the restaurant manager for you, Miss Cromwell," she said as she took a mobile phone from her jacket pocket and punched in a few numbers. "I have Miss Olivia Cromwell who is requesting me to make changes to seating assignments that I don't feel I can do. Will you please come up here?" She closed the phone, and turned to tell the hypnotist that the restaurant manager was on his way, but she was gone.

The manger arrived. "She was here when I called you, and then she was gone after I was done talking with you."

"What did she want?" he asked.

Adriana gave him the details.

"Wow," he responded. "Perhaps she's taken one too many of her own potions."

That caused Adriana to laugh, the first time she'd done that on this cruise.

"I'll go look to see if I can find her," the manager said as he turned toward the tables. "You did the right thing to call me, even if she disappeared before I got here." He walked through the dining room with a broad smile, greeting people here and there as if he were just casually making the rounds. Convinced she wasn't there, he headed back to the entrance. "She's not in there," he told Adriana. "I'll talk to Becky and ask her to get to the bottom of this. She comes under entertainment, and that's Becky's area. Don't you worry about it." The manager smiled as he headed toward the cruise director's office.

26

Sunday, July 14

Later That Evening

"No; playing Craps doesn't interest me that much. Sure you can play the odds and make some money that way, but you really have no control once the dice are thrown. At least in Black Jack I can apply some skill in my play; not that it works all the time." Well-dressed in a handsome sport coat, shirt, and slacks, John Phillips looked like a Ben Affleck in his late 40s. He had a beautiful head of hair and a neatly trimmed mustache; he looked as if he had just stepped out of a leading role in a Hollywood blockbuster film of years gone by.

"Dealer busts; players win," the casino dealer announced as he turned over a seven to go with the nine and six that were already showing.

"Thank you," Phillips said as he slid a red five dollar chip to the dealer.

"Thank you for the tip, sir," the dealer said.

"Thank you for the great cards," Phillips responded. "Cocktail, please?"

"Certainly, sir," the dealer said as he raised his right hand in the air and clicked his fingers twice. His eyes never left the table and his left hand firmly held the single deck of cards.

Sitting in his preferred third-base position, the players' last spot before the dealer, John Phillips was enjoying the evening. He was doing well at the table; there were other friendly (and good) players also at the table, and he'd had a great day in Civitavecchia. The stacks of green and black chips in front of him got everyone's attention as they walked by the only single deck table in the small casino. Single deck Black Jack typically has better odds for the player, thus the table minimum was set at $25, with a maximum wager of $2,000.

"Another gin and tonic, Mr. Phillips?" the attractive server asked as she approached from the players' side of the table.

"Yes, thank you," he replied as he looked into her eyes and smiled. He held out his room key for her.

She couldn't help but return the infectious smile. "That's 7053, right?"

"I'm glad you have it memorized," Phillips said in a teasing tone that made her blush.

"Cocktails for anyone else at the table?" she asked as she scanned the other players. There were no other takers so she turned and walked to the bar with the silver tray neatly balanced on an upturned left hand.

The man to Phillips' right turned to John and said, "You certainly made her blush."

"Just teasing," Phillips replied. "All the cruise lines have a no fraternization policy and besides, I'm too old for her." As the dealer put the cards in front of the four players, John remarked to his neighbor, "All right; you got a Black Jack. Good job!"

As the dealer placed the winnings, $37.50, next to the player's single green chip, the player said, "I wish I'd kept that other stack out there."

"I never complain about any winnings," Phillips said. "Those cards could have just as easily gone to the dealer and you would've lost that stack. Look at mine, fifteen. Not much to do with them but let the dealer bust."

The dealer turned over his hole card, another seven to go with the face-up seven.

"No trips," Phillips said, indicating that he didn't want the dealer to turn up a third seven for a total of twenty-one with triple sevens. A black ten made the dealer's total twenty-four.

"Dealer busts; players win," the dealer announced as he paid the two players who still had cards on the table. Two black chips were placed next to Phillips' $200 bet and John pushed another red chip to the dealer.

"Thank you, Mr. Phillips," the dealer dutifully said.

"You're welcome; change please," John replied as he slid a green chip toward the dealer. The dealer pulled five red chips from his tray and placed them on the table as he placed the green chip in the tray.

"Your gin and tonic, Mr. Phillips," the cocktail server said as she approached the table from his left side. "Bombay Sapphire as you prefer, sir," she added with a professional smile as she placed the drink in the metal holder near his left arm." She put the two receipts in front of him.

"Thank you, dear," he said as he took the top chip off the new stack of reds and placed it on her tray. He then signed the top copy and put it and the pen also on her tray.

The server was about to leave the table when John said, "Wait a second, please. My treat for you gents at the table since the table's been quite generous to me." He looked up at her and said, "Anything they want; my tab."

"Certainly, Mr. Phillips," she replied she went to the other three players who were now quite willing to have a drink since John Phillips was paying for it.

The dealer shuffled the cards, slid the red plastic cut card part way into the deck, and then offered the cards to John to cut. As he placed the cut card near the top of the deck, he said, "Thin to win." The dealer cut the cards, placed the top card face down in the discard area and then waited to deal until each of the players had ordered their free drink.

"Thanks, pal," said the player at the opposite end from John, who nodded his head as the other players also thanked him.

"Bets, please," the dealer said as he stood and waited patiently for the players.

Most casinos have a standard of how fast they want the dealers to deal; after all, the house does have the advantage, so the more hands that are dealt, the more the casino wins in the long run. The casino manager on the *Royal Holiday* preferred a *guests first* policy; he'd rather the players feel comfortable rather than rushed. The casino still turned a significant profit, plus the passenger reviews were among the highest in the industry for onboard casinos.

John Phillips signed the bill for the drinks and he gave her a green chip for her tip this time.

"Thank you very much, Mr. Phillips. And here's a glass of champagne for you, compliments of our manager," the server said as she placed the flute next to his gin and tonic.

"Thanks," John said as he raised the champagne glass and looked over to the casino manager and nodded his head in appreciation for the kind gesture. He didn't really like to mix the bubbly champagne with the gin and tonic, but he wanted to show his appreciation and drank it.

Player number two was the first to leave the table, followed shortly by the player in first position. As the player to John's right announced he was leaving since he had no more chips, John also headed off for the evening. It had been a good night for John.

27

Sunday, July 14

Earlier That Evening

The three men walked down the passageway; the cabin steward, the hotel director, and head of security, Clive Stewart. As they reached cabin 7043, Stewart said to the steward, "Go ahead," and the cabin steward knocked on the door several times. There was no answer. The steward looked at Clive who nodded his head. The cabin steward slid an electronic key into the door lock, the green light flashed, and he opened the door slightly.

"Mr. Jacobs; are you here?" the steward called out. No answer. "Mr. Jacobs?" he repeated. Same result, and so the cabin steward opened the door fully and entered the cabin while holding the door for the security manager and for his senior manager.

"Don't touch anything," said the head of security as the men looked around the room. Putting on a pair of latex-free gloves, Clive slowly opened the bathroom door, stepped inside and pulled the shower curtain to one side; nothing seemed amiss. He stepped back into the room and looked at the hotel director.

The director looked at the cabin steward who said, "It looks just like I left it this morning, except for when I came for the evening turndown and left tomorrow's paper and chocolates on the bed."

"Okay; you can go back to your regular duties," the hotel director said to the steward who turned around, opened the door and left cabin 7043 as fast as he felt he could and still keep his dignity. *At least they didn't find a dead body inside that I'd have to clean up after.*

Clive continued to look into drawers, under the bed, inside the closet; any place where there might be a note or some clue as to Tyler Jacobs' disappearance. As a former police detective, Clive Stewart knew that most people left behind some indication of their motive for going away, but this cabin was clean.

"What was he reading?" the hotel director asked as he pointed to a ship's library book on the nightstand.

With gloves still on, Clive went to the other side of the bed and picked up the book. "*Angels & Demons* by Dan Brown. He's the fellow who wrote *The DaVinci Code.*"

"Yeah; I've read them," responded the director. "How far did he get into the book?"

Clive Stewart fanned the pages but didn't see a bookmark or any other indication of where Jacobs stopped reading the book. "No telling." Stewart set the book back on the nightstand and pulled a mobile phone from his coat pocket. He pushed four digits, the number for accounting. "Hello, this is Clive Stewart; has there been any activity for cabin 7043 today?"

After a short pause, he said, "Okay, thanks," and closed the phone. He turned to the director. "His card has not been used on the ship today, at least not since he used it to exit this morning. I'll notify the captain that Mr. Jacobs is officially missing. I'll have this cabin secured so no one on your staff is to enter without my explicit permission. Is that okay with you?" The cabins were under the domain of the hotel director, but ship security was Clive Stewart's, so it was always a delicate situation when a cabin would have to be secured. But these men were professionals and they weren't worried about stepping on each other's toes.

"It's fine, Clive. I'll pass it along to the crew. I hope he just forgot what time it was and that there's nothing actually wrong with him."

"I'll take it from here if you want to head back," Clive said as he wanted to do just a little more looking around. As the director left the cabin, Clive made sure everything looked as it did when they'd entered ten minutes earlier. He went to the cabin door, but didn't open it. Instead he reached inside his coat pocket for a small camera the size of a shirt button. He slid the switch on the side of the camera, faced it toward him and spoke into the camera. "This is head of security, Clive Stewart. It's approximately 21:10 on Sunday, the fourteenth of July. This is being placed in cabin 7043."

He then removed the covering on the adhesive backing, reached up into the corner above the door, and pressed on the camera to secure it to the wall. *Now let's see who comes in here.*

28

Sunday, July 14

Nearing Midnight

The music in the Sky View Lounge on Deck Twelve was as lively and as energetic as those on the dance floor could take. A couple of the ship's dancers showed some good moves, but they were there more to motivate others to get up and dance than to show off. They were too professional for that.

Olivia Cromwell was conducting her own show at one of the large round tables where she would place a trance on an agreeing subject. One of the stipulations in her contract was that she would not put anyone in a hypnotic trance who wasn't aware of what she was doing, or if the person didn't want to be hypnotized. She'd been tempted at times to hypnotize certain people without their knowing it. But rules were rules.

The laughter at her table indicated that most people were enjoying her act. She had people doing imitations, singing along to the music, speaking in foreign languages and reciting classic poetry. She'd pull them out of the trance after a few minutes, even sooner if they'd been drinking.

At the other side of the lounge, Cyril was performing some magic tricks with cards. People always wanted to know how he did it, to which he would say, "It's magic." After all, if a magician gave away his secrets, then he wouldn't be able to attract a crowd. The one trick that always amazed everyone, even the most skeptical, logical person involved was having someone write their name on a card, and that card would somehow end up in that person's pocket. Cyril would shuffle all the cards, keeping them in plain sight all the time. But that signed two of clubs, or seven of hearts, or whatever they picked would show up in the person's pocket. One lady, sipping on a glass of white wine, was trying to figure out how the four aces ended up on the top of the four piles of cards, and she was the one who divided the cards into stacks and turned over the top cards. *It's magic.*

29

Monday, July 15

8:45 AM

"Good morning, and welcome to the theater," Shore Excursion manager Walter Peterson said as passengers began to assemble in the theater for the day's activities. "Come down to the stage on my left, your right, with your shore excursion tickets to get your bus sticker. We're a little ahead of schedule right now, so just go ahead and relax once you have your sticker. If there's a group of you and you want to be on the same bus, then bring all the tickets down at the same time. Otherwise you might end up being on different buses."

There was a small amount of laughter in the audience. "And it's still too early in the cruise for that; maybe later on," he added, to which there was more laughter.

"For those of you going to Mt. Etna, it's always windy and cool up on Silvestri Crater, so I'd suggest that you take a jacket along with you. And if you're going to be in Taormina this evening, the onshore breeze can also get cool as it whips between the buildings, so taking a jacket is also a good idea."

Some more passengers began to make their way into the theater so the manager began his pitch again. "Good morning, ladies and gentlemen. If you've just come into the theater..."

Peterson's instructions were being repeated by his staff members at the entrance to the theater, so most of the passengers knew what to do as they entered. They kept to the right and walked down the aisle to the stage to get their bus stickers. The process was going smoothly.

30

Monday, July 15

9:05 AM

"Good morning, ladies and gentlemen," the announcement began in the same way the captain began all his announcements. "This is your Captain, Konstantinos Christopolous, speaking to you from the Navigational Bridge. As you might have noticed, we had to slow down for some unexpected traffic as we were entering the channel this morning. That's why we're a few minutes late, but I don't think that should impact your activities here today. We are now securely docked here in Messina on the island of Sicily and we've been cleared by the local authorities so you may proceed ashore as you like."

"Thank you very much, Captain Christopolous. This is Becky, your cruise director, and we've been told that the weather here today in Messina is going to be absolutely beautiful. It might get a bit warm in the afternoon, but we suggest that you take a jacket with you if you're going out past six as the evening breezes can get a little cool. Remember that all-aboard time is at 8:30 and, as such, only the Grand Dining Room and Oceans Café will be open for dinner this evening."

In his office next to Guest Relations, head of security Clive Stewart checked the computer to see if there had been any sign of Tyler Jacobs; there hadn't been. He also scanned through the footage from the camera he'd placed in Jacobs' cabin; no one had been in there since he was there about twelve hours ago.

31

Monday, July 15

9:15 AM

The first few tour groups were being released in the theater with instructions to follow their escort to the Central Lobby, through the ship's exit and down the gangway to their buses. As one of the groups was going down the stairs, one person commented, "I wonder where Tyler was for dinner last night. Did he say anything to you about going to one of the specialty restaurants?"

"Nothing," her husband replied. "He might have felt that our table was too boring with three married couples, him and an empty chair. Maybe he moved to another table with younger people or some other singles."

"That's probably it," the wife responded as they continued toward the exit. "Get a water for me, too," she added.

"Yes, dear," the husband said as he picked up two bottles of water and put them into his backpack. This slowed the line as he then had to dig his room key out of his wallet.

The process of boarding the bus was smooth, partly because the ship booked a maximum of forty passengers on a bus that could hold fifty-five. Cruising with one of the smaller lines had its advantages—not being crowded on the tours was one of them.

Fernando Moretti waited at the end of the line and then introduced himself to the tour guide after everyone else had stepped up into the bus.

"You're not a crew member, are you?" the guide asked.

"No; I'm a speaker, but I've escorted quite a few times," Moretti replied. "So if there's anything in particular you want me to do, just let me know. Otherwise, I'll pretty much stay at the back of the line to keep them moving."

"*Grazie*," the guide said. "You won't have much to do until we get to Taormina, and even then, people are essentially on their own. So your job should be pretty easy today."

"I like that," Moretti said. "If we're set to go, I'll go up and introduce myself."

"Sure," the guide said as she saw her manager and went to hand over the forty-one tickets, forty for the guests plus one for the escort.

Fernando stepped into the bus and introduced himself in Italian to Luigi, the bus driver. After a brief chat, the two men shook hands and Fernando turned to face the seats. "Good morning, or *buongiorno*, to all of you. I'm going to be your escort on the tour today, and for those of you who haven't been to one of my talks, my name is Fernando Moretti.

"We have a great driver today; his name is Luigi, and he and I are *paisanos*, meaning that we're like brothers from the same village. So I know he's going to drive extra careful for us today. I've been on quite a few of these tours and I know that several of you are going to want to get that one extra picture taken, but that slows down the entire group. My job is to stay at the back and use this paddle if necessary to get you moving a little faster to catch up with the rest of the group." He raised the escort paddle as many of the passengers laughed.

"So the ones who didn't laugh are the picture takers, right? I'll keep a watch on you."

There was more laughter, except from a man with a camera and long lens strapped around his neck.

"It's going to be a long day as we visit Mt. Etna and then the tiny town of Taormina," Moretti continued, "so let's all get along and we'll all make it back to the ship just fine. Okay?"

"Okay," was the mostly unanimous response.

The tour guide climbed into the bus, saw the thumbs-up from Moretti and said something to Luigi. The tour was underway.

32

Monday, July 15

10:15 AM

All the early morning tours had departed, so while it appeared that there should be a brief lull in the activities for the shore excursion staff, they were busy counting the tickets and getting them posted to various accounts. The ship's theater was still needed for managing the departure of the remaining tours, so Zumba was being held in the Sky View Lounge. Bingo had to be played in the theater, so it was scheduled for two o'clock.

It was one of those rare times when the cruise director and her staff didn't have any obligations. Assistant cruise director Larry Allen had taken his laptop ashore to the port's crew lounge where he could access a free wi-fi connection. He wasn't the only crew member inside the lounge; it was packed with the galley stewards who didn't have to be back on duty until eleven. The cabin stewards were still busy with their morning chores, but most of them would show up shortly after they were done.

"Good morning, Becky," Walter Peterson said as the cruise director entered the office.

"Hey, Walter," Becky replied. "May I take a look at the tour listings for this afternoon?"

"Sure," the Shore Excursion manager replied as he handed her a clipboard with three sheets of paper, one for each of the afternoon's tours. "Did you want to go on one?"

"Maybe," Becky replied as one of the excursion staff looked up from his desk. "Larry's covering for me this afternoon, so I'm free until six." Becky looked at the listings that showed the names of the passengers who were booked on each of the tours. She looked at all the sheets then handed the clipboard back to Walter.

"Did you see one that interests you" he asked. "I could use an escort on the walking tour of Taormina. That one always gets spread out. You don't have to escort if you don't want; you could just go if you want."

Her lips turned up slightly. "Sure," Becky said. "I'll escort that one."

"Thanks," Walter said. "Maybe with you along, we can get everyone back on board today."

Becky looked concerned. "Have you heard anything more about the fellow who didn't make it back yesterday?"

"No," the manager said. "Apparently, security checked his cabin and there was nothing to indicate anything strange going on. Maybe he'll show up today, although I hate to think what that's going to cost him to get here from Civitavecchia."

"Well, I'll bring everyone back for you, Walter," Becky said as he handed her an escort ticket for the one o'clock tour.

"Thanks; I appreciate it. Have a good time and don't eat too much of the pizza or ice cream."

"Thanks, Walter," the cruise director said as she left the office.

33

Monday, July 15

2:00 PM

The short drive from the cruise port into the hillside town of Taormina was right after lunch. Even though it only took twenty-five minutes, most of the passengers feel asleep to the hum of the bus's engine. The tour guide was undeterred as she'd been doing this for years and it was always the same. Put a group of passengers on a bus right after eating, and they fall asleep. Along the way, she described the old town, the city walls and the ruins. She waited until the bus stopped in Taormina then she told everyone that they could either meet right there at six o'clock to go back to the ship or they could wait until eight o'clock. That meant they could either go back to the ship to eat or they could have dinner here in town.

As the thirty-three passengers got out of the bus, Becky stayed near the back of the group where she could keep an eye on all of them. No one was going missing while she was a tour escort.

The tour guide stopped and climbed up on a convenient pedestal. "Come closer," she said. After they all gathered around her in a semi-circle where her back was against the building, the guide continued. "This isn't a self-guided tour, so you're supposed to be following along with me. But if you do get separated from the group, and that's easy to do with all the little side streets and interesting shops, this is where we'll meet at five forty-five if you want to go back to the ship at six. Otherwise, be here at seven forty-five and you'll be on the last bus back to the ship. I won't be able to keep track of all of you, and neither will Becky as it's a holiday today. A lot of the locals are here for shopping and eating too. What time do we meet here?"

There were various responses; some of the passengers said five forty-five, others said seven forty-five, and it was clear that a few weren't even listening to the guide! *Why don't they just go on the Self-Guided Walk if they don't want to be a part of a group?*

The guide stepped off the pedestal, opened her bag and then handed each person a map of the town. She stepped back up, opened a map for herself and then gave a brief orientation of the area. Becky was listening to the guide and didn't notice when one couple turned and started off on their own.

"If you get disoriented, all you have to do is go into a shop, show them this map and ask for directions to the flag pole here. All the shopkeepers know 'flag pole,' even if they don't speak much other English. They're used to having visitors like you here and you'll find that they're very friendly."

The guide hopped down and started to lead the group down a narrow cobblestone street. As she passed by Becky, Becky told her, "We've lost two already."

"That's okay," the tour guide said. "No one's ever gotten lost in this town; it's too small," she said as she continued down to point out a sweater shop on the right side.

Becky stayed at the back and tried to keep everyone moving along, but it was as futile as trying to herd cats. One of the young men on the tour, Phil Watson, was near the back of the group and he started talking with Becky as they walked along. He asked how long she'd been a cruise director, how long were her assignments, etc. She normally shied away from these questions and the people asking them, but Phil seemed different. He was interesting and he actually listened to her as she talked. *He's a nice guy,* she thought. The tour reached the main town square which was packed with many locals, including children, plus several other tour groups.

Chaos, or at least a lack of continued organization, was about to set in.

Each tour guide was trying to talk loud enough to be heard, which tended to raise the overall noise level. The pastry shop on the near corner was too tempting for some to pass by without going in. The ice cream shop on the opposite corner had a line out one door, while satisfied customers exited the other door with their double and triple scoops of various flavors precariously perched atop brown sugar cones. A street acrobat added to the confusion as people were gathered around him.

Phil and Becky were talking quietly away from the rest of the group and Becky could account for only about twenty of their original thirty-three. So much for keeping the group together, but then there wasn't much she could do about it.

The guide finished her talk, one that very few could hear let alone understand, and then she turned and headed away from the pastry and ice cream shops. She lost more of the group with that move. Becky and Phil continued in her direction until they saw a little narrow lane heading off to the right. "Want a drink?" Phil asked.

"I should stay with the group," Becky said.

"What group?" Phil responded. "Over half are already off on their own. So long as we're back at the flag pole on time, that's all that's going to matter."

"Okay," Becky said. Phil seemed like a nice guy. "But just one."

"It's a deal," Phil said as he headed down the lane toward a flashing outdoor sign and pointed to a sidewalk table for two.

There really wasn't room for a sidewalk, per se, but the café still had four little tables set outside.

"White wine," Becky said as the waiter arrived.

"Beer on tap," Phil said as the man looked at him.

"*Grazie*," the waiter said as he headed inside.

It must have been slow inside because the waiter returned within a minute with their drinks and a small bowl of mixed nuts for them.

"*Grazie*," Becky said to the waiter, remembering that she always told passengers to speak some of the local language if they could.

"*Prego*," the waiter said as he smiled at the attractive cruise director.

"Excuse me," Phil said. "Too much water," he said sheepishly as he headed inside.

Becky took a sip of her wine and then quickly reached down inside her purse. Phil was gone for several minutes before returning with a relieved look on his face. "I couldn't figure out how to flush it," he said.

Becky laughed.

Becky's one drink turned into two and Phil's beer glass became a large glass for the second round. The shade from the nearby building provided a nice relief from the hot sun and the cold drinks were definitely refreshing.

"We should probably head back up there and see if we can find any of the group," Becky said as their conversation had slowed down.

Phil's face looked flush; was it from the heat of the day? Or from the beer? Or...

34

Monday, July 15

3:00 PM

The tour would have been up to Silvestri Crater several hours earlier had it not been for the petroleum truck that caught fire on the only road up the mountain. The resourceful tour guide and driver found a side road to go into a small village where they had lunch. The guide kept in contact with local authorities, but they had to let the fire burn itself out due to the flammable materials involved. Once it was out and the one lane was cleared, the passengers re-boarded the bus and they headed back up the mountain. As they passed the blackened wreckage, everyone could see that it was a miracle that the fire had not spread to the hillside.

One positive, and perhaps the only positive, of being late was that they were the only tour group when they arrived. "Yes, it looks nice outside, ladies and gentlemen, but I can assure you that there is quite a cold breeze. I'll give you a couple minutes to put on your jackets before Luigi opens the doors."

Luigi pushed the buttons to open both the front and the rear doors. She was right. The wind was really blowing hard and it was cold! "There's a nice fireplace inside the restaurant and they have a snack and a beverage waiting for you whenever you get in there," the guide said.

The sign, when translated into English, roughly said **Silvestri Craters Altitude 1,986 meters**; they were half way to the top of Mt. Etna. This was as far up as the tour went, but the wind and the temperature even at this elevation meant that it had to be brutal at the top of the volcano. A few people went past the restaurant to walk around one or two of the craters that had been there for hundreds of years. Most, however, went right inside the restaurant and grabbed the closest spot by the fireplace.

The snack was a delicious pastry and the beverage was a choice between a glass of white wine, hot coffee or cocoa. Only a few chose the wine; Luigi, Fernando Moretti, and the tour guide chose the hot coffee. As Fernando looked out the restaurant window, he noticed one man crossing the road and heading over to the Mt. Etna lava flow. The man was hugging his jacket tightly around his chest and the collar was turned up to help protect him from the cold and biting wind.

After everyone had their snack and beverage, they were all inside the restaurant where it was warm and calm. Fernando stood up and asked, "Would you like to head back down the mountain where it's a bit nicer so we can still have enough time in Taormina?"

It was a foolish question, of course. No one wanted to stay up there; not even the one who went to the lava flow across the road. So they all headed back to the bus and Fernando counted to make sure that everyone was there. "Forty plus me," he told the tour guide as he boarded the bus.

"I hope you enjoyed our quick little stop up here, and that you were able to get your Mt. Etna pictures and souvenirs," the tour guide said into the bus microphone as Luigi started driving back down the mountain. "Thank you all for staying together, and now we'll have about an hour ride down to Taormina. I'll turn off the microphone for those who want to rest along the way. The good news is that we'll still have enough time once we get there for those who want to have dinner in town. And for those who want to have dinner on the ship, you'll have an hour or so in town for souvenir shopping or just walking around until a bus will take you back to the ship."

35

Monday, July 15

6:30 PM

"Hello, everyone. This is Becky, your cruise director, with just a quick reminder of the activities around the ship tonight." Becky's voice didn't sound as confident and lively as it had been before; it had been breezy outside and several people had come back coughing and with a sore throat.

Becky cleared her throat and continued. "You're free to go back ashore, but just remember that all-aboard time is eight thirty and then tonight's show in The Royal Theatre begins at nine o'clock. We have a special comedian for you tonight, so get ready to laugh. We'll be in Valletta, Malta, tomorrow morning and I'll talk with you again. Until then, have a great evening no matter what you choose to do on the beautiful *Royal Holiday*."

A couple hours later, the cruise director popped a throat lozenge into her mouth and cleared her throat several times before clicking the switch to the ON position. "Ladies and gentlemen; I'm sorry to disturb your evening. Will Mr. Phil Watson in stateroom 4050 please report to Guest Relations on Deck Three immediately. Again, that's Mr. Phil Watson in stateroom 4050; please report to Guest Relations on Deck Three immediately." Becky flipped the switch back to the OFF position and cleared her throat again.

36

Tuesday, July 16

8:00 AM

"Good morning, ladies and gentlemen. This is Becky, your cruise director. I apologize for my voice this morning, but I think I got a sore throat in town yesterday. For those on the upper decks or in the lounges, you can see that we're tied up on the starboard side here in Valletta, the capital of Malta. I've spoken with our captain and he said that we've been cleared by the local authorities; so guests may now go ashore at their leisure."

She paused to clear her throat. "If you're on one of our fantastic shore excursions, please check the time on your ticket to see when you should be in the theater to get your tour sticker. Just a reminder that the all-aboard time is four thirty today, so please make sure you're back on board by then. For those of you staying on the ship, please check your daily paper for the listing and times of all the activities we have on board for you today. And then tonight, we have a special musical guest for you. You saw him on the Grammy Awards and he's here with us for one night only, but he's agreed to put on two shows so that everyone will have a chance to see him. You won't want to miss Mr. Blake Adams live in the Royal Theatre tonight at seven and then again at nine. Thank you for your attention, ladies and gentlemen. I hope you have a wonderful day here in Valletta." Becky switched off the microphone and doubled over in a hard coughing fit.

Down in the theater, passengers started walking down the aisles with excursion tickets in hand. "Come on down, ladies and gentlemen," Water Peterson said as passengers started coming into the theater. "You all know the process now, don't you? Come down with your tour tickets and we'll give you a corresponding sticker for your bus tour or one of the walking tours here in Valletta. Once you have your stickers, please take a seat on the other side of the theater until we call your sticker number." The Shore Excursion manager accomplished a smile on his face as he greeted the passengers even though he'd had a late night; he didn't drink, but he just didn't get his normal amount of sleep.

"If you're on one of the walking tours, or you think you might go back out on your own after the bus tour, make sure you stop by our desk on Deck Three and pick up a town map. You won't need it to find the ship, but the map does point out the highlights you won't want to miss. One of the little secrets that we've put on there is the hidden entrance to St. John's Co-Cathedral. Use that entrance and you'll cut about thirty minutes off your time waiting in line for tickets."

"Do you have any of those maps in here?" a male passenger asked.

"No, I'm sorry we don't have them here. They're all at our desk on Deck Three," Walter replied.

"Could you go get them for us?" the same passenger asked.

"We're all tied up right now," Walter replied. "But I guarantee that it won't take you more than an extra five seconds as you're walking by the our desk on the way to the exit on Deck Three."

The highly demanding man turned to his wife, "What happened to the service on this ship?" His wife just forced a smile.

"Good morning, folks," Walter began his spiel again as more passengers came into the theater.

The overhead chimes sounded.

"Ladies and gentlemen, may I have your attention, please. This is your First Officer speaking and I want to alert you to a drill for the crew only that will be taking place starting at nine o'clock this morning. I repeat that this drill will be for the crew only, and it will be announced as such once it commences. There will be various drill activities going on around the ship and I ask for your courtesy. For the safety of the crew members involved, please don't interfere with any of the crew during this time. All crew members who are involved in the drill will be wearing an orange vest so that will be your indication that they're participating in a drill. If you need anything from housekeeping during that time, please call Guest Relations who will be able to direct your request to someone who can assist you. Oceans Café and the Pool Grille and Bar will remain open during the drill, but all other food and beverage concessions will be closed until the end of the drill which should be around eleven o'clock."

The First Officer paused, and then continued. "Again, ladies and gentlemen, there will be a drill for the crew and for the crew only starting at nine o'clock. Please disregard any emergency signals that you hear at that time. In the extremely unlikely case that there is a real emergency while the crew drill is taking place, the captain, and only the captain, will make such an announcement over the public address system. Thank you for your attention, ladies and gentlemen. I hope you enjoy your day here in Valletta, Malta."

Walter and his staff continued to hand out tour stickers during the announcement. He'd forgotten about the drill; he was planning to catch up on his sleep. That would now have to wait.

37

Tuesday, July 16

8:20 AM

In a scene eerily similar to what they did on Sunday evening, head of security Clive Stewart and the hotel director were walking down a passageway with a cabin steward. As they reached cabin 4050, the director said, "Go ahead."

The cabin steward knocked on the door, for which there was no response. The cabin steward looked at the hotel director again, who nodded his head. The steward knocked on the door again. Same thing, no response.

"Key," the normally talkative director said.

The cabin steward took his pass key and inserted it into the electronic lock, saw the light turn green and he turned the handle. He opened the door slightly. "Mr. Watson, are you in here? Mr. Watson?" he repeated when there was no answer.

"Wait," Clive said. "Put on these gloves," he instructed as he handed each of the men a pair of gloves. His were already on, so he pushed the door all the way open and held it as the other men put on their gloves.

The blinds were still drawn closed; the light over the nightstand was still on. The daily paper was on the bed, as were chocolates. "It's just as I left it last night," the cabin steward said. The hotel director opened the bathroom door slowly, sensing there might be something amiss in there, but there wasn't.

"Nothing's been touched," the cabin steward stated the obvious.

The hotel director thought for a moment and then said to the cabin steward, "You're excused from the crew drill; please tell your supervisor I said so. I'd like you to stay in your area in case I need to call you."

"Yes, sir," the cabin steward said as he took off the gloves and left.

"He should have left the gloves on to open the door," the hotel director said.

"It doesn't matter," replied Stewart. "If he was indeed the last one in here last night, as it appears he was, then his fingerprints were already on the door knob and everywhere else in the cabin."

"Good point."

"Let's check the drawers and everywhere for anything that seems out of place," Stewart said. "But this is really looking like Sunday night up on Deck Seven."

"This isn't good," the director replied, also stating the obvious. "Any use of his room key?"

"I already checked with accounting and there's been nothing charged to his room since dinner on Sunday. And security shows that the last time his key was used was when he checked off the ship at ten forty-three yesterday morning." The head of security was becoming all too familiar with the checks to run on a person's room key.

The two men spent another ten minutes in the cabin carefully opening drawers, the closet doors, looking inside the medicine cabinet, under the bed, etc. Nothing. There was absolutely nothing where it shouldn't be and it didn't appear that anything was out of place.

"Let's go see the captain," Clive Stewart hesitatingly said.

38

Tuesday, July 16

8:40 AM

"I'll get the door," the head of security said to the hotel director. "You can take your gloves off so it doesn't look suspicious to any of the guests."

"Good idea," responded the director who removed the gloves and handed them to Clive Stewart.

As the hotel director stepped out into the passageway, Clive put the man's gloves in his pocket and said, "Just a moment, there's one more thing I want to check," as he let the door close. He quickly took another button-sized security camera out of his coat pocket, switched it on, removed the tape backing and placed it up in the corner of the entry way. He then opened the door, held it open with his right foot, removed his gloves, put them into his coat pocket and stepped out into the passageway.

"Has anything come up with the other missing man?" the hotel director asked discreetly as they headed toward the forward bank of stairs.

"Nothing," Stewart responded. "I thought we might've gotten a phone call or something. Certainly, he didn't decide to just skip the rest of the cruise. Unless…"

"Unless something bad happened to him," the hotel director completed the sentence.

"Yeah, and maybe a second one now?" Clive questioned.

The two men greeted several passengers coming down the stairs as they were heading up to the ninth deck. The men were used to taking the stairs, so they weren't winded by the time they'd climbed the five levels. "Are you ready for this?" Clive asked.

"I don't think you can ever be ready for this," the director responded, "but I don't know how much of it was in or out of our control."

They went to the starboard passageway and turned left. When they reached the door marked SECURED AREA – AUTHORIZED PERSONNEL ONLY, Clive put his secure key into the cipher lock and then entered his four-digit code. The lock whirred; the blinking red light turned solid green and then there was an audible click as bolts slid from their locking positions.

The ship's First Officer looked at them and said, "Why aren't you down at your positions getting ready for the drill?"

"We have to see the captain immediately," the head of security responded.

"What is it; I'll tell him," the First Officer said, wanting to exercise his power as the Officer of the Day and senior officer on the bridge.

"Sorry; this is a security matter between the two of us and the captain." Clive continued to stand his ground. It was definitely a security matter, and the captain would be furious if he found out about it from anyone else but him.

"Follow me," the First Officer said reluctantly. The two men followed him to the captain's private office.

"Come," the captain responded when the First Officer knocked twice on the secure door.

"Thank you," Clive said as the officer went back to his position on the bridge. Clive opened the door and held it open for the hotel director. "Good morning, Captain," the head of security said as the captain got out of his chair. "Sorry to bother you," Clive continued, "but we have a problem. Two problems, in fact."

"Very well, come in and have a seat," the captain said. Clive let the door close on its own; the pneumatic hinge closed the door quietly and securely. "What are the problems?" the captain asked as he sat back down.

The hotel director looked at Clive, who spoke. "One of our passengers has gone missing in each of the last two ports."

The normally calm Greek expressed shock. "What? We're missing two passengers? How come this is the first I've heard about it?"

"That was my decision, captain," Clive continued. "When the first passenger didn't check back on board Sunday evening from our stay in Civitavecchia, the hotel director and I checked his cabin for anything that looked suspicious, and we found nothing. I even installed a secret camera in there and no one's been in that cabin since we were there Sunday evening."

"But you said two passengers," the captain interjected.

"Yes, Captain. Another passenger didn't return last night from our stay in Messina and we just finished checking his cabin. Same thing; the cabin was just as the steward had left it the night before. There's been no activity on their room keys since they checked off the ship."

"What about your hotel staff?" Captain Christopolous aimed that question at the hotel director.

"These two passengers were on different decks; the first was on seven and the second was on four. They're different cabin stewards and their stories check out completely. The missing passengers are both male, single passengers. They checked off the ship, but never returned. I don't believe there's anything to do with my staff or the security staff, Captain. The strange thing is no one has contacted the ship or the cruise line to ask how to reach us."

"That makes it sound like foul play ashore; nothing that could be prevented here, sir," Clive added.

The captain's face tightened as he clenched his jaws together. He then stood, which meant for the other two men to also stand. "One passenger missing is too many," he said in a stern voice. "But two means that we're all out of a job. Now I want tighter security."

"With all due respect, Captain," the head of security responded, "we can't control what happens on shore."

"I want someone from security on each excursion," the captain answered.

"We don't have that many to go ashore and still maintain our security level in and around the ship," Clive said.

"We won't have a ship to worry about if we don't find those men, and we'd better not lose any more. Do you understand, Mr. Stewart?"

"I don't have enough security personnel to do that, Captain, unless we limit the number of shore excursions that are off the ship at a given time."

"You know we can't do that. You either find the personnel to secure each excursion, or I'll find someone who can. Is that clear enough for you, Mr. Stewart?"

"Yes, sir," Clive Stewart answered, still not knowing how he was going to carry out the captain's order and not disrupt any of the passenger activities.

"Dismissed," barked the captain.

"Aye, aye, sir," both men said as they turned and left. They left the bridge without saying anything to the First Officer.

39

Tuesday, July 16

9:00 AM

"A secret camera in the cabin?" the hotel director asked as the two men walked down the stairs.

"You saw his reaction," Clive said. "What if he'd asked if we'd done everything possible and I'd not done that? I might need to borrow some of your senior people to help out with security on the excursions. I'll let you know how many after I meet with Shore Ex and explain this to them."

"Just let me know," the director said right as the chimes announced the beginning of an announcement.

"The following is a drill and a drill for the crew only. All passengers are kindly requested to ignore the alarms and other announcements unless it is from the captain, and only from the captain. Thank you for your cooperation."

The ship's whistle blasted out the general emergency signal of seven short blasts followed by one long blast.

"Oh, crap. That's just what I didn't need right now," Clive Stewart said as he hastened his pace to the shore excursion office on Deck Three. He arrived there just as Walter Peterson was leaving. "I need to talk; now," Clive said.

"We've got this drill," Walter said, and I have to get to my station."

"That can wait," Clive responded. "I've got a direct order from the captain and it involves you. Who's your drill supervisor? I'll call him."

"The hotel director," Walter answered.

"Consider it done; let's go someplace private. Is your office empty?"

"Yes," answered Walter as the two men headed back into the shore excursion office. Meanwhile, Clive quickly called the director and told him why Walter wouldn't be at his drill station.

"You want me to include someone from security on each of the tours? You're crazy," Walter exclaimed. "We're already pushing our luck by having an escort on some of them. Now you want me to tell the tour outfitters that we have to have at least one extra person that we're not paying for? Sorry, that won't work."

"You think I like this? It means I have to pull people from security here on the ship and in the port. But if you don't believe me, call the captain. He just ordered me to do exactly that." Clive just stood there and waited for the seated Walter to make the next response; he didn't say anything.

"Look, what I'm going to tell you is highly confidential, and at this point only the captain, the hotel director, and I know this. So if I hear it from anyone else, I'll know you told them. And if that happens, I'll march you right to the captain and request that you're thrown into the brig or fired on the spot. Got it?"

A concerned look came across Walter's face. "Okay," he said, not quite sure what he was about to hear. He also wasn't sure that he wanted to hear it.

The head of security laid out the stories of the two single male passengers who'd gone missing in the two ports they'd visited so far. "If this continues, or if this news gets out, which it will if passengers keep disappearing, we're sunk; and that's not a good word to use in the cruise industry. So let's figure out how we get someone from security on each tour."

"But, some have already left," Walter countered.

"Contact the tour company and just tell them that you need to know where each tour is, where they're going and then get our security detail to each tour. Use taxis to get them out there; I don't care. How many have gone?"

"Most of them; fifteen or sixteen should already be on their way. And then we have another nine or ten scheduled for noon."

"I'll contact port security and get us a secure room to use as a staging point off the ship," Clive said. "Call me once you have the details on all the tours and then I'll meet you at the exit; my people will already be off the ship and ready to deploy. Contact the people who were going to be escorts on the afternoon tours; tell them there's been a sudden change, but they're not going to be able to go. Tell them you'll make it up to them later."

"How will I do that if I have to put one of your people on all the tours from now on?" Walter was feeling hemmed in.

"I have no idea right now," Clive said. "We have to deal with the current problems first. Where do you want the ten people for the later tours to go?"

"Have them report here at eleven thirty," replied Walter.

The announcements for the crew drill continued, but Clive and Walter were experiencing their own fire drill at the moment.

40

Tuesday, July 16

10:30 AM

The conversations going on inside the main ballroom of the Palais des Congrès in Paris, France, were as varied as the many fields within the study of mathematics itself. English was the default language being spoken, although others were being used among friends of similar nationalities. The selection of Paris as the site of this year's International Mathematics Symposium rankled some researchers who felt that the breakthroughs coming out of Beijing were far more deserving. The central committee, citing air pollution and the visa requirements for China, selected Paris because of its international appeal and the ease of entry and exit travel.

The morning's first session consisted primarily of highlighting some of the key discoveries and new theorems that made the most press in the academic journals the previous year. String Theory was once again at the top of the list where research continued to be promising, although the results and their applications continued to fail in their delivery. But so long as there was grant money available from governments and private foundations, the research and the promises of the "big breakthrough" would continue. That's the way the cycle worked in scientific research and the mathematics community was no different from the other sciences.

Jacketed and white-gloved waiters scurried about during the intermission to refill each table's water pitchers and coffee carafe. The audience consisted primarily of men, although there were more women attending each year; their main concentrations seemed to be more in practical applications rather than in theoretical research. Many participants took advantage of the schedule break to use the restroom and some went outside to smoke. France was still a smoking country but it had joined with most of the western civilizations that banned indoor smoking in public places.

"We'll resume in five minutes; thank you," came an announcement from the stage. *"Cinq minutes, je vous remercie,"* the speaker repeated as a courtesy. The overhead lights flashed several times, as did the ones in the hallway. Most would be back on time; some would be making a phone call, others checking email or getting in one more cigarette.

Although not the main table in the room, table number two held many dignitaries and people being honored for various contributions to the study and practicum of mathematics. Alfred Dunningham and his wife Sylvia were two of the eight guests at that table. They'd arrived in Paris two days ago having flown nonstop from San Francisco. The symposium was a three-day event, and while Alfred planned to attend most of the three days, Sylvia planned to use the free time to scour old bookshops for large-format historical picture books. They'd spend a few more days in the City of Light before flying back to San Francisco on Sunday. It was primarily a business trip, although there was time built in for leisure. This morning's session was their primary reason for attending.

The lights dimmed, which had the desired effect of ceasing most of the conversations around the room. The emcee got out of his chair and approached the podium. "Thank you, ladies and gentlemen, *mesdames et messieurs*. It is now my distinct pleasure to introduce one of our colleagues who takes a different approach in his use of mathematics. But before I invite him up here and present him with his award, let me tell you a little about him just in case there are some of you who've never met him.

"Alfred Dunningham earned his PhD at Stanford University and has been a Professor of Mathematics at the University of Northern California for over ten years. He and his wife Sylvia live on a small parcel of land in Napa, California that is known as the second best grape-growing region in the world. I think you all know where number one is."

The speaker paused for the laughter.

"While his classes are always filled to capacity as he's providing wisdom to today's youth and tomorrow's visionaries, his contributions to the world at large come about through his seminars and through his work with detective agencies around the globe. Last year for example, and the reason that he has been selected for this year's McLandish Award, he was highly instrumental in working with the New South Wales Police Force in Sydney, Australia, to discover the person responsible for committing four gruesome murders in highly public locations. Unfortunately, the killer chose suicide over the justice system. But it was Professor Dunningham's ability to see mathematics in everyday occurrences and events that led to solving the mysteries that had struck fear into the hearts and minds of the people of Australia's largest city. Please acknowledge Professor Alfred Dunningham."

Although the emcee applauded vigorously himself, the rest of the audience responded with only a warm greeting. The theoretical researchers felt that practical applications of any form of mathematics were only a necessary byproduct of their own hard work and commitment. The real kudos should go to the researchers, not to those who taught, and especially not to those helping police departments.

"Congratulations, dear," Sylvia Dunningham said as her husband stood up and walked to the steps at the left side of the stage.

The emcee handed Dunningham an engraved glass plate and an envelope as he approached the podium. "Congratulations, Professor," he added.

"Thank you very much," Dunningham responded. He thought about saying *merci beaucoup* instead, but he wasn't French; neither were most of the people in the room. He waited for the emcee to get to his chair at the side of the stage before continuing.

"This is an outstanding honor; I am deeply moved to be this year's recipient of the McLandish Award and I thank the International Symposium of Mathematics for inviting me and my wife to this gathering of amazing people. I know that many of you in this room feel that the importance of mathematics is heightened when there has been another discovery, a breakthrough in an age-old dilemma, or a new theorem that answers one question, and possibly asks a new one. And I agree with you. When I was in graduate school, I felt that there was nothing nobler than to conduct theoretical research. That work is valuable; there is no question about that. What I do is far different from what you researchers do. But I think that we are all doing something that is similar; we are searching for answers with the ultimate goal of making the world a better place."

He paused as there a small smattering of applause. He had no notes; he typically spoke without them. He smiled and nodded in acknowledgment to a few of his friends around the room. Alfred Dunningham had an ego just like every other person in attendance; he just didn't let it define who he was.

"I remember one of my first teachers when I was very young. My hometown was very small, and so our school had only one classroom per grade. As a result, we had a wide variety of children in our class, including me. But one thing I've never forgotten is something our teacher said to us one day when there was a disagreement over something that turned out to be quite trivial. I can't recall her exact words, but she said something like this, 'Getting along with others when they don't agree with you makes for a better world.' I liked that saying back then, and I still like it today."

Many of the people in the room stood up as they applauded vigorously; a casual observer from the outside might have thought that Dunningham was giving a civil rights speech or a talk on equality. And here he was, talking about mathematics.

"I would like to share this honor today with my research friends at table number eight who hoped to be sharing their joys and celebrations and discoveries in their home country. But I'm glad they were able to come here to Paris, and so I gladly share this with them." The group from Beijing stood in unison, bowed and then applauded Dunningham for his generous and courageous statement.

"*Xie-xie*," their leader said as he bowed once more in respect.

"Thank you again," the professor said as he left the stage and returned to his table.

41

Tuesday, July 16

11:45 AM

The sun was bearing down intently as the throngs made their way up and down the various streets and alleyways of the capital city of Malta. So full of rich history, this Baroque city had become a popular vacation spot for Europeans and a stopping point for most Mediterranean cruises. Once a critical port for merchant vessels, it now offered its services as a flag nation for cargo and cruise ships and it was a growing area for movie production. The views from the twinned Upper Barrakka Gardens and the Lower Barrakka Gardens provided a stunning picture of the magnificent Grand Harbour.

"Come over this way, into the shade," the tour guide said as she motioned her group out of the sun. The Churches, Basilicas & Cathedrals Tour of Valletta had already been inside five magnificent buildings. The best one, St. John's Co-Cathedral, was being saved for last. The guide continued as everyone gathered close in to her. "You're on your own to wander around and have lunch for the next ninety minutes. The large square behind us is very popular, which also means it gets very busy at lunch time. My suggestion is to go to your left for two streets and then turn left. The little square there won't be busy and you'll find a great assortment of foods and drinks for a lot less than you'll get right here."

"Where do we meet up?" one anxious voice asked.

"We'll meet right here under the bell tower at exactly one fifteen; that's eighty-nine minutes from now according to my watch. By the way, the popular scam going on right now is the 'dropped ring' scam. Someone, usually nicely dressed to look like a busy professional, will tap you on the shoulder and ask if you dropped a ring. The scammer will show it to you and when you say, 'No,' he'll say something like, 'Wow, this is really nice; it's got to be worth at least two hundred Euros. I thought it was yours, but I'll make you a deal. How about eighty Euros, and we both come out ahead?' The truth is that the ring is imported junk and not worth even one Euro. Just say no and keep walking. If he keeps bugging you, then yell, 'Stop trying to cheat me with your fake ring!' He'll disappear in a second."

She stopped for emphasis. "Okay, see you at one fifteen."

A middle-aged couple, both a little overweight and wearing matching khaki pants, waited for everyone else to leave before they approached the guide. "Hi. What's a souvenir that would really be emblematic of the area?"

"Glass or lace would be the two items that are really special here," the guide answered.

The wife looked at the husband. "Lace," she said. "Where'd be the best place for that?"

The guide thought for a moment. "Right next to that little square where I said you should go for lunch is a small shop called Lovely Lace. Go in there and tell them I sent you; they'll give you a really good deal. I don't get anything for sending you, but they're just nice honest people who make and sell fantastic items."

"Thanks," the wife said as she hooked her arm into her husband's and starting walking to the little square for lunch and lace.

"You're welcome. Enjoy lunch," the guide said as she headed down a different little alleyway to a secluded café where she would enjoy a few moments of quiet time along with a free glass of red wine.

"Hey, how are you doing?" Greg Brighton asked as he saw some fellow passengers enjoying lunch and beer at another outdoor café. "I'm Greg; we sat at the same table in the dining room the first night."

"Oh, yea," the man replied. "Are you on a tour today?"

"No," Greg said. "I did all my research at home and I've got it mapped out where there are some really awesome secret places here in town. St. John's is a pretty cool cathedral with those two Caravaggio paintings, but I'm going to some places where the tour companies refuse to take you. Besides," he paused as he lowered his voice, "I've found a way to sneak into St. John's and take some photos of those paintings. Want to come along? They're not far from here." Greg sounded extremely convincing, but the couple wasn't convinced.

"Thanks," the wife said. "We've already paid for this tour, so we'll just stick with it. Don't forget that we're supposed to be back onboard a little earlier today; I think it's four thirty."

Greg showed them his map. "Yep, I've got the time written right here. You sure you don't want to come along? It'll probably be the coolest thing on this entire cruise."

"Thanks, Greg. Let us know how it is, though. Okay?"

Greg took the hint and left. *They don't know what they're missing*, he thought as he re-oriented his map and headed west. He headed west according to his map, but the sun was on his right side…

42

Tuesday, July 16

3:40 PM

Walter Peterson and Clive Stewart were out on the dock as the tours began returning to the ship. Try as they might, they weren't able to get security personnel to two of the tours that were the first to depart that morning. Both men were relieved when the buses for those tours returned with the same number of passengers as when they'd left the dock. That was one bullet dodged. Stewart was more concerned about the tours that went out into the countryside of Malta than he was about the ones right there in Valletta. The town was small, meaning it was hard to get lost; plus you could see the ship's stacks from just about any place that wasn't hidden behind a tall building.

The next group of buses pulled into the small lot. Each of the security personnel that did make it to one of the tours had been instructed to keep everyone on the bus until the head of security came on and verified the count. A few passengers talked among themselves. "What's that all about?" one said.

"The head of security? I thought the guide and the escort did the counting," another one said.

Bus three checked in fine, as did all the rest of the buses.

"I'd be interested to hear what your people have to say about being on the tours, especially if there were any particular comments about security," Peterson said.

"So will I," Stewart replied. "For now, I'm just glad that all the buses returned with the right numbers."

"In all my years of doing this," the Shore Excursion manager began, "I've only seen one or two people not make it back on the same bus. And that's counting a couple thousand tours."

"This is definitely a different situation; there's no question about that," the head of security responded. "Ah, here comes the first walking tour. Hold your breath."

Thirty-one passengers left on the tour, and thirty-one came back. The process was repeated for the rest of the walking tours, and the respective numbers matched each time.

"Well, the numbers matched on each tour, so that's good," Walter said to Clive.

"Numbers are one thing, Walter; but they don't tell the whole story," Clive said as he and Walter began walking to the ship's gangway. "What I need you to do now is to check your system to verify that everyone who left on a tour came back."

"But the numbers matched, Clive."

"And that's all we have so far, Walter; numbers. We need to make sure that the names match, also. How long will that take?"

"Assuming everyone checked back in, it's only about five minutes of work," Walter answered.

"They should have all checked back in. My people were instructed to tell everyone that they had to check back in from the tour even if they wanted to go back out into town."

"I like that," Walter said. "Besides, there's not much time for them to do anything in town anyway since all-aboard is in less than an hour."

"Right," Clive responded.

The two men went straight to the shore excursion office once they were aboard. Walter signed in to his computer and brought up the file showing that day's tours. Every passenger on a tour was listed along with the tour. When passengers exited the ship, their name would be marked with the exit time.

Upon return to the ship, their entry time would then automatically be added to their name. Until the return time was posted, the passenger's name would be highlighted in red. Thus, it was an easy check for Walter. Any passenger's name that was highlighted in red had not checked back aboard the ship. He started with the first tour; no red. Same for the second tour and the third. All the tours were checked, and all the passengers had returned to the ship.

"Great; thanks, Walter," Clive said. He then added, "Are we set for the next ports?"

"All I need are the names of your people and I'll get them on a tour," Walter said.

"Great. Thanks," Walter said as he left to make the call to the captain that all passengers on tours had returned safely to the ship. The captain was pleased, although somewhat facetiously, to hear that they made it through one day with losing a passenger in port.

43

Tuesday, July 16

4:38 PM

The passenger gangway had been pulled in and onshore preparations were being readied to cast off the lines so *Royal Holiday* could get underway promptly at 5:00 PM and leave Valetta for its next port. Clive Stewart was in his office determining who from his staff would be the security escorts on the tours in Santorini on Thursday. At least tomorrow was a sea day so the issue of passengers on tours wasn't an issue.

His mobile phone started vibrating on his desk and then it started ringing. He opened the phone. "Clive Stewart," he said.

"Mr. Stewart, are you near the Central Lobby?" the voice asked.

"Yes, I'm in my office," Stewart replied.

"Will you please come to the check-in area? Now," the voice added for urgency.

"On my way," Stewart responded as he closed the phone, put it into his coat pocket and headed out for the check-in area, less than one minute away. "What's the problem?" he asked the security officer there.

"We show that one passenger did not return to the ship. It's Mr. Greg Brighton in cabin 4099. The system shows he left at ten forty-three with all the tours, but he's not checked back in."

The head of security looked at the computer and cabin 4099 was showing red; Greg Brighton had checked off the ship, but not back on. "That can't be right; all the tour passengers checked back on; I saw that an hour ago."

"I don't know, sir," the security man said. "Maybe there's a glitch somewhere, but the system says he didn't come back aboard. What do you want me to do? Should I call the bridge?"

"No; don't do anything. If the bridge calls you, delay them. Tell them the system's re-booting," Stewart replied. "I'll be right back," he said as he headed directly toward the shore excursion office.

As he went through the door, Walter looked up at him. "I don't need that list yet; tomorrow's a sea day. Remember?"

"We've got a problem," Clive said. "Remember when you said all the tour passengers checked back in?"

"Right," Walter answered.

"We're missing a passenger. Cabin 4099 didn't check back in according to the security system in the lobby."

Walter turned to his computer screen; he made a few clicks of the mouse. "What was that cabin number?"

"It's 4099. The name's Brighton, Greg Brighton."

"There's no one from 4099 booked on any of the tours for the entire cruise. Your missing passenger wasn't on a tour today."

"But the security system shows he left at the same time as several of your tours. Maybe his ticket was listed under a different cabin number." Clive Stewart didn't have a good feeling about this.

"I doubt it," Walter said. "We've never had a mix-up like that. And remember, everyone who left on a tour came back; you saw that for yourself. Just because he left at the same time as the tours, that doesn't mean anything. Anyone could just leave the ship then. Have you checked his cabin or paged him?"

"I don't like this," Clive said as he hurried out the office, went up the flight of stairs and headed aft to cabin 4099. He nearly ran someone over. "Excuse me," he said to a couple with wine glasses heading topside to watch as they sailed out of Grand Harbour.

"Sorry," the man said. "I hope nothing's wrong," he said to his wife. "I think he's with security, and he sure seems in a rush."

"Let's take the elevator so we don't spill any wine," the wife said, more interested in getting to the upper decks.

Clive Stewart knocked rapidly and loudly on the cabin door. "Mr. Brighton," he called. He knocked again. No answer. Just then the cabin steward came walking his way.

"Anything wrong, Mr. Stewart?" the steward asked.

"Have you seen the passenger?" he asked.

"Not since this morning," the cabin steward replied.

"The system shows he didn't check back in; I'm going into his cabin," Mr. Stewart said as he retrieved his pass key and inserted into the door lock. The light turned green and he turned the door handle. "Mr. Brighton, this is security. Are you in here?" Still no answer.

Both men entered the cabin and let the door close. The cabin was empty. The cabin steward opened the bathroom door, stepped inside and then back out. "He's not used the head since I cleaned it this morning," the steward said. "And the bed's still perfect," he added.

"Call me if you see him, or if anyone else attempts to enter that cabin," Clive said as he left the cabin and hurried back down to Deck Three.

44

Tuesday, July 16

4:55 PM

Head of security was on his way down to his office when he called the hotel director to inform him of the missing passenger. "Meet me at the Deck Nine forward elevators right away; we've got to tell the captain in case he wants to stay in port," Clive Stewart said. He then rushed back into the shore excursion office; Walter was still there.

"Is he in his cabin?" Walter asked.

"Cabin hasn't been touched since this morning. Let's go; we've got to tell the captain right now," Clive said.

"Why me?" Walter protested. "Every passenger who left on a tour came back; why's this my problem?"

Clive closed his eyes and let out a deep breath. "I'm not asking you, Walter. Let's go," Clive said in a stern voice.

"Ridiculous," Walter mumbled as he got out of his chair. Clive was already out the door and walking briskly toward the forward section of the ship.

Clive opened a crew door, held it for Walter, and said, "Let's use the crew elevator; it's faster."

As they got to Deck Nine, they exited the crew area into the passageway and continued forward to the passenger elevators where the hotel director was waiting for them. "Nice security," the director said as Clive approached.

"We can't baby sit them all," Clive responded as he led the all-too-familiar way to the secured bridge area.

"What's this all about?" the captain asked as he turned at the sound of the opening of the secure door. "We're getting ready to cast off the remaining lines. Why aren't you at your stations?"

"Another passenger is missing, Captain," Clive said, getting right to the point. "And I didn't know if you wanted to stay in port since it's still early enough in the day."

"What?" Captain Konstantinos Christopolous yelled. "I told you to put a security detail with each tour. Did you do that?"

"Yes, sir, we did," Stewart replied.

"Ready to cast off the bow lines, Captain," the First Officer announced.

"Very well; cast off the bow lines," the captain answered. "Make ready to be underway," he continued in a calm manner.

"Aye, aye, sir," the First Officer replied. "Cast off the bow lines," he repeated into the ship's phone. As he stood in the Flying Bridge, he saw the bow lines being uncleated and tossed toward the ship. "Bow lines are cast off; we're free from the dock, sir."

"Very well," the captain responded. Managing the operational aspects of the ship required a cool head, and the captain maintained his cool. "First Officer, you have the con. Take us to sea," the captain said as he relinquished command of the bridge to his second-in-command.

"Aye, aye, sir," the First Officer responded, following standard shipboard protocol. "I have the con."

Captain Christopolous turned to the three men who'd interrupted the departure procedures; his angry look returned. "My office; now!" he barked.

The three men followed the captain into his office and remained standing as he sat down behind the desk. "Well?" he asked. "What happened to your security, Mr. Stewart?"

"There was no problem with the security, Captain," Clive began, "even though we weren't able to get the detail to two of the tours that were already on the other side of the island."

"Then what happened?" the captain asked in a calmer voice. "What happened on the tours?"

"All the tours came back with the right numbers and all the passengers who exited the ship for a tour checked back in," Walter said. "We had everyone check back in from the tour as soon as they got back to port. We told them it was a new procedure and that they could go right back out, but they had to check in first. There was a little grumbling, but everyone went along with it."

"If everyone came back from the tours, how come you're missing one person?" the captain asked.

"He wasn't on one of our tours, Captain," Walter again answered. "In fact, he's not registered for any of the ship's tours for the entire cruise. He could have booked his own tour through Cruise Critic or somewhere else. But he wasn't on one of ours."

"Three passengers missing in three ports; how many people know about this?" the captain asked as he scanned the three men.

"Just the four of us in this room, Captain," Clive responded. "Each of the respective cabin stewards knows that one of his passengers is missing and a few of the security officers manning the check-in system know that one is missing. But as far as I know, we're the only ones who know about all three of them."

"So you think this fellow just walked off the ship on his own, not on a tour, and didn't come back? That doesn't make sense." The captain was trying to apply logic to the situation.

The hotel director finally offered an answer. "That's the only logical explanation we have right now, Captain. The cabins haven't been touched since they were last serviced by the cabin stewards. We've received no phone calls or emergency messages to tell us anything else. What would you like us to do, Captain?"

The captain brought his arms to the desk, placed his elbows on the top and then rubbed his temples with his thumbs. Looking directly at the head of security, he said, "Alert the local police here in Valletta. And let's keep this just between us."

"What about the police in Civitavecchia and Messina?" Clive asked.

"Those Italians," the Greek captain murmured. "I wouldn't trust them with this information. After all the bad press they got after one of their own ships ran aground, they'd have fun with this in the media. No, just Valletta," he continued. "That's all."

The three men turned around and headed for the door. Two of them had gone through the door when the captain called Clive Stewart back into the office. "Call Interpol," he said quietly.

"Aye, aye, Captain," Stewart replied and he left to join the others as they waited for him. "Sorry," he said as he met back up with the other two and they left the bridge to go to their respective offices.

45

Wednesday, July 17

10:30 AM

The seas were a bit choppy and there was a cool breeze on the exposed areas of the decks. They'd been relatively close to shore on the previous days, but now they were in the middle of the Mediterranean Sea, completely open to all the elements. The pool area was fairly protected, enabling the sun bathers to relax in the sun.

Fernando Moretti made his way across the pool deck to the forward stairs and walked down to the fourth deck. He heard the Zumba class music even before he got to the open door of the theater. He could tell that the pace of the music was slowing down, so the exercise class would soon be over. There weren't as many participants as on the day of his first talk and the aisle closest to the podium was empty. He walked down the aisle, smiled at the instructor who looked his way, and he sat down in the front row. It would only take him a couple minutes to get set up; it was going to be a good day.

The music stopped and so did all the awkward gyrations on the stage and in the open space in front of the stage. "Thanks, everyone," the Zumba instructor called out. "You're doing great. Now go have a refreshing smoothie to rehydrate your body."

She walked over to the podium to disconnect her equipment. "Sorry we're late again," she said. "The CD wouldn't play, so I had to go and get a different one."

"It's not a problem," Fernando said as he stood up. "You really give them a good workout. How many do you think you'll still have in here by the end of the cruise?"

"We already lost the most that we're going to lose. There might be one or two more that stop, but these people look like they're the serious ones." For as good as shape as she was in, even the Zumba instructor was sweating quite a bit. "You ought to give it a try sometime," she said.

"I would, but you're always right before me, and that just doesn't work." Fernando really had no desire to do Zumba, so it was good that he had a ready reason why he couldn't attend.

"We could always arrange for a private session when it would work for you," she said.

Is she coming on to me? "Thanks; I'll let you know," he said as he opened his bag and removed the laptop. As he was connecting the cables, Scott Eaton, the stage manager came down the aisle.

"Do you need any help, Mr. Moretti?" Scott asked.

"I'm fine for now, Scott. Sound check in a minute?"

"Sure thing," Scott replied. "Just let me know when."

"Will do," Fernando answered.

"Well then, if we can't do Zumba, how about dinner?" the instructor asked, continuing her advance on the handsome Italian.

"I'm not sure that my wife would think that's a great idea," he said without even looking up.

"Oh," came the disappointed reply from the rejected suitor.

Fernando opened up the file for today's presentation, *Olives: More Than Just for Oil* and gave a thumbs up to Scott in the sound booth. The background music began. *Perfect.* Now if only Fernando really had a wife here to watch.

46

Wednesday, July 17

2:15 PM

"That's odd," a man said to his wife as they looked at the screen in the Central Lobby that showed the ship's course. "We were heading almost due east and now we've turned about thirty degrees north. Maybe the captain is going to take us near his hometown after all."

"Maybe he's changing direction just like the airplanes change altitude when they've hit a rough area," his wife said as she noticed that the ship's heading was almost directly toward Athens, Greece.

"I didn't think the water or the waves were that rough, but we are heading directly into the wind," he continued. "Oh, well. Let's go see if we can find those lucky Bingo cards." The two held hands as they headed forward for the theater and today's Bingo game.

The whirring sound of helicopter blades increased as they got closer to the ship. The forward deck had been secured and the area around the helicopter pad had been thoroughly inspected and cleared of any loose debris. Those in the Sky View Lounge on the twelfth deck had the best view of the landing as they weren't distracted by the noise or the strong blasts of air.

The rumors began flying when people saw the helicopter approach and then slowly lower itself and land on their cruise ship.

"Maybe it's a special performer for tonight's show."

"Probably one of those Hollywood-type celebrities."

"I hope it's more lobster for dinner."

The helicopter blades kept spinning even though the bird was firmly on the ship. They were spinning in more of an idling fashion, and the sound was a deeper sound as the blades' pitch had been increased to create downward force, thus securing it to the deck without having to tie it down.

A former military pilot who was watching the action correctly observed, "He's getting ready to take off again or he would have shut down the engines." He was right.

One man in a dark green jumpsuit got out of the helicopter, grabbed the suitcase that was being handed to him from the open door and quickly walked to the crew door which was being held open for him. Instead of lifting back off, the helicopter stayed right there, continuing its idling.

The deck's crew door was opened again and two medics pushed a gurney out toward the helicopter. The rear door was opened and the medics lifted the stretcher with its occupant off the gurney and onto the floor of the helicopter. The door was closed and the two medics rolled the gurney back to the crew door.

The pitch of the blades changed and the helicopter slowly lifted from the ship's deck and headed straight along the current direction of the ship, directly into the wind.

The former military pilot knew what just happened; they evacuated someone who needed medical attention that was not available on the ship. *Sure hope he makes it*, he thought.

47

Wednesday, July 17

2:30 PM

"Resume heading of zero eight five," Captain Christopolous ordered.

"Heading is now zero eight five, Captain," the First Officer replied.

"Very well. Maintain our course per the plan," the captain said.

"Aye, aye, sir," came the response from the officer who was actually "driving" the ship.

Just then, the secure door to the bridge opened and the head of security and the man in the dark green jumpsuit entered. The captain turned to look.

"First Officer, take the con," he commanded.

"Aye, aye, sir," was the response. "I have the con," the First Officer continued so those on the bridge knew who was in charge.

"This way," the captain said to the two men who'd just entered his sanctuary. Heads turned to see who'd just arrived. They knew Clive Stewart from security. But who was the other man?

Nothing else was said until they entered the captain's office and the door was closed.

Clive was the first to speak. "Captain, this is Antoine Moreau, Interpol from Paris. Moreau, this is Captain Christopolous." The two men shook hands and then the three of them sat down.

"You're from Paris, but you were in Greece, my home country?" the captain asked.

"I was wrapping up a case there, Captain. I was planning to head back to Paris tomorrow. What's going on that needs Interpol out here in the middle of the Mediterranean?" The Interpol agent wasted no time in diving right into the case.

The captain looked at Stewart who took the lead.

"We've had one passenger go missing, disappearing so to speak, each day we've been in a port. We left Barcelona last Friday; our first port of call was Civitavecchia on Sunday. One passenger, a single male from a cabin on the seventh deck exited the ship using his room key, but he never checked back in. Our next port was Messina on Monday; another single male passenger, from the fourth deck this time, went on one of our tours, but never made it back. And then yesterday we were in Valletta; a single male, fourth deck again but not on a tour, exited the ship with his room key, but never made it back on." Clive Stewart stopped to let that information sink in.

"I'm assuming you've checked their cabins for any leads or other information on where they might have gone or why they didn't return," the agent said although it was phrased as more of a question.

"Precisely," Stewart said. "No one's been in their cabins, with the exception of me, the hotel director, and the cabin stewards once we noticed they were missing. I installed a security camera in each room and I was the only one who knew about the cameras until I mentioned it to the captain and the hotel director. But no one's been in their cabins; they're just as they were the last time the stewards made them up."

"That is a bit unusual to have one passenger missing each port." Moreau thought for a moment before he continued. "What do you want me to do, Captain?"

It seemed pretty obvious to the captain what he wanted the Interpol agent to do, but he knew that 'obvious' wasn't part of the lingo for spooks. "I want you to find out what's going on, and then stop it," the captain said.

"Very well, Captain," Moreau said. "I'll need unbridled access to all areas of the ship and to all the security features you have on board. Is that acceptable?"

"Do I have a choice?" the captain asked.

"Not unless you get that helicopter back here right away while it still has enough fuel to make it back to land with me on it." The Interpol agent wasn't playing hardball; it was just how he worked. If you wanted his help, you played by his rules.

"Mr. Stewart here will make sure you have access to everyone and everything that you need, *Monsieur* Moreau." Captain Konstantinos Christopolous typically had the last word on his vessel; this was the first time that someone else, a Frenchman no less, actually had the upper hand.

"It's nice to meet you, Captain," Moreau said in a genuine tone as he stood up to shake the captain's hand. "We'll get to the bottom of this."

"Thank you; I hope so," the captain replied.

"Let's go down to my office to get you situated," Stewart said to Moreau and the two men left the office and the bridge and made their way down to the security office on Deck Three to continue their discussions.

48

Wednesday, July 17

2:30 PM

From the outside, you might be able to tell; but from the inside, you wouldn't know that this grand masterpiece, Paris's Musée d'Orsay, was an old train station next to the Seine River that had been slated to be demolished. She was saved and now she's one of the world's finest homes for Impressionist Art.

"That was really sweet of you to share your honor with the Chinese," Sylvia Dunningham said as she and Alfred were entering the Orsay with their museum pass. The line at the ticket window wasn't too long, but they were able to skip it completely, just as they would do tomorrow at Le Louvre where the lines were always long.

Professor Dunningham smiled as his pass was scanned and he stepped into the massive main hall. "It was my way of telling the organizers that they made a mistake by not holding the meeting in Beijing, where it deserved to be held."

"But the weather is so much nicer here, and it's easier to get from place to place. Besides, we'd need an interpreter in China," Sylvia responded in a mild protest.

"We'd have been fine," Alfred said as they headed to the right. "Did you notice what their table number was?"

"No, I don't even remember what ours was," she replied.

"Eight," the professor responded. "Eight is considered to be a very lucky number in China. Do you remember when they held the Summer Olympics there a few years ago? Opening Day was held on August 8th. Thus it was 8-8-8 for August 8,

2008. That wasn't a coincidence and I don't think it was a coincidence that they were at table eight yesterday."

Numbers. Everything revolved around numbers for Alfred Dunningham. His special tea at home had to be brewed for just the right amount of time – the length of the first movement of Beethoven's *Moonlight Sonata*. He solved the Famous Sites Murder case in Sydney the previous year by using the numbers 4, 3, 2, and 1. What numbers and sequences would he notice today? How would numbers factor into the rest of their stay in Paris?

The exhibits on the ground floor were interesting, especially the architecture ones and the glass-covered diagram of Paris that you could walk on. Today was planned as a leisurely day but he was anxious to go to the top floor where the key Impressionist paintings were displayed. It was one thing to see pictures of the paintings in articles and books and magazines, but their impact and the feelings that they evoked truly came out when seeing them in person.

Sylvia and Alfred made a good pair as they were both compatible and complementary. While everything had to have a reason and a purpose for Alfred, Sylvia was able to just enjoy things as they were. It wasn't that she was a simple person; she had a Master's degree in English Literature. She could have done more professionally, but she was quite content to be Mrs. Alfred Dunningham and to manage the care of his roses and their five acres of Shiraz grapes when he was wherever he might be in the world providing help "through mathematics."

The halls on the middle floor held some interesting works, although they weren't why most people came to the Orsay. But Alfred was patient; he wanted Sylvia to be able to enjoy the experience as much as she wanted. They would soon get to the top floor and he could then soak in the creations of masters such as van Gogh, Cézanne, Whistler, Monet, Renoir and the list went on and on. But there was time and he wasn't in a rush; great things were best enjoyed slowly and not on a timetable. Today would not be a day about numbers.

The exterior of the Gare d'Orsay had not been altered much since Jacques Duhamel, Minister for Cultural Affairs, ruled against plans to build a new hotel in its place in 1970. The old train station couldn't expand its tracks to hold the newer, longer trains, plus the commuter routes were being replaced by the highly efficient Metro. No, Gare d'Orsay had lost its value as a train station. But now as a museum, it was extremely valuable in what it did for the art world.

A lot of work was required to transform the interior to an art museum, but that work was accomplished while retaining much of the charm of the old station. Standing on the fifth floor platform, one could almost hear the trains and the conductors of years gone by. The arched glass ceilings invited light to come inside the museum, just as they'd done for decades for the train station. Gare, now Musée, d'Orsay was a magical place indeed.

"Would you like a coffee and pastry, dear?" Alfred asked as they arrived on the fifth floor.

"That would be a nice way to get off my feet for a bit," Sylvia replied, happy to see her husband in a relaxed mood. She looked through the guidebook while Alfred got in line for two American coffees and two pastries. One of the photographs in the guidebook caught her attention and it wasn't one of the paintings. *I bet Alfred will like this.*

He returned to the table carrying a tray with the coffees, pastries and the small change from his ten Euro note. He was happy that so many of the European Union countries had adopted the Euro as their currency, but he fondly recalled coming to Paris when France was still using the Franc. Of all the places he'd been to, he wished France were still on the Franc; it just seemed so "French."

"The coffee smells delicious; thank you," Sylvia said as she closed the guidebook.

"The pastry choices were too many," Alfred said as he offered them to her; she chose the one with the chocolate drizzled along the top. "*Bon appétit*," he added.

"Mmm; it's gorgeous." That was all Sylvia could say as she was thoroughly enjoying the rich but flaky chocolate pastry. Her eyes were closed as she devoured it with her mind and then she licked her fingers when she was done. "Wow; this is heaven, isn't it?"

"If it's not, it's pretty close," he replied, happy that she was enjoying herself on this trip.

"Oh," she said as she remembered what she'd seen in the guidebook. "I saw something I think you'd enjoy looking at," she added as she thumbed through the book. "Ah; here it is." She held the book open as she turned it and slid it across the table to Alfred.

"Yes," Alfred said. "The old clocks on the outside of the train station." He read the article. "I didn't know you could view them from the back. Those would be interesting to see." He picked up the receipt from the tray and placed it in the guidebook to mark its place.

The couple sat in plastic chairs and savored the coffee, its aroma and its flavor. "Shall we go find the clocks?" Alfred asked once Sylvia had finished her cup.

"Sure; let's go," she said as she picked up the guide book and he put the cups and plates on the tray and then emptied the items into the waste container on their way out of the small café. "This way, dear," she said as Alfred had turned right when he should have turned left at the exit. "They're on the north side facing the Seine."

"Ah, yes," he said. Sense of direction wasn't one of his perfected skills.

Sylvia opened the guide book to the marked page. "The closest one is over here," she said as she looked at the clock's location and compared it to the sign board. Alfred followed his wife as they made a series of turns; there it was!

"How interesting!" Alfred exclaimed as he marveled while watching the clock movements in action. "Is that Sacré Coeur I can see through the glass?"

Sylvia took the mini-binoculars from her purse and looked through the clock glass. "It sure is," she said. "What an amazing shot; do you want to take a picture?"

"Sure," Alfred replied.

Sylvia put the binoculars back in her purse and pulled out her camera. She selected the electronic zoom and the magnificent basilica on Paris's highest point came into clear view. Just as she pressed on the button to take the picture, Alfred heard a slight noise as if a door were being unlocked. He looked to his right where there was a glass door to a small outside balcony. The light on the door handle turned green for five seconds before returning to red.

"What are you doing?" Sylvia asked as Alfred stepped over the door and attempted to turn the handle, but it wouldn't budge. The red light meant it was locked.

The professor looked at his atomic watch; it was just 4:37. He closed his eyes in thought.

"What is it?" she asked.

"If I'm not mistaken," he began, "when that clock was at the exact time where the minute hand was precisely as far away from the six as was the hour hand on the other side, the lock on that door over there automatically unlocks. That must be how the workers get outside to clean the face of the clock." He paused for a moment. "My watch is accurate to the tenth of a second, but I didn't look at it exactly when I heard that lock open. I bet that if we were here in about fifty-four minutes, I could prove my theory."

"The museum closes at five, dear," Sylvia said.

The disappointed professor replied, "I want to come back here tomorrow to see if I'm right."

"Do you think the workers understand that math stuff?" Sylvia asked.

"Of course not, even though it's a simple algebraic calculation. If my calculations are correct, that lock clicked open at precisely fifty-five point four seconds past thirty-six minutes past four. But they'll have a table of times when the lock changes from red to green." Alfred scanned the area for such a sheet of paper. None was visible, but there was a rectangular area on the wall that wasn't faded; he walked over to that spot and did a rough measurement with his outstretched hand. "Roughly eight by eleven, which would match the A4 paper size of 8.27 by 11.69 inches. Interesting."

After they'd returned to their hotel room later that afternoon, Alfred performed the algebraic calculation and he had been correct. The time at which the minute hand would have been as far from the six as the hour hand was from the six would have been 4:36:55.4. Apparently, numbers would be a part of the day after all.

49

Wednesday, July 17

3:30 PM

"Good afternoon, ladies and gentlemen; this is Becky, your cruise director, and I certainly hope that you're enjoying this wonderful day at sea. Yesterday we were at the amazing island and country of Malta and tomorrow we will be on the most spectacular island of Santorini, Greece. You'll want to make sure your camera batteries are fresh as you'll encounter one great photo opportunity after another. Also, make sure that you are wearing comfortable and sturdy walking shoes for two reasons. One, you're going to do a lot of walking unless you're booked on the bus-only tour of the island. The other reason is that we'll be dropping anchor about a half mile off shore and using our tender boats to take us to the dock area. If you've never been on a tender boat before, don't worry, you don't have to climb down rope ladders or anything like that.

"We do have a special treat for you today; Cyril the magician will be giving a matinee presentation at 4:30 in the ship's theater. If you haven't seen him perform his magic with cards, get ready to be amazed. I've heard from several people already who've said that he's the best they've ever seen. No cameras or video recording are allowed during the show, but he'll invite a few people on stage to see if they can figure out how he does his magic. That's at 4:30, just one hour from now in The Royal Theatre on Deck Four."

Down on Deck Three, Clive Stewart had created an identity for Antoine Moreau so that the Interpol agent would have access to everyplace and everything on the ship. His accent was clearly French, so the thought of having his new identity be anything but French was out of the question. He was now Pierre Dubois, the new Chief Marketing Officer at Holiday Cruise Line, PLC, the ship's owner. Since only a few people had actually seen Moreau, and he was wearing a dark green jumpsuit at the time, the transformation to Dubois, wearing slacks and a sport coat, was simple.

In keeping with his role as the cruise line's CMO, Pierre Dubois was given cabin 1028, a suite with full amenities. He had unlimited free internet access, using either the wireless signal or the special wired connection that was hastily enabled in his suite. The actual signal was still a wireless signal given that they were at sea, but a certain amount of the bandwidth was separated and isolated for the wired connection that was available to only a few individuals.

There was a knock at his door and Dubois went to see who was there. He looked through the peephole and saw a tuxedoed waiter. He opened the door and saw that the man was carrying a tray with a bottle of wine and some appetizers. "Good afternoon, Mr. Dubois, my name is James and I will be your personal butler. May I come in, sir?"

"Certainly, James," Dubois said as he held the door with his right hand and stepped back to allow the butler in.

"Your refrigerator is stocked with water and soft drinks. If there's a particular wine or liquor that you'd like, please let me know and I'll bring it right away," James said as he pulled a card from his right jacket pocket and handed it to Pierre. "Would you like me to open the Sauvignon Blanc for you, or shall I just place it in the refrigerator?"

"Actually," Dubois answered, "I don't drink so you may take it back with you. Sparkling water, Perrier preferably, will be just fine."

"Very well, sir; it will be my pleasure," James said. "May I check the contents while I'm here, sir?" he asked as he stepped toward the refrigerator.

"Of course," Dubois replied.

The butler set the tray and the wine on a nearby table and opened the three-quarter size refrigerator. The Frenchman's favorite sparking water, Perrier, was already inside. As he closed the door, the butler placed a magnetic card on the front of the refrigerator. The card had a four-digit number to call to reach the butler. The card was thicker than most magnetic cards and the colorful dots seemed a little out of place.

"Your water should already be chilled, Mr. Dubois. If there's anything else you need, my number is also on the card there on your refrigerator. Should I make dinner reservations for you or would you like to have dinner here in the suite?"

"I'm not sure right now," Dubois responded. "I'll let you know or I'll just manage for myself."

"Very well, sir; I'll remove the wine and do let me know if there's something I can do," James said as he gathered up the wine and his tray and left the suite.

Antoine Moreau was beginning to like being treated as a high-level corporate executive. He normally felt tolerated, but now felt appreciated and valued. This was good; he had a fantastic suite, his own butler and complete privacy.

50

Wednesday, July 17

6:45 PM

The sun had set almost thirty minutes ago, but its brilliance continued to be reflected in the ship's wake; those near the Grand Dining Room's floor-to-ceiling windows that ran the width of the ship's stern had a great view of the reflection. The waves rippled as they moved out from the wake that was a perfect straight line from the propellers to the horizon. The conversations at the larger tables varied as the passengers talked about their day's activities, while those at the tables for two held more personal conversations or just engaged in small talk.

At a round table for six, James Phillips was enjoying the company of the two couples at the table. There was an open place that was occupied the first evening, but the single lady must have moved to another table or was dining elsewhere on the ship. "Got a little sun today, James?" one of the men asked.

"I forgot the sunscreen and I left my cap in the cabin. I wasn't planning to be outside that much, but the breeze made it feel as if it wasn't that hot. I sure hope it doesn't peel; there's nothing worse than seeing a bald head that's peeling." James Phillips took his hand and rubbed it gently on the top of his head; the sunburned skin felt warm to the touch.

"Maybe you could get a toupee," the other man at the table said.

"I tried that once," James said. "It didn't look good at all. I don't know if it's the shape of my head or if I just got a really bad toupee, but I looked like a bad hair day that went totally bad," he continued.

The two couples laughed. One of the women then said, "Well, you better make sure to wear your hat from now on; I'd hate to see you stuck down in medical because of a bad head burn." The other woman, feeling some of the effects of her second glass of wine, laughed so hard that heads turned at the nearby tables.

"Not so loud, dear," the embarrassed husband said quietly as he patted her on the shoulder. The wife couldn't stop; she had an incessant case of the giggles.

"Speaking of medical," James said, "I wonder how that young man is who was taken off by the helicopter yesterday. He must have needed some pretty urgent care." The change of subject seemed to work for stopping the giggles at the table.

"I saw the helicopter heading toward us, but I didn't know what it was for," the man next to James said.

The one with the knowledge and with the attention of the other four people at the table, James, took over. "I was up in the Sky View Lounge taking a break from the sun, but apparently not enough of a break. I heard it coming in from the left front of the ship. It landed and a man got off with a suitcase and then a couple minutes later, two men rolled a gurney out to the helicopter that was still running and loaded a man in a stretcher into the open door. A minute later it was taking off and heading back in that same direction, about forty-five degrees left of the bow."

"I've heard of ships pulling into the closest port to drop off a sick passenger, but I'd never heard of a helicopter coming out and getting them." The woman with the giggles had managed to regain her composure.

James continued, "We're more than a hundred miles from shore, which could take the ship at least three hours in each direction. If he was that critical, the helicopter could cover that distance in much less time. I wonder if he was married or traveling with someone; I didn't see anyone else get on the helicopter with him."

"It had to be bad for them to send a helicopter out here; those aren't cheap and most insurances don't cover them," the neighbor said.

"Yeah," James said. "Hey, did anyone catch the card magician in the theater today? I thought he was pretty good."

The man opposite James responded. "You know, I saw him the other night in the lounge and I watched him carefully on one trick. It's the one where the aces end up as the top card on each of the four piles."

"What'd you see?" James asked, somewhat interested in magic himself.

"What I noticed in the lounge was that he did that as his first trick, meaning the deck of cards hadn't been touched yet. I didn't know what he was doing until the four aces were turned up one at a time. Then in this afternoon's show, I sat down near the front and watched as he started with the same trick. With all the tricks he has available to him, doesn't it seem strange that he would start with the same one?"

The people at the table, including James, agreed.

"He'd announced that it would be the first one by asking people in the audience who played cards and who knew what the top card in the deck was? That clued me in that he was starting with the aces trick again. As I watched him, I figured out why it was his first trick—the deck of cards had to be stacked in a certain order."

"But he shuffles them, doesn't he?" James asked.

"Yes, but…" the man paused.

"But what?" Everyone at the table wanted to know.

"The key is that he doesn't shuffle the top cards down into the deck, so the top group of cards, and it only has to be four, the four aces, stays on the top of the deck."

"But he let that gal divide the cards into four stacks, move cards around and so forth. How could Cyril know where the aces were all the time?" the other man asked.

"I agree; that's what I thought also," said the man explaining the trick. "I went back to my cabin and got out a deck of cards. It took me a while to remember it all and get it figured out. You want to see me do it?" he asked.

Everyone at the table wanted to see that trick done, so the man pulled the deck of cards out of his pocket and performed the trick. All four aces ended up being the top cards on the four stacks. Proud of his accomplishment, he then showed them how it was done. He kept the aces face up the whole time so everyone could see where they were in relation to the other cards. The tablemates were impressed.

"Let me see if I can do it," James said, and the man handed the cards to James. It took him a couple tries to get it right; he had to make sure he wasn't too thorough in shuffling the top cards down into the rest of the deck. He finally got it right; James was now a card magician.

51

Thursday, July 18

9:00 AM

"Good morning, ladies and gentlemen. This is your captain, Konstantinos Christopolous, speaking to you from the Navigational Bridge. As you can see, we are anchored here off the beautiful Greek island of Santorini. The local authorities have cleared us for arrival, however the docking area on the island is having some work done and they need to clear away the heavy machinery before our tender boats can arrive there.

"You may have noticed the helicopter that landed on the ship yesterday and then took back off a few minutes later. We had a passenger with a severe medical situation that required getting him to a facility that could provide the proper care for his condition. We did have to turn the ship off our normal course to make sure we were within the helicopter's range, but we were able to make up the time last night. And now here's Becky, your cruise director."

"Thank you, Captain Christopolous, and let me add my greetings to you here in Santorini, Greece. For those of you going ashore today, when you see the many white buildings and blue roofs and cupola tops, those images will be forever in your memory as the typical picture of a Greek island. As the captain said, we have to wait just a few more minutes before we can begin to board the ferries, but all our tours will still run their full scheduled length."

Many of the passengers who weren't on an early tour were on the upper decks enjoying the sunshine. The *Royal Holiday* wasn't the only cruise ship anchored off Santorini today. A ship that appeared to be half the size or smaller had already set anchor and had its tender boats in the water, but none were heading to the dock.

James Phillips was seated at a table on the pool deck trying out some of his newly learned card tricks to those who would sit down or just stand and watch. Even though the table was in the shade, he was wearing his hat. He still wasn't that fond of the toupee idea. He'd faithfully practiced the tricks last night in his cabin after being shown a couple of them at the dinner table. Just like Cyril, he started with the four aces trick and his 'audience' clapped when the fourth ace was turned up.

Trying to fill the time that was now created due to the delay on shore, Becky had asked Fernando Moretti to give a bridge talk about some of the highlights of Santorini. Most of what he talked about was repeat information to those who'd been to his presentation yesterday. Since he always had more to talk about than the time he was allotted for his presentations, he was able to add a few interesting items that he'd not covered yesterday.

"Thank you, Fernando Moretti," Becky said as she signaled to him to wrap it up. "Just a reminder that all-aboard time tonight is eight thirty, which means that the last shuttle from the gondola pier is at eight o'clock. There will be only one last shuttle boat at eight o'clock so it's advisable to get to the pier well before that. And that's the only place where the tender boats will be bringing passengers back to the ship except for those designated bus-only highlight tours that will come back from the same place where the tender boat takes you.

"Ladies and gentlemen, the captain has informed me that we just received word that we can now begin shuttling passengers to shore. If you're not on one of the ship's excursions, you will need to go to Guest Relations on Deck Three to get your priority card. We'll start boarding those just as soon as we get our scheduled tours off the ship. Please wear comfortable, but sturdy closed toe shoes today as we don't want anyone to slip boarding the local ferries or while you're walking around the island. Do remember to take a bottle of water with you as the forecast is for warm temperatures and only a slight breeze. Enjoy your day, ladies and gentlemen, and we'll see you back onboard the *Royal Holiday* this evening."

52

Thursday, July 18

9:20 AM

"Did you hear what the captain said?" a surprised Doctor Khalid said to his nurse as they sat in the empty medical facility.

"You mean about the patient they evacuated yesterday?" she replied.

"Yes; there wasn't anyone who's been in here that we haven't taken care of," the Cairo-trained doctor answered. He continued, "There was that one man in Civitavecchia who looked like he'd been in a fight, but there's not been anyone with a severe medical condition that we've not been able to properly handle. I think I'll call the captain to find out what he meant by that."

The doctor had just picked up the telephone when the door opened and a smartly dressed man walked into the facility. The doctor placed the phone back into the cradle. "May I help you, sir?" the doctor asked.

"Hello, Doctor Khalid," the man said as he approached him and put out his right hand. "My name is Pierre Dubois, and I am the Chief Marketing Officer for the cruise line," he said as he handed the doctor a business card. Even Antoine Moreau was impressed with the speed at which Clive Stewart had prepared his on-board identity, complete with name tag, photo identification and real-looking business cards. Of course, if anyone ever called the phone number on the card, the person answering the phone would have no idea who Pierre Dubois was. That might be a problem later on, but Clive Stewart was more concerned about solving the current problem—why are passengers disappearing from the ship?

"*Bonjour, Monsieur* Dubois," the doctor greeted the Frenchman. "Are you not feeling well today?"

"Thank you, doctor. I'm feeling just fine. I'm spending time on all of our ships looking for ways that we can improve what we deliver to our guests and I'm talking with all the department heads to find out what ideas they have for improving the overall customer experience." Moreau/Dubois was playing the part of a marketing executive very well.

Khalid and Dubois spent the next forty-five minutes talking about ways to improve the image of medical facilities on the ships and why that would be important. Dubois took notes especially when the doctor answered the questions about the prescriptions that had been dispensed so far on the cruise.

The main door was thrust open as a woman staggered into the facility and immediately vomited on the open floor. "Nurse!" called the doctor as he stood up to help the woman maintain her balance.

The nurse appeared and the two medical personnel helped the woman into one the examining rooms. The nurse reappeared, wiped up the floor and then sprayed it with a disinfectant. "Please tell the doctor thank you for his time," Dubois said as he left the facility.

Doctor Khalid began treating the woman and he completely forgot that he was going to call the captain.

53

Thursday, July 18

10:10 AM

About ninety passengers got off the local ferries as each one pulled up to the concrete dock. The handsome helpers looked quite smart in their white uniforms that accentuated a natural dark skin color. Most of the women wore a large smile as the muscular men held out a hand to help them out of the boat safely onto land. One of the single women, in her early thirties, threw her arms around the young man and gave him a big kiss to the delight and cheers of the other passengers. Blushing and with fresh lipstick now on him, the young man smiled and continued to assist everyone as he greeted them with, "Welcome to Santorini."

The tour guides raised their paddles high in the air next to the buses with their corresponding numbers. Tours one, two, and three were on the first tender and a new boat arrived at the dock about every eight to ten minutes. The sun was beginning to peek over the hill behind the dock; it was going to be another warm day on this island that was visited by most cruise ship passengers who came to Greece. The line of taxis was long by Santorini standards; most of the taxis on the island would normally be around Thira Airport when it was time for planes to land. On days when the cruise ships arrived, the taxi drivers had an unwritten understanding which ones would service the airport and which ones would be down at the dock. After all, this was a small island and they all had to get along with each other. Besides, for most of them driving a taxi wasn't their only source of income. Some of them owned a small restaurant or bar that they would tend to if the taxi traffic was slow and others grew olives or other foods that they sold to the markets.

It was getting warm and most passengers were wearing short sleeves. The seasoned travelers had a lightweight jacket tied around their waist or in their backpacks as they knew the evenings would get cool, especially right near the water. Tour bus number one pulled out of the dock area and began its tour, Highlights of Santorini. Bus two, on the same tour but on a reversed route, left seven minutes later. Bus three, on the same route as number one, had to wait as four of its passengers weren't on the first ferry.

Despite the delay in boarding the ferries, the day was off to a great beginning. On the ship, Clive Stewart was pleased because the port today was a small island; he had security personnel with each tour and he would have extra personnel at various locations on the island ready to respond to any problem.

54

Thursday, July 18

10:30 AM

Pierre Dubois knocked on the third deck door of security. *"Bonjour, Monsieur* Dubois," Clive said as he opened the door, not knowing who else might be around and who else might hear him.

"Good morning, Mr. Stewart; do you have some time for me?"

"Of course; please come in," Stewart responded as he held the door open for the man to enter and then he shut the door. The area was now secure. "How's it been going?" Clive asked as the Interpol agent sat down on the opposite of the desk.

"It's been fine," Moreau answered. "I've not encountered anyone who's not thought I was the marketing fellow that you've made me out to be." Moreau paused for a moment and then continued. "Now what would happen if someone actually went online and looked up the chief marketing officer for the cruise line? What then?"

Prepared for that question, Clive Stewart responded quite easily. "They'd find that Pierre Dubois, CMO, was a married man about fifty-five and a resident of Lyon, France. His picture would be a bit fuzzy, the resolution being blamed on the antiquated software being used by the cruise line. Why? Have you been out there to see if there was a resemblance?" Clive Stewart already knew the answer to his own question. He was good at what he did because he was usually able to predict the questions that might come his way. And knowing what those questions might be allowed him to be prepared with the answers. Clive could easily move into other corporate arenas or private consulting, but being head of security on an "under the radar" cruise line provided him with a lot of advantages plus access that wasn't available to anyone else. He liked his job; he loved the perks.

"No," Moreau replied. "I was just wondering." He just lied, and he did it with a very honest-looking face. "I'd like to go over the details of the three missing passengers; let's see if there's a pattern or clue that we can use to bring in others to help us. After all, I do have access to the most sophisticated investigative systems in the world."

"I know that *Monsieur* Moreau, and that is precisely why I asked to get you involved." Clive Stewart wasn't completely accurate with that last statement, but he wanted the Interpol agent to be on his side. As bad as it would be for the cruise line if the word got out that it was losing one passenger each day it was in port, it would be equally bad for the head of security whose job it was to safeguard the passengers as well as the assets of the ship. No; it would be worse for him. The cruise line would always rebound as other lines had done and other businesses had done after they'd suffered a horrible business and ecological disaster. But Clive Stewart would be fired in shame and it would be extremely difficult for him to get another position in security. He might be able to get a job as security in a shopping center but he wouldn't have the same perks as he had on the *Royal Holiday*. He needed to get this situation under control, and he needed Interpol's help.

Clive Stewart continued, "Last Sunday was our first port of call in Civitavecchia. Tyler Jacobs, a single male passenger in cabin 7043. He wasn't on a ship's tour, so all that we have is that he exited the ship in the morning but we have no information on where he went. All we know is that he never returned and we've not heard from him.

"The next day we docked in Messina and another single passenger, Phil Watson in cabin 4050, didn't return from his tour in Taormina. It was one of those tours where the guests had free time on their own in town; then they were supposed to meet back at a certain point and time to get on the bus back to the ship. There were several meeting times available so it wasn't until it past the all-aboard time that we knew he was missing.

"Then the following day on Tuesday we were docked in Valletta. By then, because we'd already had two passengers missing from the previous two ports, the captain had ordered that we have security personnel on each tour. But Valletta is such an easy walkable town from the pier that lots of passengers just went out on their own. Starting that day we also required that every passenger on a tour had to check back in on the ship even if they wanted to go back to town. And everyone from a tour did check back in after the tour; they were all accounted for at all-aboard time. The one passenger who was missing was Greg Brighton, another single male passenger from cabin 4099."

Clive Stewart paused; he'd given the Interpol agent all the details of the missing passengers. But Moreau was skeptical that he'd just received ALL the information. "Is that everything you know about these passengers?" he asked.

"Of course; I have no reason to hold anything back from you," Clive responded.

Moreau had done many of these investigations before. What he'd just heard from the ship's head of security about the missing persons couldn't be all the available information. "Are you telling me that no one else knows anything about these three men who coincidentally each went missing one day after another?" Moreau just stared at Stewart.

"You're asking me a question that is impossible for me to answer," Stewart replied. "Obviously, if someone else had something to do with their disappearance, then that person would know something. But I would have to know who that someone was so I could then go interrogate him."

"Or her," Moreau corrected.

"Him or her," Stewart said, the tone of his voice getting stronger.

Moreau continued, "You said that this Mr. Watson was missing from a tour in Messina. Have you talked with everyone on that tour to see if anyone remembers anything particular about him, or why he might not have returned?"

"No, I haven't," Stewart replied. "I didn't want to cause any alarm in the passengers that it wasn't safe to go on one of our tours."

"Well, it's quite obvious that it isn't safe, right?" Moreau questioned.

"I don't know that it's the tour, or if it's not the tour, Moreau," Stewart replied. "I'll have to run that by the captain before talking to thirty or more passengers about a missing person. I don't think he's going to like that."

"Do you think he's going to like it when the media reports that he's losing one passenger in every port?" Moreau was playing hardball, but that was the only game that was going to get any answers.

"I'll talk with him," Stewart said, not liking the prospect of having to go to the captain one more time with this problem.

55

Thursday, July 18

Late Afternoon

The afternoon tour bus stopped at the hilltop spot and everyone got out to take in the views. "Everyone calls this island Santorini," the tour guide began. "Santorini is actually the name of the islands that are remaining from a massive volcano. This island is technically Thira, which means that if you flew into here, you would be landing at the airport there to the east that's called Thira National Airport. It's not a very busy airport but it does handle both international and domestic flights totaling almost eight thousand flights per year. That's not a lot compared to the many airports you might use, but this is an island community of under twenty thousand people, and those flights bring in about four hundred thousand people per year. Most of them are coming for a week holiday, maybe two weeks. The tourism business is very important to us."

She paused as she led the group to the other side of the parking lot and then she continued her descriptions. "As you look north you can see how this island starts to curve around to the left. And then when you look south, you see it curving to the right. So this island is the largest remnant of the volcano caldera. The big one out there to the west is Therasia, and it's the only other inhabited island in this group, although there are only a couple hundred full-time residents." She stopped to let the passengers take in the views. Beyond the few islands was nothing but water. "Well, what do you think so far?"

"It's beautiful," several people replied. There were also responses of Gorgeous, Amazing, Wonderful and Fantastic.

Many of the passengers were taking pictures, although the prettiest sights were still to come. Some stepped away from the group to experience the quietness that was infused with the rustling breeze as it rose from the water to the top of the hill.

As the tour guide started walking back to the bus she said, "Let's go to a restaurant with an equally amazing view and have some appetizers and wine." Most of the group was automatically following her.

The security person assigned to this tour stayed back as he glanced around to make sure that no one was wandering off, not that there was any place to go from up here. The passengers climbed into the bus and security then boarded and counted from front to back; it was the right number and he gave a thumbs-up to the guide who was standing near the driver.

The doors closed and the bus started heading down the windy road. The driver was about to make a wide right turn when a small car coming up the hill also entered the sharp turn. The bus driver braked and then put both hands in the air, palms up, for the driver of the car to see. The bus wasn't going anywhere so the driver of the small car put it into reverse and slowly backed up, conceding the road to the bus. As the bus driver drove past the small car, the bus driver honked the horn; a few passengers in window seats at the rear of the bus on the left side saw the car driver's interesting response.

"We'll be at the restaurant in about five minutes," the guide interrupted the quiet, pulling a few out of their short naps. "We have tables assigned to us so just look for our bus number when you go inside. There are some washrooms on the main level and there are more down the stairs at the back of the room. The appetizers they'll be bringing out are all local delicacies and I'll come around to explain what everything is. There'll be water on the table and one of the servers will come by to offer you a local wine. It's probably not like what you're used to on the ship, but it's pretty good for growing on island soil. After you're done, you can wander around the grounds and look at the flowers and see how they grow their vegetables; I think you'll find that interesting. Any questions?"

"How long do we have?" came from a voice halfway back on the bus.

"We have exactly one hour here."

Just then the driver turned off the paved road into a rocky parking lot with three other tour buses already parked. "As you can see," the guide continued, "this is a popular restaurant for the tours, so I know you'll like it."

Even though they were now the fourth busload in the restaurant, there was plenty of room and the opened windows allowed a fresh breeze to move through the interconnecting rooms. Most of the passengers headed directly to the washrooms where lines formed leading out of both the men's and the women's.

The security person walked up to the guide and started talking with her. "Are there some larger industries on the island or is most of the business tourist related?"

"Tourism is our main source of income especially since they shut down the pumice quarries back in the eighties. We do have a thriving wine industry, but it's mostly for local and tourism sales. Some of it goes to the mainland, but I don't think any of it's exported since we just can't grow that many grapes with our limited rainfall."

"That's interesting," security replied. "I noticed the drip system for the plants; that's one way to make sure that the precious water goes right where it's needed. What are our plans for the rest of the day?" he asked.

Looking around to see if the passengers were coming back from the washrooms and going to the designated tables, the guide said, "We'll go have a little walk around a typical area, by some houses, markets and an old church. Then we'll head to Thira where you're on your own to take the gondola down to the ferries and back to the ship. We should be in the main part of town in two to two and a half hours."

'On your own' wasn't something that the security man wanted to hear. Once the passengers were turned loose, he would lose control, and there would be no way for him to make sure that all of his passengers made it back to the ship. Sensing a prescription for problems, he decided to have a glass of the local wine.

After lunch and the walk through the small village, the bus took the passengers into the main square in Thira and the tour guide gave them directions on where to find the best places to eat or have a glass of wine, to find authentic souvenirs and how to get to the gondola that would take them down to the ferries. "Remember," she began, "the last ferry leaves at eight o'clock and so that means you should be in line for the gondola by seven o'clock. With another ship in, the wait for the gondola gets long and you don't want to miss your ship."

Yes, please don't miss the ship, the security man thought.

The sunset was spectacular as most passengers found tables with amazing views of the water below, their ship, the other islands and the beautiful setting sun. A cool breeze picked up shortly before the sun went down but the effects of the breeze were offset by the wines that were being enjoyed by many.

Knowing there wasn't much he could do to make sure that all of his passengers made it back to the ship, the security crewman walked down the narrow alleyway to the gondola. He did recognize some from his tour—or were they other passengers that he'd seen on the ship? It was getting dark rather quickly but he was able to see the winding path going down the hill to the ferry landing. There were a few people on donkeys going down that way and he also saw a few people walking down that tricky slope.

He decided to take the gondola down the hill even though there was still sufficient time. He'd be at the ferries to help if needed and he'd be sure to get one back to the ship. As he rode down in the open windowed car, he could hear a few people singing as they walked down; it sounded as if they really had enjoyed the local wine.

56

Thursday, July 18

8:40 PM

"Clive Stewart," the head of security said as he answered his mobile phone. "What? I'll be right there." He closed his phone. "Another one," he said to the Interpol agent as he got up from his desk and headed to the door. Once out into the passageway, Moreau became Dubois and he followed Stewart past Guest Relations to the check-in area.

Clive went right to the computer and looked at the screen. The name Tony Lockwood in cabin 7012, was highlighted in red. "What do we know about him?" Clive asked.

"There'd been nothing unusual up to today," the security guard said. "He left this morning on one of the tours and he's the only one who left but didn't check back in."

"Has anyone checked his cabin?" Dubois asked.

The security guard was surprised that the other man, not the head of security, asked that question. "Yes, a detail already went there, but the cabin steward said it was just as he'd left it this morning after cleaning it. It didn't look as if anyone had been in the cabin since the steward was in there."

"Who from security was assigned to his tour?" Stewart asked.

"It was Roberts. I've already called him to come down here and what he told me didn't really surprise me. He said that all the tours were turned loose in town and just told to make sure they made the last ferry back to the ship."

"That sounds like a disaster just waiting to happen," Dubois said as he looked at Stewart who just nodded his head. "Do we send someone back for him?" Dubois asked, forgetting that the ship's tenders weren't used, so it would require a new set of local approvals just to lower a boat into the water.

"That's not an option," Stewart replied. "We use the local ferries here." Stewart paused, then said to the guard, "Call ashore and find out if there are any ferries en route to the ship or if there are any of our passengers waiting there."

"Yes, sir," the guard said as he went to the ship's phone and called to the ferry dock. He returned two minutes later with the answers. "The last ferry for our ship has already returned to the dock and there aren't any of our passengers waiting there."

"Thank you," Clive said and he turned to return to the office. "Oh, Roberts," he said as he saw the security person who'd been assigned to Tony Lockwood's tour. The two men talked and it was just as the other guard said: the passengers were turned loose in town so there was no way to keep track of them. There was nothing the security man could do. Clive Stewart agreed with him, although he knew the captain was not going to agree.

Clive thanked the man and he and Dubois returned to the security office. "Any thoughts before we call the captain, Moreau?" Stewart asked as he sat down, hoping for any ideas.

"It is very strange that these passengers would just leave the ship and willingly miss getting back on board. I've heard of it down in the Caribbean where someone just wanted to escape, but one in each port doesn't make any sense to me." Moreau stopped; he was telling things to Stewart that he already knew.

Clive Stewart called the captain, who was, of course, upset. He screamed through the phone at the head of security who just took the verbal abuse. Nothing he could say would alter the way the captain was thinking. He just hoped that the Interpol agent would be able to help him come up with a solution before they got back to Barcelona in eight more days. Clive held the phone away from his ear, not to let Moreau hear but to protect his left ear from the yelling.

Clive placed a quick call to the Guest Relations manager.

"Will Mr. Tony Lockwood in cabin 7012 please contact Guest Relations immediately? Once again, Mr. Tony Lockwood, please contact Guest Relations on Deck Three immediately. Thank you." That was the fourth such announcement on the cruise; how many more would there be?

57

Thursday, July 18

9:00 PM

Becky Anderson peeked between the stage curtains to see a half-empty theater. Normally full, the draw of tonight's show was not strong enough to outweigh the busy and tiring day that most passengers had ashore. It wasn't a reflection of *Final Act*, a highly talented musical duo; it was hard for them to compete with a comfortable bed for passengers who probably had one too many glasses of local wine and whose feet were tired from all the walking.

She closed the curtain and turned to the couple. "Sorry it's not a full house for you tonight. This is a port that really takes it out of the guests. But I know that those who are here will really enjoy your show."

"We started out playing to crowds of maybe a dozen, so we're used to it," the man said.

"Thanks," Becky said as she picked up her microphone and walked through the curtains, smiling and trying to look upbeat. "Good evening ladies and gentlemen; how was your day in Santorini?"

The weak response prompted Becky to go with a different approach. "You're going to have to help me out," she said, "since many of your fellow passengers got too tired out today or had a little too much of the local *vino*. So how about if you do two things for me? First, would you gather here in the center section and make it like a cozy nightclub for our fantastic act tonight?" Most of the people moved right away;

peer pressure got the remaining few stragglers to move down near the front and in the center.

"Excellent," the cruise director said as the last person sat down. "You are a good audience," she continued, placing emphasis on the word *are*. "Now the second thing I want you to do is to make noise like three people. Let's give it a try." She turned her back, walked toward the curtain and then turned back around.

As she was walking forward, she started again, "Good evening, ladies and gentlemen? Did you have a good day in Santorini?"

The loud response was overwhelming this time. It sounded like a full-house audience this time. "That's great; thank you!" Becky said excitedly as she smiled. "Now, I want that same level of enthusiasm for the next hour as a highly talented husband and wife duo are going to entertain you with amazing music and song. So, please give that same warm, almost piping hot, welcome to *Final Act*!" The thunderous applause was fantastic as the curtains opened for the duo to begin. The lights were dimmed in a circular fashion so the performers could see only some of the audience and none of the many empty seats.

58
Thursday, July 18
9:00 PM

"Come," the captain barked upon hearing the knock on the door. He leaned back in his comfortable chair, although he wasn't feeling too comfortable at the moment. All it would take would be one passenger to get wind of what was happening and send it out on social media and his career would be over. Actually, it wouldn't even have to be a passenger; it could be a crew member who could sink his ship, figuratively speaking.

The door opened and Clive Stewart and Pierre Dubois entered. Stewart shut the door and he and Antoine Moreau approached the captain's desk. They didn't sit down immediately.

"Have a seat," the captain instructed and the men sat. There was silence. "We now have four missing passengers; is that right?"

"That's correct, Captain," Stewart answered.

"What do we know?" the captain asked.

Clive Stewart cleared his throat and then began. "There are a couple similarities, and then there's a lot we don't know. But here is what we do know, starting with the similarities. First, one passenger has failed to check back in on the ship in each port of call. Second, each missing passenger is a male traveling solo. Unfortunately, that's where the similarities end."

"Certainly that's not all we know," the captain stated.

"Correct, Captain. The first and third missing passengers were not on tours, while the second and fourth were on ship tours." Clive Stewart wanted to give all the information to the captain, and he was going to do that. There just wasn't much information to give.

"Remind me again how we lost passengers while they're on one of our tours," the captain said sarcastically.

"Our second port was in Messina and some of the tours were in Taormina where people had free time to walk around the town; then they were supposed to be back at a certain meeting place at a given time to get on a bus back to the ship. Our fourth port was today here in Santorini, and just like Taormina, the passengers were turned loose in town and told to take the gondola down to the ferry dock because the last ferry for our ship left at eight o'clock." Clive Stewart waited to see if the captain had anything to add or to ask; he didn't.

Clive continued, "So even though we had security with each of our tours, once the people were set free in town, there was no way to keep track of them. I did check with each of the security personnel on today's tours and they had all of the passengers accounted for all the way up until they were set loose. I'm not suggesting that we change the way Shore Excursion does their tours, because every other cruise line does the same thing. So it's not the tour and it's not the process. This has to do with something else."

Antoine Moreau sat silently in his chair. Patience was a key virtue in his profession and he used the time to process the information. He thought he'd come up with something but he wasn't going to mention it until it was the right time.

"And we know nothing about the background of these four men who are missing?" the captain asked.

Clive Stewart looked at Moreau, giving him the nod that this was a question for him to answer. Digging into a passenger's past was a very sensitive subject and one that would raise a lot of questions if discovered. Cruise lines didn't typically have the assets available to them to do that type of investigative work. Holiday Cruise Lines, PLC, did have those assets in place; now that they had Inspector Moreau on the ship. It was Moreau's time to tell the captain what he'd found.

"As you know, Captain, Interpol is primarily an agency that looks into international crimes and other affairs. So it's definitely a rarity that we come on a ship to help solve an intriguing mystery that doesn't seem to have any criminal intent. We have, however, looked into the backgrounds of Tyler Jacobs in cabin 7043, Phil Watson in cabin 4050, Greg Brighton in cabin 4099, and Tony Lockwood in cabin 7012. In one respect, I'm happy with what we found, but in another, I'm not." Moreau stopped; he wanted that to sink in.

It did, and quickly. "And what did you find?" Captain Christopolous asked.

"Absolutely nothing," Moreau responded. "Everything we saw on these four young men came up clean. One of them had a traffic ticket and another was behind on his student loans, but these are decent young men. As Mr. Stewart said, an interesting point is that each one of the missing passengers is a male passenger sailing solo on your cruise. Is that significant?" He paused. "I don't have the answer to that question right now, but it certainly creates an additional data point."

Clive Stewart was enjoying not being the center of the captain's attention. He knew it wouldn't last for very long, but he'd take what he could get. He liked Captain Christopolous, but he wished the captain would see things from a logical point of view at times. What was it about the Greeks; why did everything have to be about emotions and feelings?

"So is that all we have?" the captain asked.

"I'm afraid so, Captain," Stewart said reluctantly.

"Actually, it's not," Moreau interjected to the surprise of the ship's head of security.

"What else do you have, Moreau?" Captain Christopolous leaned forward in his chair, expecting to hear a revelation, something that might turn this fiasco into a solution.

Stewart was stunned; this was news to him. He leaned back in his chair, even though there wasn't much room to lean back into. What was the Interpol agent keeping from him?

Antoine Moreau got up from his chair and went over to the whiteboard on the wall to the right of the captain. He picked up a marker and then wrote the four cabin numbers in order of the disappearance of the passengers:

7043

4050

4099

7012

"As those cabin numbers appear, they mean absolutely nothing except there was a single male passenger in each one of them and he is now missing. The captain is no doubt aware of the major contributions that the early Greeks made to the development of mathematics. So let's take another look at those numbers."

Moreau then added the individual digits of each number:

7043 7 + 0 + 4 + 3 = 14

4050 4 + 0 + 5 + 0 = 9

4099 4 + 0 + 9 + 9 = 22

7012 7 + 0 + 1 + 2 = 10

"As they are," Moreau said, "those new numbers still don't mean anything. But," and he paused. "But when you look at them from a mathematician's eyes, they might mean something else. Let's take a look at each one of those sums in terms of its leading-digit modulus."

"What?" asked the captain. Stewart was glad the captain asked the question so he didn't have to.

"Modular arithmetic," Moreau began, "is something we use every day but we don't think about it. We typically use a number system based on ten. But when we use a clock, we use a number system based on twelve. So if it's nine o'clock and you add five hours, you don't get fourteen o'clock, you get to two o'clock. Why? Because while nine plus five is fourteen based on the decimal, or tens, system that we're used to, we have to count to see how many units past twelve we get to when we add five to nine. So we have nine, ten, eleven, twelve, one, two. In the case of a clock our modulus, or the number at which we start counting again, is twelve.

"So let's look at those sums and see what they are if we use the leading digit, or the deck number, as the modulus."

7043 $7 + 0 + 4 + 3 = 14$; $14 - 7 = 7$; $7 - 7 = 0$

4050 $4 + 0 + 5 + 0 = 9$; $9 - 4 = 5$; $5 - 4 = 1$

4099 $4 + 0 + 9 + 9 = 22$; $22 - 4 = 18$; $18 - 4 = 14$;

$14 - 4 = 10$; $10 - 4 = 6$;

$6 - 4 = 2$

7012 $7 + 0 + 1 + 2 = 10$; $10 - 7 = 3$

"Here's what I want you to notice," Moreau continued. "When we summed the cabin number digits and then used the deck number as the modulus, we end up with this sequence." And he wrote it on the board.

0 1 2 3

"Does that ring a bell?" Moreau asked.

The captain just sat there, so Stewart jumped in. "It's a normal sequence of numbers starting at zero," Clive said with a shrug.

"You're right about that," Moreau said. "But that's not its only significance. I don't know where you were sailing last year, so you might have never heard of this. There were some murders down in Sydney, Australia, and they were getting front-page attention in the newspapers because of where they were committed. The police weren't coming up with anything and then they brought in this mathematics professor from the United States who made sense of it all. It all had to do with numbers, and I think that's where we are."

"What do you mean?" the captain asked.

"Notice our sequence, 0-1-2-3," Moreau answered. "That was the same sequence in those murders and I think it plays an important role here."

"So you're saying that this mathematical linkage that helped solve those murders in Sydney is the same linkage that's tied to our disappearing passengers?"

"Yes, Captain," Moreau said. "That's exactly what I think."

Stewart smiled; he was off the hook for answers.

"And so what do you think we should do, *Monsieur* Moreau?" the captain asked.

"I think the answer is quite clear, Captain Christopolous. You need to bring in this mathematics professor; he's helped solve mysteries elsewhere in the world and I believe he is just the man that you need." Antoine Moreau was clearly laying the responsibility on the master of the vessel.

"What do you think, Mr. Stewart?" the captain asked.

Not having solutions of his own, Clive Stewart had no other choice. "I think *Monsieur* Moreau has found a very workable approach, Captain."

59

Thursday, July 18

10:00 PM

"What do you think, ladies and gentlemen; wasn't that a fantastic performance? Applaud one more time and let's hear it once again for *Final Act*." Cruise director Becky Anderson was trying to get a good response for the highly talented duo. It wasn't their fault that they were scheduled to perform just thirty minutes after all-aboard time in a port that always returned tired passengers. The audience, as small as it was, did the best they could do. The stage crew managed the lights to focus on those who were in attendance, while keeping the lights off the vacant seats.

The curtain opened again and the gracious couple smiled and bowed. They had put on a great show; those who chose to relax rather than seeing the show were the ones who missed out.

Becky shook their hands and then went to the front of the stage. "Even though their name is *Final Act*, maybe we'll be able to convince them to do one more show. What do you think?" The audience once again responded to give an energetic applause to the highly talented duo. One couple in the front row stood up and then the rest of the audience followed suit to give them a nice standing ovation. Becky stepped to the side to let the couple be the center of focus. They stood and bowed and showed their appreciation for what they knew was a small crowd by clapping their hands as a way of saying Thank You to the audience.

The applause slowed and the audience sat down.

"Thank you so much," Becky said. "We'll let you know when we're able to schedule them and I hope you tell all your friends what a fantastic show they put on tonight. Agree?" The applause was polite, but not as strong as before. "Tonight we have late night dancing in the Sky View Lounge starting at ten thirty. Then tomorrow is an absolutely fabulous day with our first Art Auction at Sea taking place in the Sky View Lounge. We'll have a beautiful day at sea and you can come and view and bid on some fantastic works of art; it all starts at ten thirty in the morning. There'll be coffee, tea, and pastries, so if you want to sleep in and then come on up, they'll have something for you. Plus there will also be champagne and mimosas to get you into the auction spirit.

"Then at two o'clock you're not going to want to miss our galley tour where you get to see exactly how all your wonderful meals are prepared. Not only that, but you'll be able to snack on some of the tasty items as you walk through. Make sure you bring your camera because you're going to see some creative displays that you'll want to try at home for your next dinner party.

"Then tomorrow night is our second formal night of the cruise. So make your plans to get your hair done and dress up as there will be music all around the ship and photographers will be taking pictures all night long. I think they're closed right now, but tomorrow morning you can make reservations to have your formal photos taken at a time that best suits you.

"Well, ladies and gentlemen, you've been a great audience tonight, and I truly mean that. Whatever you do around the ship, do enjoy it and have a great evening on the *Royal Holiday*."

The small crowd which all stayed to hear Becky's announcements, gave her a nice round of applause.

60

Friday, July 19

9:00 AM

"Yes, I'll hold," Captain Konstantinos Christopolous said as he waited to have his call patched through to Paul Martin, Holiday Cruise Line's Chief Executive Officer, who was vacationing in the Netherlands. "Get ready for some fireworks," the captain said softly to Clive Stewart and Antoine Moreau.

"Hello, this is Paul Martin," the voice came on the line.

"Good morning, Paul. This is Captain Konstantinos Christopolous on the *Royal Holiday*, and I have a serious problem to discuss with you. I have you on speaker phone from my office on the ship and in the office with me are Clive Stewart, our head of security, and Antoine Moreau from Interpol."

"Interpol?" Martin asked in disbelief. "What's going, Konstantinos?"

"Let me assure you that there's nothing wrong with the ship or it would have already been blasted all over the media," the captain said hoping to calm the CEO. "But the problem we do have will really cripple us if we don't get it resolved immediately. That's why we brought Interpol on, and that's why we're calling you this morning."

"Get to the point, Kostas," Martin insisted.

"Of course," the captain resumed. "We've been to four ports on our current fifteen-day voyage and one passenger has gone missing each day we've been in port."

"You've lost four passengers?" Martin screamed.

"Yes, it looks that way, Mr. Martin," Clive Stewart jumped in. "But from what we've been able to uncover, they've disappeared while on shore; it had nothing to do with the ship. Two of them were off on their own and the other two were on tours where the passengers were turned loose in town and told to meet at a certain time or place."

"Who's speaking?" the CEO asked. "And how is that supposed to make it any better?"

"I'm sorry, Mr. Martin. This is Clive Stewart, head of security. I agree that it's not better knowing those circumstances, but you can't control people when they're free adults in the port. We had security personnel on the tours in the last two ports and each passenger was accounted for up to the time when the tour was over in town."

"Well, Mr. Stewart, what is your solution and what is Interpol doing?" Paul Martin typically liked phone calls from the ship captains; this definitely wasn't one of those calls.

"*Bonjour, Monsieur* Martin," Antoine Moreau interjected, using his French to diffuse the tense situation. "My name is Inspector Antoine Moreau out the Paris Interpol office. I came aboard the ship a couple days ago because these disappearances do have an international connection. My resources have looked into the backgrounds of these four people, all single male passengers, but we've found nothing that would provide a clue as to why they didn't return to the ship. I have, however, uncovered a pattern that I think may help us, and that is also the reason for our call to you this morning."

"Kostas, who's in charge there and what do you want?" Martin wanted be able to go to breakfast with his wife, and then head out into the countryside. Being a CEO had plenty of perks, but being accessible even on vacation was not a perk; it was a requirement.

"You know that I'm completely in charge here, Paul," the captain replied as he took offense to the CEO's implication that he wasn't in charge of his ship. "You've always stressed the importance of utilizing the best possible resources, and that's what I'm doing. Now I'd like you to listen to Inspector Moreau's proposal."

"As I was saying, *Monsieur* Martin," the agent continued as if he'd not been interrupted. "I've uncovered a numbers pattern that I think can help us. Did you read about those murders in Sydney, Australia, last year where the police brought in this mathematics professor to help them? The numbers pattern I've found is similar to the pattern that the professor uncovered as he pinpointed the murderer."

"So?" Martin interjected.

"So," the captain took over, "we're going to call the professor and you're going to convince him to come on the ship and work with us to solve these disappearances."

"How are you going to locate this professor?" Martin asked.

Moreau smiled as he began. "That is where the power of Interpol comes in handy. Professor Alfred Dunningham lives in California in the USA, but our resources found that he's currently in Paris attending the International Mathematics Symposium. It turns out that he's there to receive an award for the work he did last year down in Sydney helping the police force. He's in his hotel room right now and we're going to call him. Please stand by." The Interpol agent didn't give the CEO any opportunity to object. Moreau knew he wouldn't hang up; good CEOs wouldn't abandon their employees in times of need. And this was certainly one of those times.

"Yes, hello," the voice at the other end said.

"Good morning, Professor Dunningham," Moreau began. "I realize it's a bit early, but I ask that you bear with me for just a few moments."

"Who is this and how did you get my number at eight o'clock in the morning?" Dunningham responded.

Moreau pushed the button to patch in Paul Martin's line so that there were now three lines connected. There was a slight click as Martin's line was re-engaged. "Professor," Moreau continued, "my name is Antoine Moreau and I'm stationed in Paris, although I'm not there right now. You see, I'm an Interpol agent and I'm on a ship in the Mediterranean Sea where our captain has great need of your services."

"*Merci, Monsieur* Moreau," the professor replied in a slightly mocking tone. "But I'm on vacation and I don't appreciate being tracked down. So as you French say, *Au revoir.*"

"Please professor, wait," Martin said. "My name is Paul Martin, and I'm the CEO of Holiday Cruise Lines, and there's been a terrible problem on one of our ships. That is where the Interpol agent is right now, along with the ship's captain and head of security. Will you please just listen to them? That's all I can ask."

Dunningham sat in the hotel room's desk chair and exhaled. "I'm listening," he said with resignation in his voice.

"Thank you, Professor," the Greek captain said. "This is Captain Konstantinos Christopolous on the *Royal Holiday* and as our CEO Paul Martin just said, we're encountering a rather strange problem and the Interpol agent who came on to help us has uncovered something that he says you'd recognize."

"Yes, Captain," Moreau took over. "Professor, remember the Sydney murders you helped to solve last year? Of course you do, that's why you're in my beautiful city of Paris right now to be honored for that work. I'll be as brief as I can be, so let me explain what's happened and the pattern I've found." The Interpol agent went on to describe the disappearance in each of the four ports where the ship had been. He then said what they knew about the passengers and their respective room numbers. "I remembered your work in Sydney last year, and so I took those room numbers and using the leading digit, which is the same as the deck number, I used that digit as the modulus of the sum of the digits. The pattern that emerged from that was 0-1-2-3. See how that ties in with the Sydney murders that you solved?"

"Yes, I see that, Inspector," Dunningham replied. "That's good work."

"And?" Moreau asked.

"And what?" Dunningham answered. "I told you that's good work, but if you're thinking that your disappearances are being done by a copycat of the Sydney murders, then that's way too obvious. You know this as well as anyone, you can find patterns in almost any set of numbers; it's the understanding of the pattern and its relevance to the particular situation that counts. So unless you can tell me how 0-1-2-3 plays into the disappearances, you really don't have anything."

Captain Christopolous knew that was the only chance to get the renowned professor involved, so he had to step in and be very direct. "Professor Dunningham, just as the Sydney Police Force needed your help, that is where we are right now. This isn't just about my ship or Mr. Martin's cruise line; it's about the cruise industry. If this problem doesn't get solved and the word gets out that it's not safe to go on cruises, the entire industry will suffer hundreds of millions of dollars of losses. I am begging you; we need you to join us on the ship in the Mediterranean."

"Professor," it was Paul Martin. "We've booked you and your wife two first class tickets on Cyprus Airways out of Paris today for a direct flight to Cyprus where you'll be met by a chauffeur and treated to the finest possible accommodations. I know this is a terrible inconvenience, but we wouldn't ask you — no, we wouldn't plead with you — if this weren't of absolute critical importance. Please help us and you and your wife will be able to sail with us any time you want completely free of charge."

There was silence on all three phones except for the tapping of a pencil; that was the professor.

"And I'll arrange for your seminars to be given in the best places in the world, wherever you want to go," Moreau added as an enticement.

"Gentlemen, please," Dunningham broke in. "You don't have to offer me bribes. That's probably a bad word. My wife and I want to enjoy the last couple of days here in Paris. You certainly understand that, don't you, Inspector?"

"Of course, I do," Moreau answered. "We're asking you to think of all the people whose lives will be affected if we don't get to the bottom of this. It's not just the four people who are missing, but what about the bigger picture?"

"Sometimes I wonder why I even bother to answer the telephone," Professor Dunningham said as he resigned himself to the natural conclusion of this conversation. "What time's the flight and how will I get all the other details?"

Clive Stewart breathed a sigh of relief as Moreau gave him the flight information and told him that an agent would be at his hotel in thirty minutes to help them with any necessary departure incidentals and then drive them to the airport.

"We could have reached him even if he didn't answer the hotel phone," Moreau said once they'd all hung up the phones.

61

Friday, July 19

Late Morning

"I hope you're all enjoying our sea day today," came Becky's voice public address system. "The captain has told me that we should have very smooth water and only slight breezes today, so it's going to be a gorgeous day here on the *Royal Holiday*. Here's a quick reminder of some of the activities going on around the ship today. In about ten minutes time we'll have our first Art Auction at Sea up in the Sky View Lounge on Deck Twelve. That will be starting at ten thirty. At two o'clock our executive chef will be opening up the galley for all to come through and see how many of the culinary delights are made. Cameras are welcome, and please wear closed toed shoes as the galley is a working environment.

"Then tonight is our second formal night, so get all dressed up and join in the festivities going on throughout the ship. Please remember that all public areas, except for Oceans Café, require formal attire in keeping with the spirit of tonight's dress code. As always, all of the daily activities, along with some special highlights, are in the daily paper so please make sure you take a look at it. Captain Christopolous and his entire crew join me in wishing you a marvelous day here on the *Royal Holiday*, and do let us know if there's something we can do to make your vacation even more enjoyable. Thank you for your attention, ladies and gentlemen."

Passengers were milling around in the Sky View Lounge, walking up and down the between the rows of paintings. Some were grouped by artist, others by genre. The art staff was busily explaining certain pieces to interested folks and telling them what the opening bids would be.

"Good morning, art buyers," the art manager said into his microphone. "Welcome to our first Art Auction at Sea. Our gallery has been in business for over fifteen years and we are proud to be the only gallery that displays and sells art on the Holiday Cruise Line fleet of ships. As you meander around, if you see a particular piece of art that you'd like brought up for auction, just place a sticky note on it and we'll bring it up when it's auction time. There's no obligation for you to bid on it, but if it's not brought up here, then no one will have a chance to bid. So it's not just for you, but you're helping your fellow passengers by placing those sticky notes on the artwork so we know what you're all interested in."

"Do you think that's a real Rembrandt?" one of the passengers asked another passenger as they looked at an exquisite pen and ink sketching that was in an elegant frame worthy of the famous Dutch painter. The sign read: **Rembrandt van Rijn**.

"I'm no art expert," said the other fellow, "but it must be real; they wouldn't put up a fake or a copy, would they?"

"They're all real originals," the art staffer said as she walked up to the two men. "One thing that a lot of people don't realize about Rembrandt is how prolific of an artist he was. He was very famous in his own time and so he sought to capitalize on that fame by turning out piece after piece to a populous that was ready for anything he did." The staffer continued, "How many people do you know who own a Rembrandt? Probably not very many, right? His works are still popular today, and we only have a few left. But you can add one to your collection today and we'll ship it to your home at no additional charge. Did you want to put a sticky note on it? Remember, there's no

obligation to bid on it, but you can't bid if it's not up there."
The attractive staffer smiled at the two men as she slowly
walked away.

"Feel free to pick up a complimentary glass of champagne
or a mimosa, ladies and gentlemen, and make sure you have a
pad of the sticky notes." The art manager was making one
more pitch to the passengers before he started the auction.
"Why do you need the sticky notes? …" He continued on with
his spiel, but most of the attendees has already made the rounds
and were now sitting down and ready for the auction to begin.

John Phillips from cabin 7053 made his entrance wearing a
light blue sport coat, white shirt and a peach-colored ascot.
Heads turned as he entered and the attractive female art staffer
snagged a champagne flute and headed over to him. "Good
morning, sir," she said as she handed him the champagne. "Do
let me know if you have questions about any of the pieces."

"I will, of course," Phillips replied. "By the way, do you
have any Jasper Johns, something in a lighter shade and not the
dark blues or reds?"

"We do, it's in pink, and it's one of his rare pieces because
as you just said, most of his are in the darker shades. Shall I
bring it out for you, Mr. Phillips?" The art staffer knew his
name; *is that a good thing?*

"Yes," Phillips replied. "I would like to see it."

Meanwhile, it was time for the auction to begin. "Okay,
ladies and gentlemen, it's time to get the auction started," the
art manager announced. "We do have a few basic items to
cover before we begin," he continued, and then he read the
rules, a legal requirement.

As the pieces were brought up, the manager/auctioneer
described the piece and then announced its opening bid. Most
opening bids were passed. Nothing was selling until one of the

Peter Max *Statue of Liberty* pieces was brought to the front. The opening bid was announced and Peter Abrahms raised his bid card. His wife, Margaret, looked at him; did the champagne have the staff's desired effect?

"Thank you for the bid, sir." The art manager continued to describe the *Statue of Liberty* series, one of the famous collections from Peter Max. "Remember, folks, we'll package and ship these items to your home, so you don't need to worry about an extra baggage fee." He was attempting to be humorous but the audience wasn't buying it.

"We have an opening bid on this highly desirable Peter Max *Statue of Liberty* painting. Who else would like to see this in their home?"

Robert Stevens turned his head to the right to look at his wife, Patricia. She saw the glance and just shrugged her shoulders. Robert took that as a yes. He raised his bid card to the delight of the auctioneer.

"The gentleman down here raises the bid; thank you, sir. Do we have any other bids?" Robert Stevens had raised his card because he really liked the painting and he knew that Peter Max was one of the most collectable and recognizable artists of the twentieth and twenty-first centuries.

Peter Abrahms immediately put his bid card in the air; he *wanted* the Peter Max painting. He had the perfect place for it in their living room and it would raise their stature among their friends. It could even be a great excuse to throw a spectacular dinner party and invite a few of the media.

"Thank you for the re-bid, sir" the auctioneer said. "Do we have any other bids for this amazing piece of Americana?"

Another bid card was raised; who was that? It was the handsome and debonair John Phillips jumping into the bidding war. "Thank you for your bid, Mr. Phillips." The art manager was mentally tallying his commission from the sale of this piece of art; he smiled.

The bidding continued with raised bids from Robert Stevens and then Peter Abrahms and then John Phillips. Phillips dropped out when the bidding reached fifteen thousand dollars. It was just Stevens and Abrahms, and a devious auctioneer, until the bidding hit twenty thousand. Robert Stevens was the last one to bid, so he was the winner.

The art manager approached Peter Abrahms after Mr. Stevens had made the arrangements to pay for his Peter Max painting. "I have one more of these that I can sell to you for the same price," the art manager quietly said to Abrahms.

"I'll take it," Peter Abrahms said, not realizing that both he and Robert Stevens had been duped by the art manager and auctioneer. The artwork was authentic, but they'd been led to believe that they had only one of that series on the ship.

62

Friday, July 19

11:00 AM

"I think it's Terminal 2D," Professor Dunningham said to the driver as the car was nearing Charles de Gaulle Airport about a half hour drive north of Paris.

"*Oui, monsieur*," the driver acknowledged.

Since receiving the phone call from the cruise line three hours ago, Alfred and Sylvia Dunningham had quickly packed their bags. He wasn't sure if it was a blessing that Paris time was one hour behind the time on the ship wherever it was in the Mediterranean Sea. As Inspector Antoine Moreau had told him, an Interpol agent did appear at their hotel shortly after the call, soon followed by another agent.

Professor Dunningham didn't know if the driver and the other man in the car were from Interpol or if they were just a hired car service. That question was answered when they arrived at the airport and pulled into a spot marked *RÉSERVÉ* (*RESERVED*). A policeman quickly approached the car as the driver was the first to get out. The driver reached inside his coat pocket, pulled something out and showed it the officer. The policeman squinted to look through the car's darkened windows, but he wasn't able to see who was in the car that warranted two Interpol agents. He did, however, motion for an airport employee to bring a luggage cart. The other agent retrieved the Dunninghams' bags from the car's trunk and placed them on the cart.

"We're certainly capable of carrying our own bags," Dunningham said.

"Our instructions, *monsieur*," was the curt reply.

Entering Terminal 2D, the two agents looked for Cyprus Airways. The airline, like most of the other airlines that were in 2D, didn't have a major presence at the Charles de Gaulle Airport. Cyprus Airways had several inbound and departing flights, but only nonstop in each direction. Thankfully, the Dunninghams were on the nonstop; it was scheduled to depart at 12:55 PM and arrive in Larnaca, Cyprus, at 6:00 PM. Allowing for the one-hour time change, the flight was a bearable four hour and five minute flight.

Continuing to say very little, the agents led the way to the Cyprus counter and the driver walked around the line, went to the First Class counter and showed his credentials. The airline employee told the male passenger she was helping to step aside and she would finish with him as soon as she took care of these passengers. The man muttered something, the Interpol agent looked at him as he opened his coat ever so slightly to show his weapon. The man thought about saying something else, but wisely opted not to.

The agent turned to his partner who pushed the luggage cart to the counter with the Dunninghams dutifully behind him. "Sorry," Sylvia Dunningham said softly as she and her husband went past the other first class passengers.

"Passports," the lead agent said to Alfred, and he pulled them out of his shirt pocket and handed them over. The airline agent checked the reservation, scanned the passports and handed them back to the Interpol agent.

"Seats 2A and 2B?" the airline agent asked as she attached *Première Classe* baggage tags to the suit cases.

"Those are fine," Dunningham replied as he retrieved the passports back from the Interpol agent.

The airline agent handed the boarding passes to the Interpol agent who looked to make sure everything was as planned. He'd been told in no uncertain terms that it was absolutely necessary for the Dunninghams to be on Cyprus Airways flight 387 out of Paris into Larnaca, Cyprus. No mistakes of any kind would be allowed. The Paris agents understood completely.

"Merci," the Interpol agent said as he turned from the counter, boarding passes in hand, and started walking toward the overhead sign that said, **Sécurité**. The Dunninghams followed him; the other agent was behind them. The passenger who'd been displaced at the counter watched the four of them leave, shook his head and then returned to the counter. He was tempted to ask who those people were that cut right in front of him, but he decided against it.

As the Dunninghams and the Interpol agents approached the security line, the lead agent walked over to the officer in charge, showed him his credentials and the Dunninghams' boarding passes. The security officer nodded his head and motioned for Alfred and Sylvia to come to him, which they did. "Your passports, please," the officer said in English.

Alfred handed the passports to the man in the blue uniform who scanned them, compared the information to the boarding passes and then handed the passports and the boarding passes to Alfred. "Have a good flight," the officer said as he opened a gate for them to pass through while bypassing the x-ray machine. The Interpol agents stayed behind even though they could have continued on with the Dunninghams. But their job was done; they'd delivered them to the airport, got them checked in and through security without any problems.

The flight announcement was first made in French and then in English: "Cyprus Airways flight 387 with non-stop service to Larnaca, Cyprus, will begin boarding in five minutes." The announcement continued with the standard notices about boarding zones and the limits on carry-on luggage. Alfred looked at his atomic watch; it was 12:18:30.4. He didn't always need to know the exact time, down to the tenth of a second, but it was handy sometimes. He did like to watch when traveling across time zones to see when it would change either forward or backward one hour, depending on the direction of travel. As he saw the exact time, he then realized that they'd planned to go back to Musée d'Orsay today to see if his theory of the door by the top floor clock and how it opened was correct. That would have to wait until their next trip to Paris.

They walked down the jetway to the Airbus A-320 when *Première Classe* was invited to board. They were greeted with a *Bonjour* as they stepped into the plane and then took their seats in 2A and 2B. Sylvia opened a magazine and Alfred took out a journal he'd been reading when that morning telephone call interrupted them.

The flight was relatively smooth; the lunch was tasty and Alfred thought their Shiraz wine was pretty good. It didn't compare to the wine from his own grapes, but it certainly wasn't the least favorable that he'd ever tasted. Touching down, the plane was brought to the gate and they stepped off into a country they had never considered visiting.

Most of the visitors to Cyprus were from other European Union countries, meaning they didn't have to go through customs. The lines were short and they moved quickly. "We're boarding our ship late as we had some other plans that conflicted with the first few days of the cruise," Alfred Dunningham said when asked why they were going to be in Cyprus for only one day. Sylvia just smiled when the customs agent held up her passport and looked at her.

The agent stamped their passports, handed them back to Alfred and they went to retrieve their suitcases. Pushing a cart with their bags, Alfred and Sylvia entered the Arrivals hall where he saw a man holding a sign: DUNNINGHAM. "We're the Dunninghams," Alfred said as he approached the man.

"Hello," the man said. "Let me take your bags," he continued as he took possession of the cart and led them out through the double glass doors. The warm dry air was quite different from what they'd been enjoying in Paris. The man pushed a button and the trunk of the black car clicked and rose to the open position. He then opened a back door for Sylvia to enter and Alfred went to the other side and opened the door himself. After putting their bags in the trunk and closing it, the man pushed the cart to a safe area and returned to the car.

"My name is Stefan," the man said as he got into the car. "I will be driving you to the hotel where everything has already been arranged for you. We'll be there in about fifteen minutes," he said as he turned on the air conditioning and then calmly drove the Dunninghams to the hotel where they enjoyed a quiet dinner and a peaceful evening.

63

Friday, July 19

7:00 PM

Formal night on the ship once again brought out many finely dressed couples. The ship's male staffers wore either a dark suit with white shirt and tie or a tuxedo. The female staffers wore long flowing gowns in a variety of colors. Flashes were going off all over as the ship photographers were busy capturing the events of the evening. Many guests had their own cameras and were asking a tablemate to take their picture.

Olivia Cromwell was on her second glass of champagne before the first appetizer arrived. The other four at the table were interested in her hypnotist act and were asking her various questions.

One of the men wanted to know if she had a long-term contract or was it just this one cruise.

The man's wife wanted to know what it was that made her decide to get into hypnotism.

"Let me tell you," Olivia began in her slurred voice. "I grew up in Chelmsford in Essex County and everyone expected me to be someone really special because of my last name. We weren't that far from London, but the Cromwells had been quite the family in Essex, so I was always being compared with what my ancestors had accomplished. Oliver, Thomas, Richard and the list goes on. Each one of them was someone special in his time and so that burden fell on every Cromwell child born in Essex."

She paused to take another sip of the champagne; she smiled as she felt it work its way down her throat. The waiter brought the appetizers but Olivia wasn't finished with her story. "I was quite rebellious when I was young because of the expectations cast on me and so I was always in trouble. I wanted to find a way to get back at some of the people, particularly a few of the boys who lived near me, so I went to the library and read what I could about magic and all sorts of other forms of trickery. I came upon hypnotism and saw that as a way of getting even so that no one would know I did it.

"One time, I put a spell on this one boy in school and told him that our teacher, an old maid, had a secret crush on him. He went up to her, threw his arms around her and gave her a huge kiss right on the lips." The table laughed as they could imagine the horrified teacher's reaction.

"I just laughed along with the rest of our class," Olivia said. "He was sent straight away to the office, protesting his innocence all the way. He never messed with me again." The other four continued with their meal as Olivia alternated between bites of food, sips of champagne and stories of how she used hypnotism to make up for a bad childhood.

64

Saturday, July 20

7:30 AM

"Good morning, Stefan," Alfred Dunningham said as he and Sylvia stepped away from the Cyprus hotel's front desk

"It was all taken care of, yes?" Stefan asked.

"Yes, it was," Alfred said. "We didn't even have to sign anything. We received a card saying someone would pick us up this morning, but it didn't say it would be you."

"I'm glad the hotel took good care of you," Stefan said as he sidestepped Alfred's last statement. Stefan signaled for the bellman who immediately came and put the Dunninghams' luggage on a cart and followed the three of them to the front door. The same black car was out front and the trunk lid was up. The bellman put the bags in the trunk and closed it as Alfred pulled his wallet from his pocket.

"It's ALL taken care," Stefan said as he tipped the bellman and said something in Greek to him. The two men shook hands and Stefan opened a door for Sylvia and then went to the other side to open Alfred's door.

"Thank you, Stefan," Alfred said as he sat down on the comfortable leather seat.

"I hope you had time to eat some breakfast," Stefan said.

"Yes, we did," Alfred responded as he reached for one of the bottles of water set between him and Sylvia. "Hmm, cold," he said as he picked it up and loosened the cap.

"If you want anything along the way, just let me know. It's about seventy-five kilometers to Limassol, so it's less than an hour if we don't stop for anything and we don't need to be in a rush to get there." Stefan started the car, turned on the air conditioning and pulled away from the hotel.

Alfred looked at his watch and started the stop watch function. It was early on Saturday morning but the open air markets were already busy. Traffic was very light on the roads and it was a pleasant drive along the southern portion of the island. Traffic increased as they entered the outskirts of Limassol. Stefan apologized for the increase in traffic.

"This is nothing compared to what we usually see in the USA," Alfred said. Stefan nodded his head.

Stefan opened his wallet and showed the port security guard something as he slowed the car and opened his window. The guard waved him on as Stefan closed the window. It was only 8:15, but it was warm; it didn't feel warm to Stefan, but he knew that most foreigners weren't used to it that early in the day. The *Royal Holiday* was an impressive sight as it came into view, suddenly appearing as they drove slowly past the large buildings.

Alfred looked at his watch. Forty-five minutes, so an average of about sixty miles per hour.

Clive Stewart and a cabin steward were standing outside the ship security area when the black car arrived. Stefan stopped the car, got out and opened the doors for his passengers. He then opened the trunk and lifted their bags out and placed them on the cart that the steward brought over.

"Professor and Mrs. Dunningham, thank you so much for coming. My name is Clive Stewart, head of security here on the *Royal Holiday*. Please follow me and we'll go right onboard the ship."

Clive turned to Stefan, thanked him, and handed him an envelope. "My pleasure," Stefan said as he placed the envelope into his coat pocket and got into the car and drove away.

"Take the bags to cabin 1024," Clive said to the cabin steward who wheeled the cart toward the crew ramp. He then led the new passengers up the ramp to Central Lobby where he checked them in with their new room keys and then escorted them to their suite on the tenth deck. "Your luggage will be here shortly and your personal butler will also be here to introduce himself and make sure that you have everything you need. Is there anything you can think of right now?"

"We're fine, thank you," Dunningham replied.

Stewart looked at his watch; 8:27. "Professor, I know you just got here, but can you meet me at the forward elevators on Deck Nine in about ten minutes?"

"I can and I will so long as you tell me which way is forward," Alfred Dunningham answered

"That way," Clive said as he pointed. "But you can also just look on any of the signs in the passageways. I'll give you a few minutes and I'll see you in ten minutes."

"Right," Alfred said as Clive Stewart left the suite.

"This is nice, dear," Sylvia said as she walked around the spacious suite.

There was a knock and Alfred went to the door. He opened the door and saw the steward with their luggage along with a tuxedoed man. "Good morning, sir. I'm James, your personal butler. May we bring your luggage in and then I'll make sure you know how to contact me if there's anything you need."

"Just the luggage will be fine right now, James," Alfred said. "We're a bit tight on time, but maybe you can come back later if that's okay."

"Of course, sir. Here's my card with my telephone number," James said as he watched the cabin steward place the luggage on a special mat on top of the bed. They left the suite and Alfred went to the bathroom to wash his face.

Sylvia picked up a magazine, opened the door to the verandah and sat in one of the deck chairs.

Alfred opened his satchel, took out his tablet and walked toward the open verandah door. "I shouldn't be long, Sylvia," he said to her through the open door.

She looked up from her magazine and smiled at her husband. She never really knew what to say to him when he was off to one of his "meetings."

65

Saturday, July 20

8:40 AM

Remembering the direction that Clive Stewart told him, Alfred Dunningham turned as he left the suite and walked the short distance to the elevators. He was pleased to see that there was a stairway across from the two elevators since he preferred to take the stairs. He wasn't an experienced cruiser, but he'd read that taking stairs versus elevators on a cruise could mean a difference of at least five pounds when returning from the cruise. The article also mentioned other health benefits.

"Hello, again, Professor," the head of security said as Dunningham arrived on the ninth deck. "Follow me, please," Clive Stewart said as he turned toward the starboard passageway without introducing the other man that was with him. Dunningham followed; he was used to eccentricities and missing details when he was working on cases.

The three men entered the bridge area and went right to the captain's office where Stewart knocked on the door. "Come," was the captain's response and Stewart opened the door and held it while Dunningham and Moreau entered the office.

"Sorry for what appeared to be rude behavior out there," Stewart said to Dunningham. "Professor, this is Inspector Antoine Moreau from Interpol. We can't let the passengers or even the rest of the crew know that Interpol is onboard, so he is acting as Pierre Dubois, the cruise line's new chief marketing officer." The head of security paused to let that sink in. He then continued, "Inspector, this is Professor Dunningham whose work you referenced." The men shook hands and then

Dunningham turned toward the captain who'd gotten out of his chair.

"Good morning, Captain," Dunningham said as he extended his hand. "You have a very beautiful ship."

"Thank you, Professor," the captain said as they shook hands. "And thank you for coming on such short notice. I assume your accommodations are to your satisfaction?" he continued as he sat back down.

"They appear to be just fine. In fact, my wife Sylvia is already relaxing on the verandah with a nice magazine. I am curious, though, about one thing. Was our cabin assignment intentional or just happenstance?"

"What do you mean?" the captain asked.

"I gave you the best suite that was open," Clive Stewart said with a slight hint of indignance.

"There's absolutely nothing wrong with the cabin," Dunningham replied. "It's just the cabin number, 1024. The cabin's on the tenth deck and two to the tenth power is 1,024. We mathematicians always see the relevance in number even when that relevance isn't intentional."

"I told you he's the man for uncovering what the numbers mean," Inspector Moreau said to Stewart.

"Well, Professor," the captain said. "I'll leave you in the capable hands of these two men and I look forward to hearing what you come up with." The three men thanked the captain and left his office and the bridge area.

66

Saturday, July 20

8:45 AM

Clive Stewart led Inspector Moreau and Professor Dunningham out of the bridge area, but not to the stairs or elevators where they'd met. He took them, instead, to the interior set of crew stairs. "Passengers are heading off the ship for their tours so this is a less- congested way. You don't mind the stairs, do you?" he asked as an afterthought.

"I actually prefer them over the elevator," Dunningham replied, assuming correctly that the question was for him. The men were silent the rest of the way down except for the occasional greeting to several crew members they encountered along the way.

The Deck Three passageway was empty as they exited the crew area and headed toward the Central Lobby, the one familiar place on the ship for the professor. Stewart opened a door on the right before reaching the lobby area and they entered his office. Dunningham immediately noticed the math work on the white board.

"Should we review the details of the four missing passengers for you, Professor?" Stewart asked as the men sat down.

"No, I can remember the details well enough, I think," Dunningham said. "My recollection is that there isn't anything remarkable about the passengers themselves, but there are some similarities. One went missing in each port where you've stopped, which makes me wonder what will happen today. And each one was a male passenger traveling solo. Now I see that you've put their cabin numbers on the board and then finding the congruence relation of the sum of the digits using the leading digit as the modulus. That's an interesting observation, Inspector."

Moreau smiled; he was proud of what he saw in the cabin numbers.

Dunningham continued. "But as I said yesterday on the phone, unless you can tell me how 0-1-2-3 plays into those men's disappearances, I'm not sure that it's relevant."

Moreau's smiled quickly faded.

Clive Stewart didn't want a confrontation between two very intelligent and strong-willed men to begin. "And that, Professor, is exactly why we needed you here. According to the Inspector, you are the only one who made sense of those numbers in Sydney last year."

"The numbers were a little bit different," Dunningham replied, "and there were some other factors that came into play. There was, for instance, the relationship between the detective and the medical examiner. Have you looked into the possibility of any personal relationships here on board? Did any of the missing passengers know each other or anyone else on the ship? Did they have anything in common such as where they went to school, what they did for a living, how stable were their financial situations? Have you dug into any of that?"

Feeling that the math professor was telling him, an Interpol inspector, how to do his job, Moreau spoke up. "We have checked with the FBI and they are digging into these men's past. We have nothing on them at Interpol and the preliminary FBI reports show nothing meaningful."

"May I see those reports?" Dunningham asked. "Sometimes, as was the case in Sydney, there are minor traces of information in them that mean nothing on their own. It's only when they're put together with other insignificant bits that a puzzle begins to take shape."

"Of course," Moreau replied. "As I said, however, there's not much in them."

"That means it won't take long for me to read them and I'll have some time with my wife. Now," Dunningham continued, "tell me what you've done to increase security on the tours so you don't lose any more passengers."

Clive Stewart went through the details of having security with each tour and that everyone on the tour had to check back in on the ship before going back out on their own. There were still two glaring issues, Clive noted, where they had no stopgap solutions. One was the passengers going ashore on their own; there was no way to maintain watch on them all the time. The other were the tours where the passengers were given free time for shopping and eating on their own.

"I don't think those issues are your problem," Dunningham said after listening to the head of security express his thoughts. "Even if your tour is completely contained, someone can go missing if he really wants to; or if someone else really wants him to disappear."

The three men continued to discuss possibilities while Dunningham took sparse notes. He'd remember most of the key information and there wasn't much new or really relevant coming out of the conversation. He said he'd review the Interpol and FBI information and get back with them later in the day. His stomach growled just at the right time for him to excuse himself to go have lunch with his wife.

67

Saturday, July 20

11:45 AM

Suite 1024

"Have you decided what you want for lunch, Sylvia?" Alfred Dunningham asked as they enjoyed the peacefulness of their suite and its verandah.

"Not yet, dear," she answered without pulling her eyes away from the interesting magazine article. "Oh, by the way, that butler James came by and checked the refrigerator to make sure it was full. He also left a cute magnet on the refrigerator door with the number to call if there's anything we need."

"Yes, I noticed that magnet when I came in; those colors are hard to miss," Alfred replied as he went to open the refrigerator to see what was inside. As he reached for the refrigerator door, an alarm went off on his watch. He hadn't set any alarms so that puzzled him. He reached for the handle again with his left hand and the watched beeped again.

"Do you have something in the microwave, dear?" Sylvia called in from the verandah.

"No," Alfred said. "My watch is beeping and I've not set any alarms."

"Maybe it needs a new battery and it's just informing you to get one before it runs out completely," Sylvia responded, being the ever practical person.

"That's not it," Alfred replied. He reached for the door with his right hand and there was no sound. Being the scientific person that he was, he removed the watch from his left arm, set it on the table and then reached for the door with his left hand; there was no sound. He put the watch on his right arm and then reached for the door with his right hand and the watch beeped. "There's something about this refrigerator door that sets off my watch," he said to his wife who didn't understand what he meant, not that she usually did.

He took the watch off his arm and looked at the watch. He'd seen that symbol before, but not on his watch. It normally meant radioactive material was present. He'd opened the refrigerator when they first entered the suite and his watch didn't make any sounds. So why would it now when he reached for the door? The magnet; it wasn't there when they first came in! Alfred used his right hand and removed the magnet and took it to the kitchen. He then returned to the refrigerator and the watch emitted no sounds no matter where the watch was. Would the magnet actually be radioactive, and would why the butler put it on their refrigerator?

Returning to the kitchen, he picked up the magnet and noticed that it was thicker in the areas of the dark circles. He pressed the circles and they felt spongy. There was one way to find out if that magnet held anything inside those circles. He placed it on a plate and put the plate in the microwave oven, pressed five minutes and Start; then went out on the verandah and closed the door.

"Why'd you close the door, dear? What if we get locked out here?"

Alfred didn't have to answer those questions as there was an explosion in their cabin, with smoke coming from the now defunct microwave oven. He hurriedly opened the door and went in to dispel the smoke before it set off an alarm.

"What happened in there?" Sylvia asked as she went inside and saw the carnage in the kitchen. "What were you cooking that blew up in the microwave?"

"That magnet our butler put on the refrigerator," Alfred replied. "Now, let's see exactly what was inside it," he continued as he used a towel to open the microwave's door. The smell of ozone told him that there had been electrical components that just burned. He pulled the plate out and there was indeed more to the magnet than just the butler's telephone number. The burnt parts were hard to completely recognize, but enough was visible. "This here," Alfred pointed out to his wife, "used to be a receiver. This magnet was actually an eavesdropping device that could listen to everything we said in here. I wonder what other little presents James left and who else he's bugged."

"Shouldn't we call security?" an alarmed Sylvia asked.

"And what if security is behind this? Who else knows that we're here besides security, Interpol, and the captain?" Alfred asked without looking for an answer from his wife. "From this point forward, no one else comes into this cabin. We'll get things at the door, but no one enters until we find out who is behind all of this."

"Won't they know something is wrong if they're not hearing us say anything?" Sylvia asked.

"Precisely," Alfred responded. "And if someone acts in a strange manner, then that will tell us who did it." Alfred walked to the cabin door, took the DO NOT DISTURB sign, opened the door and placed the sign on their door handle. "Don't let anyone in, even the cabin steward to clean the room. I need to find out who wanted to listen in on us."

"I've picked out what I want for lunch," his wife said, unfazed by what just happened. "Do you know what you want, dear?"

68

Saturday, July 20

1:25 PM

"I'll get the phone," Alfred said as he had just finished his lunch on the verandah. As a bit of a creature of habit, he'd ordered a club sandwich, with coleslaw instead of fries. "Hello," he said into the phone.

"This is Clive Stewart, Professor. We just received a call from the police in Malta where one of our passengers went missing. Can you come back down to my office?"

"I can and I will in just a few minutes," Alfred said.

"Do you remember where my office is?" Stewart asked.

Alfred thought for a moment. "Third deck, Central Lobby, behind Guest Relations."

"Exactly," Stewart remarked. "See you soon."

"Goodbye," Alfred said as he hung up the phone. He went to the verandah, picked up the plates and took them to the kitchen. He returned to the verandah where Sylvia was quite comfortable in her chair. "I'll be gone for a while. Remember, no one comes into the room. No one. It doesn't matter; we don't need maid service and we'll take care of the dishes ourselves. Just keep the door locked and don't answer it for anyone except for me; I'll use our secret knock. Do you remember what it is?"

"I do," she said proudly. "You'll knock once followed by a quick double-knock. There's a pause and then you'll knock, double-knock, knock, knock. All of that is Morse code for your nickname, 'Al.' How'd I do?"

"Marvelously, as always, Sylvia. I'll see you later," he said as he gave her a kiss on the cheek. As he stepped into the hall, he saw the Interpol agent but he couldn't remember his alternate identity.

Moreau motioned for Dunningham to come to his cabin. Alfred noticed the cabin number, 1028, and he entered the cabin. "I didn't realize we were so close to each other until you mentioned your suite number in the captain's office this morning," Moreau said.

"So how it is playing chief marketing officer for a cruise line?" Alfred asked as the two men stepped into the living room area. As they did, something caught Alfred's eye. The colors seemed out of place. Alfred pointed to the refrigerator and held his right index finger up to his lips.

A puzzled look came across Moreau's face.

Alfred motioned for the man to follow him as he opened the door to the verandah. Once both men were outside, Alfred quietly closed the door and scanned the area for more devices.

"What's with the secrecy?" Moreau asked.

"The magnet on your refrigerator," Alfred replied. "How long has that been there?"

"I came on board three days ago and the butler put it there and said it had his phone number to call if there was anything I needed. Why?"

"Your butler is James?" Alfred asked.

"Yes it is; why?" Antoine asked in response.

"He put a similar magnet on our refrigerator and my atomic watch set off an alarm when it was close to the magnet. I put the magnet in the microwave oven and it exploded of course, exposing a set of circuitry that held a receiver. That magnet is a bugging device by someone who wants to know what we are saying," Alfred explained to the Interpol agent.

"But I'm by myself and I typically don't talk to myself. Why would someone want to bug my cabin?"

"Have you called anyone from inside the cabin?" Alfred asked.

"Of course," Antoine replied. He then realized that what he thought he was saying in confidence to Interpol headquarters had been listened to by someone else. "Now what? Do I get rid of that magnet?"

"No," Alfred replied. "You'll continue on as if you don't know about it; you'll just come out here to make your phone calls. You can pretend to make calls inside the room and feed the listener with fake information. We don't say anything to anyone about the bugs and we'll see who makes the first move. Then we'll know who's behind it."

"But it was James who brought the magnet in here," Antoine insisted.

"Right," Alfred said. "We don't know if he was told to as part of customer service and someone else gave him those special magnets. He could be the culprit or he could have nothing to do with it. That doesn't mean we can rule him out, but he's certainly on the list."

"Let's inform Clive. He's head of security and he could dig into it."

"Unless he's the one behind it," Alfred countered as the Interpol agent nodded his head in befuddlement. "Let's go back in quietly and have a conversation that someone else can listen to." Alfred quietly opened the verandah door and the two men softly stepped inside, and then he slowly closed it.

"Yes, those are interesting papers, Inspector," Alfred said in a voice that could certainly have been picked up by the listener. "Your men in Interpol certainly were able to dig up more information on those passengers than the FBI could provide. I'd tip my hat to them if I wore one."

Moreau looked at Dunningham and smiled. "Yes; Interpol does a fairly decent job of tracking international travelers by their passport. I could find in five minutes every country you've been to and probably the locations you've visited in those countries."

"Impressive," Dunningham said although that was not new information to him. He'd known for many years that Interpol was extremely proficient in gathering information. Alfred winked at Moreau and then asked, "What do you think of that Stewart fellow since you've been on the ship for a few days?"

Moreau played along. "I think he's quite sharp; he'd do quite well in our agency." A devilish grin came across Moreau's face. He enjoyed the counterespionage game. "Clive's waiting for us; we'd better get going."

"Right," Alfred said as the men headed to the cabin door. Once in the passageway, Alfred began asking Pierre Dubois about the cruise line and the industry in general.

The stairs going down to the third deck were empty as most of the passengers had gone ashore in Limassol. Cyprus was not on many cruise itineraries so it was a new place for almost all of the passengers as well as most of the crew. *"Bonjour, Monsieur* Dubois," the ship's concierge said as she was headed across the Central Lobby in the opposite direction of the two men.

"Bonjour," Dubois replied as he smiled at the young lady. The two men continued on their way to the security office where they noticed the door was slightly ajar for them.

"Hello, again," Clive Stewart said to the two men as the door closed behind them.

Dunningham noticed that the white board had been erased, and new information had taken the place of the numbers. "It's Mr. Brighton that the Malta police have found?" he asked.

"Yes," Clive said. "They called just a while ago to say that they found his room key among his personal possessions when they booked him into jail."

"Did they saw why he's in jail?" Moreau asked.

Alfred Dunningham thought to himself that he would have asked a question that couldn't be answered with a simple Yes or No.

"Something about photographs and vandalism in St. John's Co-Cathedral," Clive replied.

"That's not too good," Moreau replied. "Those two Caravaggio paintings in there are priceless and are probably the greatest art treasures in all of Malta."

"They are," Dunningham said, himself a collector and one who appreciated fine art. Caravaggio's art were a bit dark for his liking, but he still appreciated them as great works of art. "So that eliminates the third one from the missing category," Alfred said, "which would take the 0-1-2-3 sequence to 0-1-3. It had a better chance with the 2 in it, although the sequence still needed an interpretation. What have you heard about the other three?"

"Absolutely nothing," Clive said. "We're still where we were yesterday. One thing's for sure; if any of this gets out on Twitter or any other social media, it won't be pretty."

"What reports do you have so far on today's tours?" Alfred asked.

"Nothing, yet," Clive responded. "But that's not bad news," he added. "I'll let you know when they start coming back. I just thought you should know about Mr. Brighton."

"Thanks," Dunningham and Moreau said as they left.

69

Saturday, July 20

4:45 PM

The pool deck was quite the scene as pool water was flying all over the place as a lively game of water volleyball had been influenced by happy hour. There were dozens of plastic drink cups around the pool and many of them were empty. During a break from the game, one of the players asked, "Does it seem like security has tightened up around here? Anyone know what's going on?"

Just then, one of the pool bar waiters rang a bell. "Last call for pool time happy hour!" he exclaimed.

Most of the volleyball participants called for the waiter to order another one, two actually since happy hour meant two-for-one. The question about increased security was quickly lost in the clamoring to order more drinks.

70

Saturday, July 20

5:40 PM

Preparations were underway on the bridge for departure from Limassol, Cyprus, as the *Royal Holiday* would have back-to-back sea days as she began her return leg to Barcelona. The next stop was the Amalfi Coast in southern Italy, a playground for the rich and famous and for the rich-and-famous wannabes. They'd be sailing in the open waters of the Mediterranean Sea where choppy waves and medium winds were anticipated. But there would still be plenty of sunshine for those who wanted to enjoy the warmth on the open decks.

All-aboard time was 5:30 and the returning passengers were tired from the exhausting day and the warmth and dryness of the area. Shore excursion manager Walter Peterson had been asked to join Professor Dunningham and Inspector Moreau in Clive Stewart's office to review the passenger list. Walter had already checked the tour logs and every passenger who left on a tour had checked back in after the tour.

As Clive Stewart was scrolling through the database, all four men were cautiously optimistic that there wouldn't be any names highlighted in red. "So far, so good," Walter said as they'd gone through the seventh deck list. Then it happened. The red highlighted line was like a flashing beacon, a beacon that foretold of impending doom. "Who is it" Walter asked.

"Juan Castro from 8055," Clive said.

Antoine thought, smiled and then went to the white board and wrote the room numbers of the missing passengers, adding the cabin number of the new member of the group:

7043

4050

4099

7012

8055

He continued as he'd done two days previously in the Captain's office.

7043 7 + 0 + 4 + 3 = 14;   14 - 7 = 7; 7 - 7 = 0

4050 4 + 0 + 5 + 0 = 9;   9 - 4 = 5; 5 - 4 = 1

4099 4 + 0 + 9 + 9 = 22;   22 - 4 = 18; 18 - 4 = 14;

                              14 - 4 = 10; 10 - 4 = 6;

                              6 - 4 = 2

7012 7 + 0 + 1 + 2 = 10;   10 - 7 = 3

8055 8 + 0 + 5 + 5 = 18;   18 - 8 = 10; 10 - 8 = 2

Antoine then circled each of the remainders: 0, 1, 2, 3, 2.

"I see where you're going, Antoine," Alfred said. "But we've already accounted for the passenger in 4099, so that gets rid of the first 2. It's good thinking, but there has to be more to it than that sequence."

"What are they talking about?" Walter asked.

"I'll explain later," Clive said. "We need to address this right now."

71

Saturday, July 20

5:50 PM

"May I have your attention please," Clive Stewart spoke into the phone that led into the ship's public address system. "Will Mr. Juan Castro in cabin 8055 please contact Guest Relations on Deck Three immediately. Once again, Mr. Juan Castro in cabin 8055; please contact Guest Relations on Deck Three immediately."

Clive then called the bridge to inform the captain, even though Captain Christopolous had a bad feeling when he heard that announcement. "Yes, Captain; I'll check with the local authorities right away."

"Ladies and gentlemen, this is Captain Christopolous coming to you from the Navigational Bridge. We're scheduled to pull out of the harbor here in Limassol in just a few minutes, but we've received reports of high winds and rough waves toward the island of Crete. Since we're going to have two sea days coming up before our next stop, we have plenty of time to get there and I've made the decision to remain in port for a couple more hours to let that rough weather pass by our intended path. Unfortunately, you're not going to be able to go back ashore here in Limassol, but all of our ship's services will be opening for your pleasure. Thank you for your attention, ladies and gentlemen. Now here is Becky with what's going on around the ship this evening."

"Thank you, Captain Christopolous, and I know the passengers will appreciate the smoother water once we do get underway." The cruise director outlined the evening's activities as well as the highlights of the next day's sea day, the first of two in a row.

"Let's hope this passenger shows up soon," the captain said to the First Officer, "or we'll have to pull in the gangway and leave port. Luckily we can make up that time or we wouldn't be able to stay here in port to see if he does show up."

72

Saturday, July 20

10:30 PM

John Phillips was enjoying another good evening at the single-deck Black Jack table in the ship's casino. Sitting once again in last position, his stacks of green and black chips were the envy of the other players. "A round for the table, please," John said as the cocktail server approached the table.

"Certainly, Mr. Phillips," she said as she took everyone's order. She knew his favorite: gin and tonic made with Bombay Sapphire Gin.

The player at the opposite end of the table was also doing well, although his stacks were red and green. "Didn't the captain say something about waves and wind tonight or tomorrow morning? I looked at the weather reports and I certainly didn't see any of that."

"Better safe than sorry," John said as he doubled down on his $200 bet. He was showing 5-4 against the dealer's 7. His next card was a king, giving him nineteen. The dealer turned over his hole card to reveal an ace.

"Eighteen," the dealer announced as he raked in the chips from the other players and then placed two stacks of two black chips each next to John's bets.

John slid a green chip to the dealer who thanked him as he struck the table twice with the chip and placed it into the money box next to him. The cocktail server brought the drinks, gave John the slip to sign and he also tipped her a $25 chip. "Thank you, Mr. Phillips," she said with a huge smile.

"My pleasure, dear," he said as the dealer was shuffling the cards. "I haven't seen you anywhere else on the ship. Do you work only in the casino?"

"Yes, just in the casino," she replied.

"What do you do when we're in port since the casino's closed then?" John continued the questions.

"That's when I study and attend class. I'm going to school online so the port days are when I'm able to get my schoolwork done."

"Accounting?" John asked.

"Nursing," she replied. "I like helping people and I've always wanted to be a nurse."

"Bet, Mr. Phillips?" the dealer asked as John was the only one at the table who hadn't placed a bet.

"Sorry," he said to the dealer as he pushed three black chips into the betting circle. He turned back to the cocktail server. "That's great; keep up the good work," he said and returned his attention to the table. He stood on his J-Q and won when the dealer drew five cards to seventeen.

"Somebody's having a good night," came the familiar voice from behind John. The voice was familiar, but he couldn't quite figure out who she was. John finally turned around to see Becky Anderson in a very attractive two-piece outfit. He knew the voice, but not the face; he looked at her name tag, which was in a rather strategic location on her blouse.

"Hello, Becky," John said as he worked to push out his chair and stand up to shake her hand.

"I'm sorry we haven't met before this, Mr. Phillips," Becky said as she smiled at the very handsome man who was also a very skilled Black Jack player. "We've been a bit busy around the ship, but I usually find out who are the top players before this. Please accept my apologies," she said as she put her left hand on his right shoulder.

"I'm the one who should be sorry," John said as he took a quick glance at the table as the dealer was showing an ace against his pair of eights. He'd let his previous winnings ride, so he now had $600 at risk. He calculated the odds in his head and he promptly pushed out another six black chips. "Split," he said as he knew he was favored to beat the dealer. The dealer dealt an ace to the first 8, making nineteen. A 9 made the second set into a seventeen, not a great hand. The dealer turned over his hole card to reveal a 5, giving him six or sixteen. Two consecutive 10s gave the dealer a total of twenty-six.

"Dealer busts," the dealer announced as he paid out the winning hands, including the $1,200 to John Phillips.

"Nice play," Becky said as she saw his stack of black chips grow even taller.

"I know you're always on duty," John said, "but do you have anything pressing you have to do right now?"

"I'm here for the passengers," Becky said coyly.

"Let's go for a walk," he said as he pushed a black chip to the dealer and picked up the rest of his chips and headed to the Cashier window.

"Sure," she said as she went with him as he cashed in $3,225.

"Buy you a drink?" he asked as they headed out of the casino.

"Sure you can afford it?" she laughed.

"I think so," he replied.

73

Sunday, July 21

9:30 AM

Antoine Moreau and Alfred Dunningham were once again in Clive Stewart's Deck Three office. Clive had cleaned the board and written what they DID know:

Tyler Jacobs 7043 – Sunday 14th – Civitavecchia

Phil Watson 4050 – Monday 15th - Messina

Greg Brighton 4099 – Tuesday 16th – Valletta (in jail)

Tony Lockwood 7012 – Thursday 18th – Santorini

Juan Castro 8055 – Saturday 20th – Limassol

"We've accounted for one passenger, Mr. Brighton," Clive said, "but then we added Mr. Castro to the list last night. Has your agency come up with anything, Inspector?"

Remembering his prompting from Professor Dunningham, Moreau relayed the information from the "reports" that he and Dunningham had discussed in his suite the previous day. "It's interesting information, but I don't see that it ties any of this together. At least we're at sea for two days, so we can't lose any more passengers."

Dunningham copied down what was written on the board. He'd continue to think about the names, the cabin numbers, the dates and the ports where they disappeared. Moreau did have a point about the remainder of the sum of the digits when using the deck number as the modulus. 0–1–2–3–2. So the next number would have to be a 1 followed by another 0.

74

Sunday, July 21

10:00 AM

"You're very lucky that you were only arrested for being drunk in public. If the restaurant owner had pressed charges for disorderly conduct in a place of business, you'd be sitting in here for three to six months. What did you say you were doing here in Messina? You don't seem like a person who'd go on vacation to Sicily." The police captain was being unusually nice to the prisoner he was releasing from jail. Perhaps it was because today was Sunday and the captain was a good Catholic who believed in doing as much good as he could on Sunday. He was a tyrant the rest of the week; but today was different; it was Sunday.

"I was on a cruise ship that docked here several days ago," Phil Watson said. "I don't know what happened to me in that restaurant. I had two beers with someone from the ship and that's the last thing I can remember. I have no idea how I got that way and I'm truly sorry for behaving so badly. Do you know where there's a decent but inexpensive hotel where I can go and figure out how to get back to the ship?"

The police captain told him of a small hotel run by his brother-in-law. "It's not far from here, but it's not that easy to find. How about if I take you there? If you just show up looking the way you do, he'd either kick you out or he'd call me to come and arrest you. Where do you think you can meet the ship?"

"That would be nice of you to take me there. I need to get online to check the schedule; I know they come back by here, but they don't stop in Sicily again," Phil said.

"And you could use some new clothes, too," the police captain said. "My brother-in-law will fix you up with our cousin who'll give you a good deal on some new clothes."

"That would help. I think the ship stops in Capri on Tuesday, so if could get a ferry, then I could meet the ship there." Phil Watson was finally able to think clearly again.

"Let's go," the police captain said as he opened the door to the bright sunny outside.

"*Grazie*," Phil said to the captain.

"*Prego*," was the reply.

75

Sunday, July 21

9:00 AM

It was four weeks into summer and the warm gentle breezes were providing the perfect timing to pick the grapes. Alfred Dunningham preferred to be at his northern California home when his five acres of Shiraz were harvested, but he knew that they would be gone when the grapes were at their peak. He enjoyed growing and walking among the grapes, but he left the harvesting and processing to the professionals. He would be able to tell how good a year it was when the cases arrived at his house several years from now.

The grapes were being tended, but Alfred's prized roses were being neglected. The automatic watering system provided just the right amount of moisture, but no one was there to dead head the roses and force new growth. Alfred and Sylvia would have been flying home from Paris today if he'd not been called to the cruise ship to help with the mystery of the disappearing passengers.

76

Monday, July 22

10:00 AM

The same three men met again in Clive Stewart's office: Antoine Moreau, Alfred Dunningham, and Clive Stewart. Clive had intentionally avoided the captain, and, fortunately for Clive, the captain had not attempted to contact him. The same information was on the white board:

Tyler Jacobs 7043 – Sunday 14th – Civitavecchia

Phil Watson 4050 – Monday 15th - Messina

Greg Brighton 4099 – Tuesday 16th – Valletta (in jail)

Tony Lockwood 7012 – Thursday 18th – Santorini

Juan Castro 8055 – Saturday 20th – Limassol

"Well, gentlemen," Clive began. "Do we have anything new to add to the board?"

Dunningham resisted the urge to say he didn't know if there was anything new because he didn't know if Clive had any new information. Thus it would be impossible for him or Antoine to answer Clive's question. But he let the temptation pass him by. "I don't have anything new," he said instead.

"Same here," Moreau chimed in.

"Keep at it," Stewart said. "Something has to show up."

"That is popular thinking, but there is no empirical evidence to support that statement," Dunningham just had to say. He was tired of everyone thinking that "something had to show up" when there really was no basis for the statement.

77

Monday, July 22

11:30 AM

The Sicilian police captain and his extended family treated Phil Watson like one of their own, despite the way that he'd been introduced to them. The brother-in-law told him he could stay for free.

"Why?" Phil asked. "I can pay," he insisted.

"You've had enough troubles, young man. We have a saying here in Sicilia that when you help a stranger in need that you're repaying the kindness that was shown to an ancestor. Our ancestors have been very blessed with kindness from so many people, so it's an honor to me to be able repay some of that kindness." The brother-in-law also made arrangements for Phil at a hotel in Capri. When Phil asked if that hotel was owned by another brother-in-law, the hotelier responded, "No, but he is part of the family, if you know what I mean."

Phil nodded his head, not sure of the meaning, but also not wanting to ask.

The cousin was nice, but not quite as generous as the captain's brother-in-law. He did outfit him in a new pair of slacks and shirt for a reasonable price and he did throw in a hat for free. The hat, combined with the slacks and shirt, made Phil look Sicilian except for the pasty white color of his skin. But he was still very presentable in his new clothes. The one big favor the cousin did was to have Phil get a good haircut and shave while the slacks were being hemmed.

The police captain stopped by the cousin's store and admired Phil's new look. "You fit right in now; you sure you don't want to stay here?"

"Your kindness is amazing, but I do need to get to the ship so I can fly home when it returns to Barcelona," Phil answered.

"Well, here's my card," the captain said as he handed a card to Phil. If you ever come to Sicily again, you give me call, okay? I want to know that everything is okay with you. You do that for me?"

"Of course, I will," Phil said, not sure if that was a polite offer from the captain or an order.

"Hop in and I'll take you down to the ferry terminal. You don't want to be seen walking, looking as good as you do."

Phil got into the police car for the short ride to the ferry terminal. The police captain got out of the car also and walked with Phil to the ticket booth. "One ticket to Capri, please," Phil said to the man in the booth.

"It's on me, Jimmy," the police captain said to the man in the booth who handed the ticket to Phil.

"How much?" Phil asked.

The man looked to the police captain. "It's taken care of kid. Nice hat."

Phil turned and looked at police captain and smiled. "Thanks," he said as he headed toward the ferry that was about to leave.

"*Prego*," the police captain replied. "Take care, and you call me next time you're here."

Phil waved and walked faster to get to the ferry. He didn't want to miss this boat.

78

Monday, July 22

11:30 AM

The open-sea winds and the light rain emptied the activities pool as well as most of the ship's pool deck chairs. Pool attendants were stacking the loose cushions on hand carts as quickly as they could, and the hand carts were taking the cushions into one of the lockers. After the cushions had been put away, the attendants began to tie down the loose chairs. The winds were picking up, and combined with the rolling waves, they were making the ship rock back and forth. The overhead clouds looked as if a downpour were imminent. Today would not be an outside day.

"Ladies and gentlemen, may I have your attention, please." The voice over the PA system was that of Becky. "As you can probably tell, we've encountered some fairly strong weather and the captain has decided for the safety of all our passengers and crew that all outside activities are cancelled for the rest of the day. We apologize for this inconvenience, but there are plenty of things going on inside the ship where it's dry and much safer. We strongly recommend that you stay indoors and not go outside unless it is absolutely necessary. This includes your verandah. Your cabin stewards will be stopping by to secure the table and chairs on your verandah, so we ask for your cooperation as we navigate through these choppy waters. Thank you very much for your attention, ladies and gentlemen."

79

Monday, July 22

1:25 PM

The tailwind helped to push the ferry along and get to Capri ahead of schedule. Phil Watson looked a bit out of place as he stepped off the ferry; his clothes were sharp, but that was all he had with him. He wasn't carrying a suitcase as most vacationers were. He didn't have a satchel or a briefcase that would be necessary if he were there for business. It was a good thing that he didn't have to explain anything to anyone.

"Mr. Watson," he heard his name being called. "I recognize the hat; my cousin really likes that style and it looks so good on you. My hotel is too far for you to walk, so I have my car here to take you." The man had not yet said his name, but Phil was getting used to that. If you didn't know someone's name, then you couldn't accuse them of doing something.

The cousin of the cousin drove to the hotel and parked the car right in front. They went inside and Phil was given his room key; it was a big key, the kind that you left at the front desk when you were leaving for the day and then asked for when you got back. "Please take a look at your room and let me know if it's okay for you," the man said politely.

"Thank you," Phil said as he took the large brass key and walked up the stairs to room number 5. He used the key to open the door and walked inside. It was light and airy and it would be just perfect, especially since he had no luggage or other things with him. He closed the door and walked back down the stairs. "It's perfect," Phil said. "How much for the night?" he asked.

The man looked disappointed as he shook his head. "It's no charge for you; my family in Sicily called and asked me to take care of you since you've had a rough few days. They did me a favor and I'm now repaying that favor to them. There's a nice café down the street if you're hungry and there's a coffee shop just next door if that's all you want. Tell them you're staying here and they'll treat you real good."

"Thanks," Phil said as he turned to go to the café.

"You can leave the key with me and it'll be right here when you come back. The wind appears to be picking up, so don't let your hat blow away," the cousin's cousin said as Phil walked out.

He turned left and passed a bar. He was tempted to go in and have a drink, but the memory of what happened the last time he was at a bar was enough to make him keep walking. He didn't remember everything that happened, but waking up in jail was a bad enough experience. He kept walking until he saw the café and he turned and went inside.

Heads turned as he entered; he wasn't from the area. "Table for one?" he inquired.

"Follow me," the waiter said, and Phil did what he said. As Phil sat down, the waiter stayed at the table. "Coffee? Wine? Beer?"

"Coffee please," Phil answered, feeling intimidated by the man just standing there at the table. He looked at the menu; there were English translations although he still didn't know what most of the items were.

The waiter brought the coffee and set it in front of Phil. He took off his hat, put in the empty chair next to him and looked up at the waiter who was just standing there quite stoic. "I'm staying at the hotel right up the block and the owner suggested I come here for lunch."

Whatever Phil said seemed to work magic. The man's expression completely changed and he walked over to the bar. He quickly returned with a carafe of red wine. "Compliments of the house," said the waiter who then began to pour some into a glass.

"*Grazie*," Phil said, getting into the Italian spirit.

"*Prego*," the waiter replied. "Did you see something you'd like, or would you like to order something special?"

"It all smells good," Phil said. "Whatever you'd recommend will be great, I'm sure."

"Right away," the waiter said as he turned and went into the kitchen.

Two older men who'd been engaged in their own conversation got up and walked over to Phil's table. They'd apparently been listening in on his conversation also. They didn't ask; they pulled out chairs and sat down. "You're staying at the hotel?" one man asked.

"Yes, I am," Phil replied as he nervously took a sip of the wine. He thought about offering some to the men, but he didn't know if that was a good thing or not.

"How long are you in town?" the other man asked.

"Just one day," Phil said. Realizing that telling the whole story could lead to too many other questions, so he kept it short. "I'm joining a ship that's coming to Capri tomorrow."

The two men looked at each other. "You haven't been here before, have you, son?" the first man asked.

"No, it's my first time but it seems very nice," Phil answered, feeling a little intimidated.

"The island is called CAP-REE, not CA-PREE," the second man added.

"I'm sorry," Phil said as he spotted the waiter coming out of the kitchen. "CAP-REE," Phil said.

"Johnny, leave the young man alone and let him eat in peace," the waiter said as he approached the table. The two men got up and went back to their table. "Don't let them bother you. They have nothing else to do all day so they look for fresh blood just like a shark in the water. You don't need to worry, though; you're covered. Chef's special; enjoy," he said as he left and took another carafe of wine to the two men. As he did so, he let them know to leave Phil alone.

The meal was delicious and washing it down with the red wine made it even better. The waiter brought him another coffee and Phil asked for check. The waiter smiled at Phil and said, "It's already been taken care of."

"What do you mean?" Phil asked.

"Just that," the waiter replied. "Your bill has already been taken care of. Now you'd better get back to the hotel as the winds are really picking up and there's talk of heavy rains."

"*Grazie*," Phil said as he stood up and retrieved his hat. He shook the waiter's hand and headed out the door. The two old men were still sitting at their table, talking away. The wind had picked up and Phil held the hat in his hand so it wouldn't blow away as he hurriedly made his way back to the hotel right before the skies opened and the downpour began.

80

Monday, July 22

4:00 PM

"It's blustery outside, but it's nice inside," the art manager said as passengers were walking into *Royal Holiday's* Sky View Lounge. "Our second Art Auction at Sea will begin in about ten minutes, so get your bid card and let us know which pieces you want brought up on stage. Remember the only ones that you can bid on are the ones you put a sticky note on. That's how our staff will know what to bring up. But don't worry, there's no obligation to buy anything. You're only requirement is to have a good time."

Many of the passengers in the Sky View Lounge were there to watch the waves as the winds were picking up and making the ship rock even more. Several paintings fell off their easels as the ship jolted as if it had hit a speed bump.

"We might as well have some champagne," one lady said to her husband. "That way we're at least feeling no pain if the ship goes down."

The man took his bid card with him and went to get two glasses of champagne. He spotted a Picasso etching and put one of his sticky notes on the frame. Returning with the champagne, the man said, "I saw a Picasso that would look nice in the living room."

"What do we know about Picasso?" she asked.

"Well, at least we've heard of him. Most of these artists are complete unknowns to us," the husband replied.

The ship kept rolling back and forth as those at the windows saw the waves breaking over the sides of the ship. The *Royal Holiday* was headed right into the eye of a storm.

The lady with the champagne leaned her head back and closed her eyes, but the ship's movement combined with the champagne started to make her dizzy. She immediately sat up.

The auction started slowly as many of the attendees were lookie-loos who had no other place to go; outside was shut down due to the weather and Bingo was the only thing going on in the theater. A very abstract yet colorful piece by an unknown French artist was brought on stage. "This artist goes by the name Jean-Marie and these works are real steals right now. This is your best opportunity to get in on the ground floor and see your art work appreciate in value as the popularity skyrockets."

The art manager was interrupted by a question. "Is Jean-Marie a male or a female?" Several in the crowd laughed.

The art manager dug through his paperwork and came up empty. "I don't know," he said sheepishly.

"Some art manager," one person said.

"A couple of you wanted this piece brought up so let's start the bidding at $100. Thank you," he said as a bid card was raised. "How about $200?"

"Thank you, sir," he said to the husband of the champagne lady.

The bidding continued between the two bidders; they were bidding on an indescribable piece of art by an unknown artist whose gender even the art manager didn't know. Champagne and high seas can make one lose sight of their senses. In this case, it was two who lost that sight. The final bid was $2,650 plus the 15% buyer's fee.

The champagne lady was shocked when she realized that she was now a co-owner of this thing.

The same two men were bidding against each other for a rather average Picasso sketching. It wasn't that the sketching was average; it just came from a large lot of 450 pieces. The bidding had reached $5,300 when champagne lady backhanded her husband so hard across the chest that everyone in the room gasped. It was shocking, but at least he stopped bidding as he worked to catch his breath.

The rest of the second Art Auction at Sea featured another Peter Max *Statue of Liberty* piece, but it received no opening bids. As the manager was taking it off the easel, the ship took a hard jolt, knocking the manager and Peter Max to the floor. Neither was terribly hurt, just the manager's pride.

81

Monday, July 22

4:40 PM

"Should we do this in order of disappearance, or start on the fourth deck and work our way up to eight?" Clive Stewart asked to the group assembled in his office. The "this" he was referring to was going into the cabin of each missing passenger, taking photographs and notes to try to get a better understanding of each passenger's character the day each went missing. The people in the office with Stewart were the hotel director, the Interpol agent and the math professor.

"Among the many things that we don't know," Professor Dunningham began, "is if there was any causal relationship or time sequencing of the disappearances. If there were, it would be harder to discover them unless we go in sequential order."

"Any objections?" Stewart asked. There were none. "Let's take the crew stairs, first up to the seventh deck," he continued as he led the way out of his office. He handed out gloves to the other men as they reached 7043, Tyler Jacobs' cabin. The hotel director used his pass key to open the door. It looked just the same as when he and the head of security were in the room right after the man's disappearance. Stewart began taking pictures and Moreau took notes based on what he saw and on what Stewart said. The Dan Brown library book *Angels & Demons* was still on the nightstand. They made other notes, seemingly unimportant now, but the items couldn't be ruled out just yet.

They looked in drawers, under the bed, they even counted the number of evening chocolates that Tyler had stashed in the desk drawer. They were being as thorough as possible. Satisfied that they saw and noted everything that was necessary, they left cabin 7043. Clive Stewart was the last one out and he reached up to remove the camera he'd placed there earlier. It had served its purpose, although it didn't provide any useful information.

They used the inner stairs again to go down three decks to Phil Watson's cabin, 4050. They used new gloves as they entered his room. His drawers were neatly organized with the socks all folded the same way and facing the same direction. The shirts were all buttoned the same way, the top two buttons and then every other one. The long sleeves were hung in one group with a small separating space from the short sleeves. All the shirts were facing to the left. The slacks were at the end followed by a suit. Neatness was abundant in this cabin, with the bathroom essentials ordered by height and the labels all facing out. Clive Stewart took pictures while Moreau dutifully took notes. Dunningham looked around but didn't see anything he thought would provide a clue to this man's disappearance; he was too much a neat freak. They repeated the exit procedure of leaving the cabin, handing the gloves to Stewart who, for some reason stayed behind for an additional five seconds before he came out.

"Do we really need to go to the next one?" the hotel director asked. "We already know the guy's in jail in Valletta, so why do we need to go into his cabin?"

"Just because he's in jail for whatever the police say he did doesn't necessarily answer the question of why he did what he did," Moreau answered. It was essentially the same answer that Dunningham was ready to provide.

The inside of cabin 4099 wasn't as neat and tidy as the previous two cabins. The desk drawer yielded information on self-guided tours and a brochure: *What the Cruise Lines Won't Tell You About Their Tours.* Stewart photographed the entire brochure, although taking it and scanning it would have provided a better copy. There was a 16GB thumb drive in the top drawer underneath pajamas that were neatly folded. They seemed a bit out of place because the rest of the clothing, his underwear and socks, were just thrown into the drawers. The shirts were clumsily hung on the hangers and the bathroom items were shoved into a corner, probably by the cabin steward. Aside from the thumb drive, they didn't find anything else that would point to a photography obsession, so maybe that wasn't why Greg Brighton was inside St. John's Co-Cathedral.

They exited the cabin and went to the rear crew stairs and took them up to the seventh deck where they walked forward to 7012, Tony Lockwood's cabin. His cabin looked to be a cross between the first two; Tony was neat and orderly, but not as orderly obsessive as Phil Watson. Clive looked under the bed and found a pair of cross training shoes. That find was corroborated with the workout shorts and shirt in one the drawers in the closet. The shoes looked new, probably purchased just for the cruise. Moreau thought the shoes would be good to wear on tours and when walking through the towns. There was some monotony in the cabins. While each man had slightly different organizing and neatness habits, there was nothing obvious to point to their disappearances.

The final cabin they had to go to was up one deck and a little aft of mid-ship. The cabin was 8055, that of Juan Castro. The striking observation as they entered Mr. Castro's cabin was the abundance of literary magazines from various countries. The man was not only highly cultured; he was also able to read many different languages. What could have happened to such an interesting man for him to disappear on the relatively small island of Cyprus? Stewart photographed the cover of each of the magazines as Moreau skimmed through each one to see if any pages were earmarked. The hotel director looked around to see if he could find any small camera that Stewart may have placed in the cabin. He didn't see one, so perhaps the one that Stewart mentioned putting in Tyler Jacobs' cabin was the only one he deployed. Dunningham looked at the magazines again and noticed that they weren't all current issues. Why would a man, apparently cultured, bring outdated magazines? Why wouldn't he bring the most current copy? Dunningham kept the thought to himself that the magazines were a ruse and that Mr. Castro was not multi-lingual as the other men thought he was.

The four men left cabin 8055 and went down to the security office on Deck Three. "I'll download and print all these photographs and Moreau will type up his notes, right? As soon as you get those notes to me, I'll assemble a packet of information for each of us. Can you get those notes done in the next few hours?"

"Yes," Moreau answered.

"Good," Stewart remarked. "Let's meet back here at 9:30 tomorrow morning and review what we have. In the meantime, if you think of anything you saw that's worth noting, please write it down and we'll add it to our package. Thank you, gentlemen." Stewart opened the door and the three other men left the office and went in different directions.

82

Monday, July 22

10:30 PM

The high waves and strong winds continued into the evening. It had been a difficult evening in the dining room as glasses toppled over and a couple waiters lost their balance as they were carrying a tray of stacked plates in to be served. Everyone was doing their best to maintain balance, decorum and a sense of humor because there wasn't anything that could be done about the weather.

What could be done was to close off the outside decks. Signs saying, "Outside Decks Closed due to Weather" were placed on all the doors that led to the outside, especially on Deck Four, the Promenade Deck. Water was splashing over the side of the ship and the water-tight doors to that outer deck were sealed. The doors on the upper decks were closed with signs on them, but for safety reasons they couldn't be locked. Security personnel and some of the deck crew made the rounds to ensure no passengers were outside. It was both foolish and very dangerous to be outside in that weather.

83

Tuesday, July 23

1:15 AM

The fax machine made its normal noises as it was being brought out of power save mode inside the ship's tiny communications center. The specialists who had the graveyard shift were doing their best just to keep all the equipment in place. The waves had been pounding the ship all night long, forcing things to roll from one side and then to the other. The winds were stronger than predicted and they would occasionally hit the side of the ship like a huge slap in the face. At least the incoming fax would give them something else to focus on besides the weather.

The single page printed and the senior specialist retrieved it. Its contents were totally surprising; although it had been a couple years since the last time he'd seen it. "What is it?" asked his co-worker.

"It's a weather alert for high seas off Capri and the Amalfi Coast; it's not suitable for tenders," the senior man paraphrased the message. "I guess we're not getting any of that Limoncello on the Amalfi Coast," he added. He walked over to the telephone to call the bridge.

"Bridge; this is the captain speaking," was the answer when the communications specialist called the bridge. It was unusual for the captain to be on the bridge at this hour of the day or the morning. But the rough weather was a good reason for him to be in the command area of the ship in case there was a need for immediate action or decisions. The fax message certainly fit that description, and it also meant that the officer in charge wouldn't have to go wake the captain to deliver the message.

"Captain, this is Communications and we just received a fax message that reads: 'Urgent Weather Alert for the Isle of Capri and the Amalfi Coast area. High waves make it unsuitable for use of tenders for the next 24 hours. Acknowledgement requested.'"

"That's not surprising," the captain said. "Very well; send the acknowledgement and then send a copy of that message to my desk."

"Aye, aye, Captain."

The captain turned to the second in command. "Send an urgent message to all departments. Prepare for continued rough seas. Stop in Capri cancelled. It will be a sea day instead as we sail north to next port."

"Aye, aye, Captain," the officer replied. "Sending message right now, sir."

"Very well," the captain said. "Get more coffee, please. It's going to be longer than we thought."

"On its way, Captain."

84

Tuesday, July 23

8:00 AM

"Good morning, ladies and gentlemen," began the loud speaker message. "This is Captain Christopolous from the Navigational Bridge. As you can tell, the waves and the winds are still quite strong even though they're not as bad as they were last night. We received an urgent weather alert early this morning for this area and we were told that the strong seas would make it impossible for us to safely use our tenders to take passengers to shore today. Now that we are in the area, the senior officers and I agree that the use of tenders would be a dangerous activity.

"The entire crew apologizes for this inconvenience, but your safety and the safety of the crew and the vessel are my most important concern. Therefore we will not be stopping off at the Isle of Capri today as had been scheduled. Instead, we will be moving farther north into the Tyrrhenian Sea where calmer weather is being reported. The good news is that we'll be docking earlier tomorrow in Livorno for the trips into Pisa and Florence. We are currently planning to be alongside the dock at 7 AM instead of the scheduled 9 AM.

"Again, I apologize that we will not be able to make our scheduled stop today, but safety is always the number one priority on any vessel on the seas. Now here is Becky with announcements on today's activities." The captain turned to the First Officer. "I'm going to my cabin to get some rest. Get us up into some smooth waters and find a calm route."

"Aye, aye, Captain," the First Officer responded as the tired captain headed toward his cabin for some much needed rest.

"Well, ladies and gentlemen, you heard from Captain Christopolous that the rough weather won't allow us to use the tender boats to get you safely to shore. The Marina Grande on the Isle of Capri isn't big enough for cruise ships, just the mega-yachts for movie stars and media moguls." Becky was trying to be upbeat and add some humor as she was also disappointed that they wouldn't be stopping at Capri.

"For all of you who had booked tours for today through our shore excursion office, you don't need to worry," she continued. "The office is already processing your refund and it will show up on your room bill this morning. Some of the services that were listed in your daily paper as being closed today will be open. An updated listing of all of the activities and services for today will be available in the Central Lobby within an hour.

"The shops will open at their normal opening time as on other sea days, as will the casino slots and tables. We're adding a special Bingo session at 1:30 this afternoon, but due to the rough weather we're not planning on any poolside games. Back by popular request, hypnotist Olivia Cromwell will once again take the stage at 9 PM. And, she has offered to do a special matinee performance at 4 PM this afternoon. Both of those hypnotizing experiences will be in the Royal Theatre on Deck Four. Ladies and gentlemen, I know that many of you, maybe even all of you, were looking forward to our stop in Capri and tasting some Limoncello. While the supplies last, our waiters will be offering a small taste of it as you enter the theater for one of Olivia Cromwell's shows today. I don't know how much Limoncello is still onboard, but get to the show early so you can get a taste of this marvelous drink.

"Once again, an updated listing of all the activities and services for today will be available in the Central Lobby in about an hour. Please stop by and pick up a copy so you can plan your day here on the *Royal Holiday*. Thank you so much for your attention and understanding." Becky's face didn't look as upbeat as she'd tried to make her announcements sound.

"Paint a smile on your face, because you're going to need it today," she said to the Guest Relations manager as she headed out into the public areas.

"Oh, Becky," one passenger called to her as she entered the lobby area.

It was going to be one of those days.

85

Tuesday, July 23

9:40 AM

"I only got one hour of sleep this morning, so let me apologize right now for my bad temper when I yell at you," the captain said as the three men sat down in the captain's office. "Aside from the rough weather, Professor, how has your wife been enjoying the cruise? Has everything been satisfactory in your cabin?"

"Sylvia's a marvelous woman, Captain. She puts up with my quirks and the occasional ramblings. The cruise has been good for her as she's not been able to do much, so she's been reading magazines. Everything in the cabin is fine, although there's a small repair that will need to be done. But it's okay for now."

"I'll send maintenance right away to take care of it," the captain said, concerned that there was a problem in the suite of the professor they flew in from Paris to solve the mystery of the disappearances.

"You never said there was anything wrong," Clive Stewart added in, a concerned look on his face.

Professor Dunningham just smiled. "I said it's not a problem for us. It can be taken care of after the cruise. But thank you, Captain."

"And what about you, Inspector, is everything okay in your cabin?" The captain was being unusually chatty this morning, a surprise given that he was on the bridge all night during the violent weather.

Polite as always, Antoine Moreau took the proper amount of time before responding to the captain. "This ship and its entire crew are the finest and the most gracious of any liner I've ever been on, Captain. It's a pleasure to be on your ship, and the suite is more than I could have expected. I appreciate your hospitality and I wish we could have met under different circumstances."

"Perhaps we can someday, Inspector," the captain replied. "Gentlemen, there is some good news with the weather keeping us out of the port today. Do you know what that is?"

There were no answers.

"We can't lose a passenger today," the captain said as he answered his own sleep-deprived question. "Well, security, you're between me and more sleep. What do you have?"

Head of security Clive Stewart handed the captain an updated report from yesterday's cabin inspections.

"Do you expect me to read all of this?" the captain asked as he thumbed through some of the hundred plus pages of notes and photographs.

"Not right now, Captain; I'll summarize it for you," Stewart said. "We were let into the cabins of each of our missing passengers by the hotel director. We all wore gloves, using a new pair in each room, so that we wouldn't leave any extra fingerprints in case more investigations are necessary."

Captain Christopolous was listening, but he was also looking at the photographs; they were good quality, but they didn't appear to reveal anything.

Stewart continued, "We looked inside drawers, the closet, under the bed and in the bathroom. The Inspector wrote down the things I was saying while taking photographs as well as his own notes. If something was locked, such as the safes and two suitcases, we didn't attempt to open them. Given that each one of these was a male passenger traveling alone, it was interesting that the cabins for the most part were quite neat and orderly."

"And what about all these photographs? Is there something particular in them?"

"No, Captain," Stewart answered. "The idea was to capture the visual image of the cabin as each one left it, realizing that the cabin steward had come in and made the bed, straightened the cabin and cleaned the bathroom. But books and magazines that were there could be important."

"And that's an interesting point, Captain," Dunningham chimed in. "The last passenger, a Mr. Juan Castro, had all sorts of magazines in his cabin. If you take a look on page, uh, eighty-five and beyond, you'll see cultural magazines in many different languages."

"An interesting man, I'd say."

"Yes, Captain," Dunningham continued, "that's what we thought, also. He appeared to be a man of culture who spoke many languages. But when you look at the covers, you'll see that most of them are old issues. If this man were truly that cultural and multi-lingual, why would he bring outdated issues? Why not bring the most current ones?"

"Very good, Professor," the captain said. "So what do you make of that?"

"I just said it's an interesting point, Captain. I haven't drawn any conclusions yet. For all we know, he was planning to take a scrapbooking class and cut out the pictures." Dunningham was making the point that just because something seemed out of place or out of character that there wasn't necessarily an immediate explanation.

The captain was hoping for answers instead of more possible questions. "So have you drawn any conclusions from all of this?" he asked.

The head of security looked at the Interpol agent. Moreau took the lead in answering the captain. "Any case of a missing person is always a bad situation. And while they seem to hit in the media harder when it's on a ship, there are actually more cases on any given day in any given country than on all the ships combined. And that's good news for you and your crew. I've had a lot of experience in this type of case where a person has just disappeared and there's no evidence of foul play. That is exactly what we have here, and there is nothing at all that anyone on your ship could have done to prevent them. Let me explain," Moreau said as he paused. He had just taken the pressure off Clive Stewart, but he wanted to add a subtle point

"Everything we saw in those cabins yesterday, and everything we didn't see because it wasn't there, as it stands right now could lead us to two equally possible scenarios. One of those scenarios is that each man planned to leave the ship and not return. By leaving his cabin just as he would on any other day, there would be nothing left behind to indicate that his departure was planned in advance. Do you see this scenario as a possibility for each of the cabins we were in?" Moreau asked as he looked toward Stewart and Dunningham.

Stewart nodded his head and Dunningham agreed and then added, "It is a bit of a conundrum. We didn't see anything that right away tells us it was planned, but then we also didn't see anything to say that it wasn't planned."

"Right," Moreau said. "Similarly, the neat cabins don't necessarily tell us that the disappearances weren't planned. We have nothing right now to tell us either way."

"What about that fellow that's in jail in Valletta?" The captain thought he might have found a flaw in the logic presented.

"We talked about that in his cabin," Stewart jumped in. "We saw nothing to indicate that he was into photography and especially so much that he would risk going to jail in another country."

"Let me summarize all of this for you, Captain." It was Inspector Moreau speaking again. "We will continue to look through the information we've given to you to see if there's any shred of a clue on these men. We saw nothing in their cabins that we could say with reasonable probability that they planned their own disappearances. Likewise, the neatness of their cabins doesn't mean that they weren't planning to run away. No amount of security, except for having a body guard assigned to every passenger on the ship, could have prevented what happened. If there is someone on this ship who is causing harm to these passengers, we'll figure that out. But Mr. Stewart's security team is not responsible for any of this and I suggest that you pull back on security because I've heard a lot of grumblings around the ship. The increased security didn't prevent the last few men from going missing, and I think it's done more harm than good."

"I am tired and I am a little grumpy," the captain began, "but I'm also a reasonable man. Stewart, stop the extra security details immediately and bring me some good news tomorrow."

"Consider it done, Captain," Stewart said as he and the other two men got up to leave. "Enjoy your rest, Captain."

"I will," the captain replied.

86

Tuesday, July 23

10:48 AM

"Your ship's not stopping here today," the hotel owner told Phil Watson as he was having coffee and scones in the lobby. "This weather is quite unusual for Capri, but the rough waters make it very unsafe for all the ships, even the ones coming to tie up in port." Phil was dressed just as he was yesterday; those clothes and his wallet and comb were currently his only possessions. It had been over a week since he'd gotten off the ship in Messina to take that walking tour of Taormina, and so much of it was still a blur. It could have been a lot worse if the Sicilian police captain hadn't taken a liking to him and made certain "arrangements" for Phil.

"I remember that the next stop is in Livorno because I was planning to go to Florence," Phil said. He was still amazed at the treatment he was receiving. Bad things happened to people, as he experienced in Sicily, but then good things also happen. He was really glad that he was currently on the "good things" side. This would be a trip that he would never forget, although there were parts he'd like to forget and there were parts he couldn't remember.

"Here's what we're gonna do," the man said. "I'm taking you down to the ferry terminal and you'll ride over to Napoli. The water's a bit rough today, so stay inside and stay dry. Once you get to Napoli, you'll be given a ride to the train station where you want to get a train to Livorno. I'll have one of my friends pick you up at the station and put you up in his house for the night. There aren't that many trains to Livorno, so he'll know which one you're on. Then in the morning, he'll take you down to your ship and everything will be just like new." The hotel manager made it all sound so perfect, like in a movie. But Phil knew this wasn't a movie; it was more like a horror story that he'd been cast in.

At the ferry terminal, Phil looked at the rough water and had his doubts about crossing the forty kilometers or so to Naples, but he had no choice. His latest new friend, the hotel manager, went to the ticket booth and talked with the man in the booth. Some words were spoken, but it seemed as if most of the conversation was with their hands. The manager leaned in and the two men exchanged hugs and kisses Italian style.

"Here's your ticket, kid," the manager said as he handed the voucher to Phil. "When the ferry gets to Napoli, and it will take about an hour and a half, a man who knows what you look like will come up to you. He's a little rough, but he means no harm. He's gonna take you to the train station and get your ticket to Livorno. He don't speak much English, so just smile at him. Good luck, kid."

"I don't know how I can ever repay you," Phil said. He put out his hand and then did something uncharacteristic. He threw his arms around the man and hugged him hard, just like he would to an uncle he hadn't seen in a long time.

"You're gonna be okay," the man said. "You ever come back to Capri, maybe with a young woman, you look me up, and I gonna take care of you." He handed a card to Phil who nodded his head and put the card into his pocket.

"*Grazie*," Phil said as he started to turn around.

"*Prego*," the man replied as he headed back to continue his conversation with the man in the ticket booth.

87

Tuesday, July 23

12:00 Noon

The thick block walls of the Orthodox Church in Limassol, Cyprus, kept the interior cool and comfortable while the noonday sun was beating down on the guests as they arrived for the hastily called wedding. A weekday wedding was quite unusual in this conservative country, but the influential father of the bride insisted that it take place as soon as all the papers could be signed and posted. The church bells were ringing to announce the joyous occasion, although word of the wedding had spread like a wildfire through dried brush anyway. As people gathered outside, they were smiling and laughing and asking questions.

"Are you serious?" one woman asked. "They just met on Saturday night and they're getting married already? Did something happen?"

"I don't know," her friend said. "All I heard was that he proposed to her and her father was happy to get her married. With his pull, he could make anything happen, but he'd not been able to find anyone to marry her. And he'd been offering a pretty nice dowry, but that wasn't enough."

"Who is he? He doesn't look from around here," the first woman said.

"Good question," her friend replied. "The one picture I saw of him he appeared to be a little dazed. Maybe he had too much ouzo and that's why he proposed to her. But when she called her father and told him, he was there right away and had him sign the proposal papers. I guess he wasn't going to take a chance that he might back out of it later on when he sobered up." The two women laughed. It's not as if they were particularly straight forward in getting their own husbands, but it hadn't happened for them in three days.

The bride's gown was elegant and flowing, a style befitting a queen. She wasn't royalty, but her dad's money was as good as being royalty. The white lace veil was a perfect match and the seamstress had worked nonstop since Sunday afternoon to make it all perfect. It was the perfect gown for the perfect wedding.

The groom, meanwhile, was sitting in an anteroom with a few muscular men nearby. The men were in suits so they could blend in with the wedding party, but they weren't there as friends of the groom. They were there to make sure everything went according to plan. The bride's father had paid for the groom's tuxedo and all the accoutrements to make him look as worthy of his daughter as possible. A smile from the groom would have made it look as if he were as happy as the bride.

There was a knock on the door and the burly men entered the room. "It's time; let's go," one of them said. The groom stood up, looking dazed as many men do on their wedding day. But his look wasn't because he was getting married. They stepped out into the central area where the bride and her party were waiting for him.

The organist began playing a processional song which meant for them to walk down the aisle. The men walked down first and stopped where instructed to by the priest. Then the women slowly came down the aisle, with the proud father and beaming bride walking together with arms locked at the elbows. When they reached the front, the father turned around and walked to the front row where he sat down.

The ceremony was conducted in Greek, which contributed to the confusion for the groom. He just stood there, being bolstered by one of the big men at his side. He knelt when he was to kneel and he stood when he was lifted up to stand. The priest continued with the incantations and blessings. The bride and groom were getting a full wedding. Her father made sure it was going to be a spectacular send off for his last, although oldest, daughter.

The vows were recited with the groom mumbling through his as he attempted to read them. The priest asked him if he took her to be his lawful wedded wife, etc., etc., and to love her forever and always. The groom looked at the man helping him stay upright; the man told him what to say.

The groom said, "I do," and he immediately shook his head and looked around. "What's going on?" he exclaimed.

Unfazed, the priest continued with the bride's vows. "And do you take Juan Castro to be your lawful husband, to have and to hold."

Juan Castro, the new husband, heard nothing more. What was he doing in a wedding? Did he just get married? He turned and started to run out of the church but the men at his side held him in place until the priest blessed them and pronounced, "…man and wife in this life and the next. You may kiss the bride," the priest added.

The new husband just stood there. The man closest to him nudged him with an elbow. "Kiss the bride," the man added.

"What is this? What's going on? Why am I here?" Castro asked again.

"Kiss the bride and we'll explain it all," the man said in a very insistent voice as he pressed a fist against Castro's side.

Juan Castro leaned forward and kissed her; he still didn't realize that she was his bride.

The father stood up in the front row and began clapping and the rest of the congregation joined in offering their congratulations to the new couple.

"May they live together forever," the father said as he turned around to face the people.

"Forever and ever," the congregation said in unison.

And then they all said, "Amen."

The father walked up to the new couple, shook the man's hand and said, "Welcome to the family, son. I know that you'll make my daughter very happy and bring me many grandchildren. Let's go begin the celebration."

Four wide, they walked down the aisle and out of the church. The father was arm-in-arm with his daughter who was clutching at Juan Castro's arm who was being led out by the muscular man. All four of them got into the back of a long black limousine to go the party that was waiting for them. The driver started the engine and the father opened the bottle of ouzo that was sitting between the four glasses. He poured two glasses: one for his daughter and one for his new son-in-law.

"Here's to a long and happy marriage and many grandchildren," the father said as he raised the bottle to his lips.

88

Tuesday, July 23

4:00 PM

The ship had moved into calmer waters now that they were following the Italian coastline and slowly sailing northwest in the Tyrrhenian Sea. Some of the outside activities had been reopened; Bingo was quite popular as it was something to do indoors and the slot machines in the casino were ringing away with almost every seat taken.

The bottles of Limoncello that had been allocated for the matinee show were quickly emptied even though each serving was only one ounce. It was a nice bittersweet reminder of the port that was missed due to the weather, one of those things that just can't be controlled. The theater was almost full as Becky looked at her watch. Olivia Cromwell had indicated she was ready, so Becky stepped through the curtain to polite applause.

Becky smiled and the applause grew louder. "Thank you," she said. "Thank you for that nice reception. I know we ran out, but did those of you who got some Limoncello enjoy it?"

The audience responded with cheers, applause, and cries for More!

"Well," she continued, "I wish I could have given you better weather instead, but you now have your excuse for taking another cruise with us—so you can see the Isle of Capri. No, it's not a free cruise. Anyway, I'm glad you're all in a good mood because you asked to have her come back on stage and she graciously said yes. So please put your hands together and help me bring back out on stage the fantastic hypnotist, the one and only Olivia Cromwell!"

The stage spotlights turned in opposite circles as the curtains opened and Olivia walked to the center of the stage. She smiled as she saw the large crowd. "Thank you, Becky. You know, it's nice not having any competition; that way I get to see half of you now and the other half at tonight's 9 PM show. How many of you believe that hypnotism is real?"

About half the audience raised their hands.

"Put your hands down. Do the rest of you think hypnotism is just a bunch of trickery? If so, raise your hands."

Only a fourth of the audience raised their hands.

"Okay, hands down. So, half of you believe it's real and about a fourth think it's trickery. Well, who hasn't raised their hand?"

About a fourth of the people raised their hands.

"Keep them up in the air," she said while she said some incomprehensible words and then clapped her hands together. Everyone whose hand was in the air suddenly stood up and started bouncing up and down like a pogo stick.

"Now who believes hypnotism is real?"

Most of the seated audience raised their hands. Some were still skeptical and others didn't want to become a human pogo stick. Olivia clapped her hands again and the bouncing people stopped. They looked around as the rest of the audience was laughing. At them.

"Why are you all standing?" Olivia asked.

The people quickly sat down.

"Is there someone sitting next to an aisle who couldn't carry a tune no matter how big of a bucket you had?" There were no aisle-seat volunteers, but there were those in a second seat who were more than willing to volunteer a non-singer on the aisle. Olivia stepped off the stage and started walking up the aisle to where someone had been volunteered. She extended her hand to a young lady in an aisle seat.

As the young lady stood up, Olivia asked, "What's your name, my dear?"

"Kristen," was the timid reply.

"Now, Kristen," Olivia continued, "this fellow next to you says you can't sing. Is that right?"

"I like to sing, but I'm not very good," Kirsten replied.

"But, yet, you didn't raise your hand when I asked if there was someone in an aisle seat who couldn't sing?" Olivia continued to pressure.

"No," Kristen said.

"That's okay, Kristen. Before you sit down, what's this fellow's name?"

"Mark," Kirsten answered.

"Thank you, Kristen, you may sit down." Olivia waited for Kristen to sit back down before she continued. "Mark. Stand up, Mark."

The hot shot stood up.

"Mark, can you sing?" she asked.

"I'm okay," he answered.

"Mark. I didn't ask how you were feeling." The audience laughed as Mark was being put in his place for volunteering his wife or his girlfriend. "Mark. I asked if you could sing. The answer is either Yes or it's No." Olivia held up her hand to stop Mark from answering.

"Before you answer, Mark, let me ask Kristen," and she looked down at Kristen. "Kristen, can Mark sing?"

Kristen looked up at Mark, then back to Olivia. "No," was the faint reply.

Olivia turned her attention back to Mark. "Let's find out what Mark's answer is. Mark, you've had plenty of time to think about it and you just heard what Kristen said. Can you sing?" Olivia stared at Mark.

"Yes," Mark said stubbornly.

Olivia turned to the center part of the audience. "Why did I think that was going to be the answer?" and the audience laughed. Turning back to Mark, she said, "That's great, Mark, why don't you come and help me." She was changing her act, but she didn't really have a script she had to follow.

Mark stepped by Kristen and followed Olivia to the front of the audience. "Look at me, Mark," she said to him. As he looked her straight in the eyes, she said some words and then took her index fingers and poked him in the fleshy part of both shoulders. He shook his head ever so slightly. Olivia then looked around the audience for a good target.

"Mark, I want you to go to the other side of the audience, and count up five rows from the front on the left side. That person in the aisle seat is secretly in love with you. Go over and sing to that person professing your mad love back."

The audience looked over, counted up five rows and laughed as Mark started walking over there. He counted the rows slowly, one-two-three-four-five. He knelt down in front of the person and started singing the worst rendition of any country and western song that had ever been done. He finished singing and then threw his arms around his new love.

"Very good, Mark," Olivia said. "Now wake up and see who your new lover is," and she snapped her fingers twice. The audience roared when Mark realized he'd just been hugging and singing to an elderly gentleman. The man took it in stride as his wife leaned over and gave him a kiss on the cheek. "I still love you even though you prefer the young men," she said.

Instead of going back to his seat, Mark walked briskly up the aisle and out of the theater. Kristen quietly got out of her seat and also left the theater.

"Any other non-believers out there before we have a lot of fun?" Olivia asked as she scanned the audience.

A balding man in an aisle seat near the back of the theater hollered out, "You're nothing but a crackpot fraud!"

Olivia's face turned crimson red as she stormed up the aisle toward the heckler. Security also headed toward the man, but Olivia got there first and she dismissed the help. She then said something and the heckler started to take off all his clothes and was jumping around the aisle like a mad man.

Olivia then yelled out, "Anyone else have any comments like that who wants to see what I can do?"

The stage manager immediately cut her microphone as two security men came back in the theater, grabbed her by the arms and took her out kicking and screaming.

89

Tuesday, July 23

4:45 PM

"This is all a big misunderstanding," Olivia Cromwell said to Clive Stewart as she began to calm down in the security office. "I was putting the man into a trance, but he said something during my incantation that must have caused the result that it did. He was just supposed to start crowing like a rooster, not start stripping. I do a family act."

"Miss Cromwell, I've talked with several of the ship's employees who said that some of your trances were crude and rather mean-spirited. I'm not sure if you should do any more shows on our ship."

"Look," Olivia countered. "I admit that I tend to pick on the men a little more than women, but it's because they're usually the ones who don't believe that this really is a gift. I'll tone it down for tonight's show; I promise."

Clive Stewart wanted to believe her as she'd been a popular entertainer both in the theater and in the lounges. He knew he didn't have the final answer, but Becky would listen to his recommendation. "Let me talk with Becky as she's over all the entertainment and I'll get back with you. For now, however, I'm going to ask you to stay in your cabin until you hear from me. You can either agree or I'll be forced to take other measures. Do you agree to stay in your cabin until you hear from me?"

Olivia reluctantly said, "Yes."

"Good," Clive said. "Now what's your cabin number?"

"It's 8062," Olivia replied.

"Take the elevator up there and wait for my call. Thank you," Clive said as he stood up and opened the door.

Olivia noticed the writing on the white board. "What are those names and dates and ports on the board?"

Clive had forgotten that the list of the missing men, cabin numbers, dates and ports they went missing in was still on the white board. That was a big *faux pas*. He quickly made up a story. "These passengers reported items lost or stolen in port, so we're just keeping track of them in case they show up later."

"What about that one 'in jail'?" she asked.

"Oh," Clive attempted a laugh. "He wasn't in jail; he stopped in the jail office to ask about taking a picture of the Wanted posters. That's where he thinks he lost something."

"Interesting," Olivia said as she scanned the list again.

"Let me give Becky a call so I can get back to you," Clive said because he wanted Olivia to leave his office. Olivia turned and walked out the door.

Clive shut the door and shook his head. He called the cruise director and told her that he thought Olivia was okay to go back on stage, but that he was going to have his people keep a very close watch on her.

90

Wednesday, July 24

8:40 AM

The 9 PM show went off without any problems and no one mentioned anything about Olivia's outburst in the matinee show. There were also no hecklers in the audience as word had quietly spread to just sit back and be polite. The rest of the evening was good as the waves were calm and there was only a light breeze blowing.

The *Royal Holiday* pulled alongside the dock in Livorno, Italy, at 7 AM and the ship was quickly cleared by the local officials. The morning tours were pulled up one hour even though they were in port two hours earlier than previously scheduled. The tours started filing off the ship at 7:50, without a security person on each tour. Security personnel were allowed to go on a tour as an escort if it didn't interfere with assigned duties. In other words, the tours were back to normal. It was hard to tell who was happier with the return to normalcy, head of security Clive Stewart or Shore Excursion manager Walter Peterson.

Becky smiled at Walter as she passed him in the Central Lobby. "It feels good, doesn't it?"

"Sure does," Walter replied not sure if the two of them were talking about the same thing. Walter knew about the missing passengers but he didn't think that Becky Anderson had been brought into the loop on that situation. "Going ashore today?" he asked.

"No today, Walter, unless you really need me. I'm really tired out from everything that's been going on. I'm going to grab a book and enjoy the sun up on twelve." Becky was looking forward to quiet time and working on her tan.

Walter went into the theater to get the next group of tours going. The routine was the same. Most of the tours in Livorno were going to Pisa or to Florence. His phone rang and he was told that the next four numbers were ready to go. "Bus number seven is now ready. Please make sure you have your room key as you leave the ship. Your bus is waiting for you on the dock." He waited a few minutes between calling each group.

As tours eight and nine were leaving the ship and walking down the gangway, one man was walking against the flow.

Phil Watson had taken the train from Naples to Livorno and was met at the station just as he'd been told. The man took Phil to his house where he and his wife treated him like a special friend. They didn't speak much English, but then Phil knew very little Italian. After dinner, the man was able to get across to Phil that his wife wanted to wash his clothes and Phil was offered a freshly pressed pair of pajamas to wear. In the morning, Phil's new clothes were hanging on a hanger including the underwear and socks. His dashing hat had been brushed and looked new. After his shower and getting dressed, he was served a breakfast that could have fed five others. Phil displayed the best manners he could and then graciously said *Grazie* to the woman he'd never see again; her husband drove Phil to the dock. It had been quite an adventure for Phil and it was just about over.

"Wasn't that the fellow that had been sitting at our table?" one of the women said as she continued down the gangway.

"I didn't notice," replied her husband. It was actually amazing that he'd even been listening to her.

Phil continued his way up against the crowd, determined to get back on the ship, especially since he was so close. Nothing was going to get in his way now. He finally made it to the top and could see a familiar sight—Central Lobby. He pulled the room key from his wallet as he approached the security machine. He inserted the card and the machine let out a screeching alarm.

"Remove your card, sir," the security officer said so the alarm would stop. "Please wait right over there," the officer said as he motioned for Phil to step to the side out of the way of traffic. The officer pulled the walkie-talkie from his belt. "Embarkation to Clive Stewart, code 7. I repeat, Embarkation to Clive Stewart, code 7."

Clive Stewart was enjoying a quiet breakfast in Oceans Café when the code 7 came across the system. He removed his walkie-talkie and spoke into it. "Clive Stewart acknowledging code 7. Out." So much for the peaceful breakfast. He carried his tray of unfinished food to the bussing area and headed to the crew stairs; it would be faster that way to get down to Deck Three, especially with tours using the main stairs.

He still had to work his way through the crowd as he reached Central Lobby because of all the tours that were leaving the ship. He went to the entrance area where he saw a young man in an outfit that looked completely out of place for coming on the ship. Clive went to the security officer who pulled up the photo and boarding information from Phil Watson's room key. Clive looked at the man; the picture seemed to match.

"Good morning, sir," Clive said to Phil. "Do you have any other identification with you?"

"Sure," Phil said as he pulled out his wallet and then got out his driver's license. That photo also matched.

"What is your room number, sir?" Clive asked.

"Cabin 4050," Phil said. "Look, I can explain, well at least some of it."

"Yes," said the head of security. "You definitely have some explaining to do. Let me have your room key."

Phil handed the key to Clive who put it into the machine. The alarm started again and Clive put his card into the officer's slot and entered a special code. The alarm stopped. "Welcome back aboard, Mr. Watson. Let's go have a chat," Clive said as he handed the room key back to Phil.

Phil followed Clive to his office and they went inside. Phil immediately noticed the writing on the white board, especially his name. "What's that all about?" he asked.

"We're going to talk about that right now," Clive said. He started asking Phil questions about his disappearance, what he was doing in Messina, where he'd been in the past nine days, how he got back to the ship. Phil had answers for the more current events, but he didn't have an explanation for Messina other than he was in a bar drinking with some Sicilians. The next thing he knew he was in a jail.

Mention of a jail sounded familiar as Clive looked at the board. That's where Greg Brighton was the last they knew of him. Phil continued with his story of the kind police captain and all his relatives who helped him along the way, eventually getting him back to the ship.

"You don't remember why you went into that bar and started drinking with the Sicilians?" Clive asked.

Phil's mind was blurry as he tried to reconstruct what happened. He remembered going into Taormina on a walking tour; it was warm and he had a couple beers. Could he remember anything else before waking up in the jail? No, that was all he could remember. He thought he saw an attractive woman in the picture, but it was all a blur. Was that woman real or was he just imagining her? No, that was all he could think of.

"Mr. Watson, you're not the only one who's gone missing." Clive pointed to the board. "I need you to keep this quiet and the best way is for you to take meals in your room and keep a low profile when you're on deck. Are you willing to do that to help me and the rest of the passengers?"

"I guess so, but what's all that?"

"That," Clive explained, "is what's been happening each day we've been in port. One passenger has disappeared and we're trying to solve that mystery. It's a very rare occurrence for a passenger to just walk away from a cruise; but when it happens at every port each day, then it stops becoming rare or even extremely rare. Something is going on and we're working to find out what that is. If you think of anything about that day in Taormina, please call me immediately," Clive said as he handed his card to Phil. He then added slowly for emphasis, "And do not say anything to anyone else about this."

"Got it," Phil said.

"Nice outfit, by the way. You'd fit in perfectly with the Sicilian mob." Clive opened the door and Phil left to go to his cabin. Clive updated Phil's status on the board.

Tyler Jacobs 7043 – Sunday 14th – Civitavecchia

Phil Watson 4050 – Monday 15th – Messina (back 24th)

Greg Brighton 4099 – Tuesday 16th – Valletta (in jail)

Tony Lockwood 7012 – Thursday 18th – Santorini

Juan Castro 8055 – Saturday 20th – Limassol

91

Wednesday, July 24

9:00 AM

Wearing his backpack, James Phillips was in line with those going on tours as they stood in the Central Lobby to leave the ship. "I see you've got your hat today, James," one of the passengers said. Several others looked in James' direction.

"I have to protect what's up here," James said as he patted the top of his head. He chuckled as did the others and he stuffed a bottle of water into his backpack

"What tour are you on today?" the same fellow asked.

"Just going out to walk around," James said. "And you?"

"We're going to Florence," the man said. "I've never been to the Academia to see the David statue. I hear it's pretty impressive."

"It is," James said. "Are you also getting to the Uffizi?"

"That and Ponte Vecchio," the man answered.

"Sounds like an awesome tour. Have a great time," James said as the lines split and he checked off the ship with his room key. The Uffizi Gallery in Florence was one of James' favorite galleries. The Louvre in Paris was awesome, but the Uffizi had genuine character. James stayed in the right line as the passengers headed into the cruise terminal.

The tour groups continued to come ashore and board the buses that were neatly lined up and waiting for them. The weather in Livorno, although it was still early in the day, was beautiful. It was the type of day that any tourism bureau would love to claim was "the typical day." The cruise was nearing its end and the weather was creating a perfect crescendo, just as the symphony orchestra would do when it was reaching the end of its classical masterpiece. The tour guides collected the tickets and once they were counted, handed them off to the tour supervisor who then gave them to Walter Peterson. It was a good system that worked smoothly most of the time.

John Phillips walked up the ramp and placed his room key into the slot. The machine beeped and the security officer squinted and looked at the display. He called his supervisor over to take a look. "Mr. Phillips, the machine is saying that you didn't check off properly this morning. I apologize for the problem. Go ahead and insert your card again."

John put his card in the slot again, the machine beeped and the supervisor overrode the beep by entering his code. John just smiled as he walked through. "Machines," he said.

"Sorry for the problem, Mr. Phillips," said the supervisor who also doubled as one of the casino managers.

92

Wednesday, July 24

10:45 AM

Clive made some phone calls to inform certain people that Phil Watson was back on the ship. His first call was to the captain who was pleased but still concerned over the others who were missing. He then called Inspector Moreau who wanted to know the details. Clive filled him in on what he'd been told and then said, "He's either holding back information or he is truly unaware of what happened to him."

"I can't imagine why he would withhold information about his disappearance," Moreau said. "You're gone for nine days and you won't say what happened to you. I don't think that's much of a possibility," the inspector added.

Clive then called Professor Dunningham. "That's good," Dunningham said. "Hopefully, they'll all just walk back on the ship because right now I don't see any pattern, but I'll keep looking into things."

"Is your wife still enjoying the cruise, Professor?"

"Yes, she is. Thank you for asking, Mr. Stewart. Do you have anything else you think I should be looking into?"

"Not right now. Thanks, Professor." Clive hung up and called Walter Peterson who wasn't in his office. Walter was on shore monitoring the tours as the buses were boarding and heading off to Pisa, Florence and the one picturesque tour that included no walking.

"A good day so far," Clive Stewart said out loud to himself.

Security on shore didn't want to let the man through. He showed them his room key and it looked valid. He opened his wallet and showed them that the name on his driver's license matched the name in the room key. They still said, "No."

Frustrated after all he'd been through, Tyler Jacobs held out his wallet. "How much money do you want? Take it all, I don't care. You have no idea what I've been through in the last ten days here in your country. I just want to get back on the ship. What do you want from me?" Tyler Jacobs' spirit was completely broken and he started crying. He had been through quite an ordeal; it was a miracle that he'd even made it back to the ship.

The two security guards were tempted with the thought of a bribe, but the man really did look horrible. His clothes were a mess; it looked as if he'd slept in them for a week. He'd not shaved and he'd probably not showered either. Both of these were actually correct. Tyler had been wandering around Rome for a week, scrounging for food and sleeping anyplace where it was dry and safe.

"Go," the two security guards finally said to Tyler as he still held out his wallet to them. One of the guards waved his hand at Tyler to indicate that they didn't want any of his money. Tyler's emotions gushed out as he finally felt that he was back to a safe place. He was almost there.

All of the morning tours had already left; the gangway was all Tyler's as he slowly walked up the sixty-four steps. His appearance was that of a homeless person who had somehow gotten past shore security. He wouldn't get past ship's security; they had a lot more at stake than the ones on shore.

Tyler put his card into the machine and a loud alarm went off. The security guard removed the key and held on to it. It wasn't the same guard as when Phil Watson came on earlier so this guard wasn't aware of what might be occurring. He pulled the walkie-talkie from his belt and spoke into it, "Embarkation to Clive Stewart, code 7. I repeat Embarkation to Clive Stewart, code 7."

"What now?" Clive Stewart said out loud as he heard the call from the embarkation lounge right outside his office. He removed his walkie-talkie and spoke into it. "Clive Stewart acknowledging code 7. Out." Clive got up and went out to the embarkation area where he saw the sorry-state of a young man. "What now?" he repeated mostly to himself.

"Good morning, sir. I'm the head of security; how may I help you?" Clive said in a professional manner.

Tyler Jacobs looked dejected as he mumbled, "Not again." His appearance was definitely not that of a passenger on the *Royal Holiday*. "My name is Tyler Jacobs," he said as he pulled out his wallet to show his driver's license. "I just want to get back to my cabin, take a long, hot shower and sleep until we get to our final place." He was exhausted, mentally and physically.

Clive Stewart looked at the driver's license. The photo looked like him, but the disheveled clothing was hard to dismiss. "What is your cabin number, Mr. Jacobs?"

"It's 7043," Tyler said without hesitation.

"Your room key, please," Clive said to Tyler

Tyler handed the key to Clive who put it into the machine. The alarm started again and Clive put his card into the officer's slot and entered a special code. The alarm stopped. "Well, Mr. Jacobs, let's go have a chat. Are you hungry?"

"I'm hungry; I'm thirsty; I'm tired; I'm confused. Can any of this wait? Do you think I'm going to go anywhere now that I'm finally back here?" Tyler Jacobs really looked pathetic. Not even the best actor in London or New York could fake the way that Tyler was right now. "Please," Tyler said with eyes that dripped with emotion and sought some empathy.

"Just a couple of questions and then I'll take you to your cabin," Clive said as he helped Tyler over to the side of the lobby. "Where have you been?" was the first question. Clive had to help Tyler from falling over.

"I was in Rome, but I have no idea why I was there," Tyler answered.

"Were you drinking?" was the next question.

"I don't think so," Tyler answered.

"Why were gone so long from the ship?" was the next question.

"I don't know," Tyler said as tears dripped from his crusted eyes.

Clive Stewart realized that there was more to this situation than a person who just headed off and didn't come back. "Let's go," he said as he grabbed Tyler's arm and led him to an elevator and then to his cabin on the seventh deck. "Would you rather eat, take a shower, or sleep right now?" Clive asked.

"I don't know," was the unresponsive answer.

"We noticed that you were reading *Angels & Demons*; does that ring a bell?" Clive asked.

Tyler Jacobs thought for a while. "I remember that the book had gotten a lot of media press after the *DaVinci Code* movie came out. I saw the book in the library, so I thought I'd read it. I don't have a clue why all of this is taking place."

Clive took out his phone and called the medical facility. "This is Clive Stewart. I need a nurse who can stay here with a male patient who's suffered some serious mental trauma. It's cabin 7043 and I'll wait here. Oh, and bring some IVs; he's quite dehydrated."

The nurse arrived at the cabin in five minutes. Clive gave her a brief description of the situation and that she should call him if there was any problem. He returned to his office and updated the information on the white board.

Tyler Jacobs 7043 – Sunday 14th – Civitavecchia (back 24th)

Phil Watson 4050 – Monday 15th – Messina (back 24th)

Greg Brighton 4099 – Tuesday 16th – Valletta (in jail)

Tony Lockwood 7012 – Thursday 18th – Santorini

Juan Castro 8055 – Saturday 20th – Limassol

93

Wednesday, July 24

5:45 PM

Walter Peterson was on the dock as each tour came back into the port. Even though the security details had been removed from each tour, Walter still wanted to make sure that his job wasn't in jeopardy. He verified the count on each tour as it came in, and each one was correct. The same number of passengers came in on each tour as had gone out on it. As far as the weather was concerned, today was a spectacular day. The very light breeze offset the warm sun and the people who took a bottle of water with them were just fine.

The 5:30 all-aboard time had passed and security was checking to make sure every passenger was on board. As the list of passengers was scanned, one name was highlighted in red. James Phillips in 7053 had checked off the ship at 9:07 in the morning, but he hadn't checked back on. "Call his brother," one of the security officers said.

"Hello," John Phillips said as he picked up the phone.

"Sorry to bother you, Mr. Phillips. This is security on Deck Three, and we noticed that your brother James hasn't checked back on the ship. Have you seen him?"

"Not since we had breakfast together this morning. He told me he was going ashore, but he didn't say what he was going to do or where he was going to go." John Phillips wasn't much help.

The security officer made a call to Clive Stewart to tell him about the one passenger who'd not returned to the ship.

"May I have your attention, please," began the announcement over the public address system. "Will Mr. James Phillips in cabin 7053 please report to Guest Relations on Deck Three immediately. That's Mr. James Phillips in cabin 7053, please report to Guest Relations on Deck Three immediately."

Clive let out a huge sigh. Two of the missing men had returned today, but now there was one more passenger who'd not returned. He went to the white board and added James Phillips to the board.

94

Wednesday, July 24

8:25 PM

Tyler Jacobs 7043 – Sunday 14th – Civitavecchia (back 24th)

Phil Watson 4050 – Monday 15th – Messina (back 24th)

Greg Brighton 4099 – Tuesday 16th – Valletta (in jail)

Tony Lockwood 7012 – Thursday 18th – Santorini

Juan Castro 8055 – Saturday 20th – Limassol

James Phillips 7053 – Wednesday 24th - Livorno

Alfred Dunningham noted the updated entries on the white board when he entered Clive's office, including the new addition. Three of the now six passengers were accounted for, although one of them was not on the ship. "What about the others?" Alfred asked. "Phillips is a new one; do you think there's much chance that the other two will show up in Barcelona?"

"You're the numbers man, Professor," Clive began. "I wouldn't hold out much hope for them returning; I just hope they're safe."

Alfred opened the file on his tablet where he'd written down Inspector Moreau's modular arithmetic and added the latest number, 7053.

$7+0+4+3 \quad \mod(7) = 0$

$4+0+5+0 \quad \mod(4) = 1$

$4+0+9+9 \quad \mod(4) = 2$

$7+0+1+2 \quad \mod(7) = 3$

$8+0+5+5 \quad \mod(8) = 2$

7+0+5+3　mod(7) = 1

Clive was the first to speak. "Well, the number fits nicely into Inspector Moreau's pattern, doesn't it?"

"You're right about that," Dunningham replied. "However, that also means that it falls into the paradox that while we don't have anything to say that this theory isn't correct, that doesn't mean that it is correct. And even if it is correct, it doesn't give us any information on why these men disappeared. There has to be more to the problem than we can see right now."

Dunningham actually saw something else, but he didn't want to say anything about it until he was able to dig deeper into it and hopefully provide an explanation for the disappearances of seemingly normal men.

95

Thursday, July 25

9:00 AM

With only one more day, twenty hours to be more accurate, until the ship reached its final port in Barcelona, the pressure was building to find solutions. Clive Stewart had a lot of resources available to him as head of security, plus he also had an Interpol inspector and a mathematics professor who was known for helping solve mysteries. So far, however, they'd come up with more questions than answers.

Inspector Moreau saw the additional name on the white board. He did the modular arithmetic and saw that 7053 fit nicely into the pattern. It was now 0-1-2-3-2-1.

"Yes, I saw that also," Dunningham said as he saw what Moreau was doing. "Unfortunately, it's still not enough." He turned his attention to Clive. "We need to check with the local authorities at the ports where the passengers who disappeared are still missing. Then let's review all the notes from their cabin visits and talk with the two who've returned. Most events don't just happen randomly; there is typically some order to their occurrences."

"I'll get those calls set up right away," Clive said. He looked at Moreau. "Inspector, has anything turned up in Interpol? Has there been any suspicious activity in the areas where our passengers are still missing?"

"There's always some activity, Clive, but nothing that our resources on the ground feel would be related to this. There is a new uprising in Cyprus, but we see these every few months. It's as if these men stepped into a black hole and disappeared."

Inspector Moreau was not painting a bright outlook for the return of the missing men.

"The Inspector and I will go talk with passengers Jacobs and Watson to see if we can learn anything more than what they told you yesterday. We'll be back here in an hour for those phone calls." Dunningham then looked at Moreau. "Does that work for you?"

"Of course," the inspector replied as he looked at the number sequence again. He so wanted those numbers to have something to do with solving the case, or cases.

96

Thursday, July 25

10:00 AM

Professor Dunningham and Inspector Moreau returned to Clive's office. They didn't say much while they were in the public areas as Moreau was so mentally into the case that he occasionally forgot about his alter ego as Holiday Cruise Line's chief marketing officer, Pierre Dubois. Dunningham would have enjoyed talking with Dubois about the use of analytics and demographics in understanding how to market their cruises. But the Pierre Dubois on this cruise actually knew very little about marketing.

"We have our first call in five minutes; it's to the jail in Malta where passenger Brighton is being held," Clive said as the returning men sat down.

Dunningham looked at his new notes. "Mr. Jacobs acknowledged reading *Angels & Demons*, that novel we saw in his cabin. What he couldn't explain was why he went to the Vatican to dig into some of the mysteries that the author presented in the book. He said he walked off the ship and went directly to the train station. When I asked him how he knew where the train station was in Civitavecchia, he said that the speaker had talked about it the afternoon before we got to Civitavecchia."

"Since neither of us were onboard the ship then," Moreau interjected, "we checked with Shore Excursions and they confirmed that this Moretti fellow who's doing the talks did tell the passengers exactly how to get off the ship and walk to the train station. So those actions check out."

The desk phone rang. "That must be the Malta call," Clive remarked. "This is Clive Stewart, head of security," he said into the phone. "Yes, thank you very much. We know this is not according to your normal procedures, but I'm glad that you realize we have an unusual situation on our hands. I'll wait as you connect Mr. Brighton."

There was a short pause.

"Hello?"

"Mr. Brighton, this is Clive Stewart, head of security on the *Royal Holiday*. Thank you for taking my call."

"Are you going to get me out of here?" the frightened voice asked.

"We're working on that, Mr. Brighton," Clive said. "I have two other men here in my office; do you mind if I put you on the speaker?"

"That's fine," Brighton replied.

Clive pushed the speaker button on the phone and the static in the line was heard by all. "In the room with me," Clive continued, "are Inspector Moreau from Interpol and Professor Dunningham who is noted for helping solve mysteries through the use of mathematics."

"Interpol?" Brighton asked.

"Yes," Clive said. "You're not the only passenger who went missing from the cruise. Now we're not releasing that information, but one of the reasons we wanted to talk with you was to learn more about your disappearance. Are you willing to share that with us?"

"Anything you want to know," Brighton said. "Just get me out of here, please." The tone of his voice clearly indicated that he was pleading for help.

"Mr. Brighton, this is Inspector Moreau. We heard that you were arrested for taking photographs of the Caravaggio paintings in St. John's Co-Cathedral. Is that correct?"

"That's what they told me."

Moreau continued. "We were in your cabin, but we didn't see anything to indicate that you were into photography. There was one thumb drive underneath your pajamas, but we didn't see anything else that said photography. Can you explain that?"

"Oh, the thumb drive. I can explain those pictures; please don't tell anyone about them." Brighton's voice had suddenly changed to remorseful.

"Your thumb drive is still there, Mr. Brighton, and we didn't look at the contents," Clive said.

"Right," Moreau added. "Why were you in St. John's and why were you taking photographs of the Caravaggios when it's clearly stated that photographs aren't allowed?"

"I don't know," Brighton answered. "I know they're famous paintings, but they don't really appeal to me."

"You didn't answer my questions," Moreau stuck to the point. "Why were you in St. John's and why were you taking photographs of the Caravaggios when it's clearly stated that photographs aren't allowed?"

A frustrated Brighton answered, "I told you I don't know why. I'm not into photography that much, but there was an inner voice that told me to go into the cathedral, take pictures of those paintings and then offer them for sale online. I know it sounds dumb, but that's it."

"An inner voice told you to do it?" Moreau asked.

"Yes; now are you going to get me out of here?" The fright in Brighton's voice returned.

"As I told you, Mr. Brighton, we're working on it," Clive responded. He pushed the mute button and looked at Moreau and Dunningham. "Anything else?" Dunningham nodded his head and Clive took the phone off mute.

"Mr. Brighton," Dunningham started, "this is Alfred Dunningham and I work with numbers all the time. I'm curious. Your cabin number, 4099, is the same as the last four digits of your Social Security number. Was that on purpose?"

There was a moment of silence and Moreau and Dunningham looked at each other. Had they uncovered something of significance?

"I'm sorry; the guard was telling me I had two minutes left. What was that you asked?" Brighton's response sent a deflating feeling through Moreau.

"Mr. Brighton," Dunningham started, "this is Alfred Dunningham and I work with numbers all the time. I'm curious. Your cabin number, 4099, is the same as the last four digits of your Social Security number. Was that on purpose?"

Brighton quickly answered, "I didn't pick the cabin; I just booked the cheapest category and the cruise line assigned that one to me about two months ago. How did you know my Social Security number?"

"Interpol knows everything about you, Mr. Brighton," Moreau said. "We know what television shows you watch, the videos you stream online, even your chat room conversations. Now are you sure it was an inner voice that told you to take the photographs?" Moreau was certain that he'd told the passenger enough information that would get him to now tell them the truth.

"Yes," Brighton insisted. "I'm not a perfect man, but I didn't break the law intentionally. I was forced to do it. Oh no, here comes the guard. Please help me." The line went dead.

"Well?" Clive said as he pushed the speaker button to disconnect his line.

"He has a few things in his past that don't look good," Moreau said. "I'm afraid to think what's on that thumb drive and why was it underneath his pajamas that were so neatly folded."

"He's scared," Dunningham offered. "He thinks we know what's on the thumb drive even though we said we hadn't looked at it. With what you told him," Dunningham continued as he looked at Moreau, "that would be enough to get anyone to start telling the truth immediately, especially when you're in jail in a foreign country half way around the world. He's telling the truth, as crazy as that sounds."

"I tend to agree with you, Professor," Clive said. "At this point, we're his best hope for getting out of that jail and he'd be an absolute fool not to tell the truth. The sad news is that there isn't much we can do for him. I've sent an email to corporate to get them involved." He went to the board and did some erasing and then he updated some information.

Jacobs 7043 – 14th Civitavecchia (back 24th) to Vatican

Watson 4050 – 15th Messina (back 24th) (drunk in bar)

Brighton 4099 – 16th Valletta (jail) "inner voice told him to"

Lockwood 7012 – 18th Santorini

Castro 8055 – 20th Limassol

Phillips 7053 – 24th Livorno

Clive sat down, pressed the speaker button and punched in the number for the Santorini port agent.

"Èla," the man answering the phone said.

"This is Clive Stewart, head of security on the *Royal Holiday*. We were in port one week ago on the eighteenth and I was told that you had some information about one of our passengers who didn't check back in on the ship."

"Just one moment, please," the agent said as he shuffled some papers, took a drag on his cigarette, and said something to someone else in the room. "Okay, I have the paperwork here. What is the passenger's name?"

"His name is Tony Lockwood," Clive answered.

"Yes," the man responded. "He was lucky he had his room card in his pocket or we wouldn't know he was on your ship."

Clive waited for more information. "What happened to him?" Clive asked.

"Oh, he's in the hospital. He was walking down the path below the gondola to the ferry and he slipped. You know that area is so bad because of the donkeys that leave their mess as they're walking up and down that path."

"Can you tell me how to contact the hospital so we can talk with him?" Clive asked.

"I can give you their number, but we already checked with them this morning and he's still in a coma. The doctors don't know how long it will be before he comes out of it."

"That's too bad," Clive said. "Do you have any other information? Did the hospital say that he's been able to say anything?"

"He's been in a coma the entire time," the agent said.

"Okay," Clive responded, not knowing what else to say. "You have the information for contacting our headquarters, so please keep them updated if you would, please."

"Yes, I will. I'd sent an email to them this morning after I spoke with the hospital. You might tell your passengers when they come to Santorini to take the gondola down to the ferry and not walk down."

"We'll do that," Clive responded. "Thank you very much."

"You're welcome," the Greek said as he hung up the phone.

Clive pushed the speaker button. The three men looked at each in silence. Clive updated the status again.

Jacobs 7043 – 14th Civitavecchia (back 24th) to Vatican
Watson 4050 – 15th Messina (back 24th) (drunk in bar)
Brighton 4099 – 16th Valletta (jail) "inner voice told him to"
Lockwood 7012 – 18th Santorini (fell; hospital; coma)
Castro 8055 – 20th Limassol
Phillips 7053 – 24th Livorno

"I guess the good news," Clive started, "is that we know where Mr. Lockwood is. I hope he's able to recover soon. That is a good idea he had about warning people not to walk down that path; I've seen it, and it is slippery and smelly. Let's call the port agent in Limassol and see if he found out anything about Mr. Castro."

Clive went through the sequence again, but there was no news about their passenger. The agent had called the police stations and the hospitals. There was no sign of Mr. Castro. He got similar results when he called Livorno, although Mr. Phillips could have gone anywhere in Italy from the port. Clive made a final update on the board.

Jacobs 7043 – 14th Civitavecchia (back 24th) to Vatican
Watson 4050 – 15th Messina (back 24th) (drunk in bar)
Brighton 4099 – 16th Valletta (jail) "inner voice told him to"
Lockwood 7012 – 18th Santorini (fell; hospital; coma)
Castro 8055 – 20th Limassol (no information)
Phillips 7053 – 24th Livorno (no information)

"Well, gentlemen, I know we don't have much more to go on, but I hope you're able to come up with something this afternoon. We have a meeting with the captain at 8:00 this evening and he's already told me he wants a solution. No more questions, no more guesses; he wants a solution." Clive was essentially delivering an ultimatum to the Interpol inspector and the mathematics professor.

97

Thursday, July 25

8:00 PM

While the rest of the crew and the passengers were getting ready for the final port tomorrow, three men were walking toward the secured door on Deck Nine. Clive Stewart wasn't sure if he'd still have a job after the meeting. Antoine Moreau was glad the cruise was ending. This case really wasn't an Interpol case. Alfred Dunningham was looking forward to getting home to tend to his roses and to find out how the grape harvest went.

Stewart entered the code and the men entered the bridge area and went directly to the captain's office. "Come," was the familiar reply when Stewart knocked on the door. The three men went in and sat down.

"Tell me that you've solved the mystery," Captain Konstantinos Christopolous said. It was a command, but he knew he couldn't force something that wasn't there. He was just hoping that this wouldn't be his last cruise with the company.

"I'll take it," Dunningham said as he went to the board.

Jacobs 7043 – 14th Civitavecchia (back 24th) to Vatican

Watson 4050 – 15th Messina (back 24th) (drunk in bar)

Brighton 4099 – 16th Valletta (jail) "inner voice told him to"

Lockwood 7012 – 18th Santorini (fell; hospital; coma)

Castro 8055 – 20th Limassol (no information)

Phillips 7053 – 24th Livorno (no information)

"Mr. Jacobs, who is back on board, went to the Vatican to research what he'd been reading in the novel *Angels & Demons*. He has no idea why we went there; he's not Catholic; he lost track of time and days; he was just obsessed with it. He seems fine now, but he has no idea what possessed him to do it." Dunningham knew he had to keep this explanation short.

He continued with the next passenger. "It's a similar story for Mr. Watson. He was on a tour and had two beers. The next thing he knew he was in jail for being totally drunk in a bar. He had no idea where the bar was, why he went in there, or anything about being taken to jail. He said he was treated very well by the police captain who made arrangements through friends to get him back here to the ship.

"We spoke with Mr. Brighton earlier today where he's still in jail in Valletta. He said an inner voice told him to go into St. John's Co-Cathedral and take pictures of the Caravaggio paintings and sell them online. He knew that it was forbidden to take pictures in that gallery, but his common sense was overpowered by that inner voice. He's a frightened young man and I truly believe he did hear that voice telling him what to do.

"We also had a call with the port agent in Santorini who said that Mr. Lockwood slipped and hit his head on that walkway below the gondola down to the ferry. He's been in a coma ever since and the doctors and nurses said that he's not spoken a word." Dunningham paused. They had information on four of the passengers and two of them were safely back on the ship. Next came the hard part.

"Unfortunately," Dunningham began again, "we have no information on the other two passengers. The port agents have been diligent in checking hospitals, police stations, etc., but nothing's turned up on either Mr. Castro or Mr. Phillips. Even Mr. Phillips' brother couldn't provide any good clues."

The captain rocked back and forth in his chair. The squeak from the springs added to the intensity in the room. "So," the captain began his summary, "two of our six passengers are back on the ship but they don't know why they did what they did. It's good that they're back, but we don't know anything of their motives." He paused for a few second before continuing.

"Okay, let's just accept that good news for now. Then the next two are still in those towns; one is in jail and the other is in a coma in the hospital. The one in jail said he heard voices that told him to do it. That sounds a little whacko to me, but we'll leave it at that. The other who we hope gets better; he could have just gone out and was on his way back. We know where he is; we just hope he comes out of the coma.

"Then our last two have just vanished into thin air, and not even the brother of one can give us any help. Is that it?" He looked at Stewart. "Do you know what will happen to us if any of this gets out to the media?"

"I'm well aware of the consequences, Captain," Stewart said. "I wish we were able to find each one of them and know why. That's the part that bothers me. Why did they go and do those things? But I guess we'll never know." He paused and then continued, "Captain, I know it won't fix everything, but I'm willing to tender my resignation to keep the heat away from you."

"I don't think that will be necessary." That statement came from Dunningham and not the captain. "We do know more, and we're very close to solving the final piece of the puzzle."

98

Thursday, July 25

8:30 PM

"Don't hold back; what is it?" the captain asked as he sat forward in his chair. Had Dunningham been withholding information?

Professor Dunningham powered on his tablet. "Do you remember Inspector Moreau's initial thoughts, the ones that led to me? There still might be something there even though I dismissed it initially. Let me show you," he said as he went to the board and started writing next to the information he'd just written.

7+0+4+3 mod(7) = 0
4+0+5+0 mod(4) = 1
4+0+9+9 mod(4) = 2
7+0+1+2 mod(7) = 3
8+0+5+5 mod(8) = 2
7+0+5+3 mod(7) = 1

Dunningham continued with his math lesson. "I told you there had to be more, and I think I've found it. Those remainders were when we added the digits together and then took the remainder when dividing by the leading digit, or the deck number." Antoine Moreau smiled; he was right!

"But, unfortunately," Dunningham continued which erased Moreau's smile immediately, "those numbers aren't going to tell us anything useful. They're interesting; thank you, Inspector; but they're not enough all by themselves."

The professor continued. "Now let's take those same cabin numbers, but rather than taking the sum of the digits, let's take the entire cabin number and find the remainder when dividing by the deck number." He looked at the file on his tablet and added to the board.

7+0+4+3   mod(7) = 0; 7043 mod(7) = 1
4+0+5+0   mod(4) = 1; 4050 mod(4) = 2
4+0+9+9   mod(4) = 2; 4099 mod(4) = 3
7+0+1+2   mod(7) = 3; 7012 mod(7) = 5
8+0+5+5   mod(8) = 2; 8055 mod(8) = 7
7+0+5+3   mod(7) = 1; 7053 mod(7) = 4

The professor smiled; this was so brilliant. "Notice that these new numbers coincide with the days of the week. Mr. Jacobs in 7043 went missing on Sunday, and that number is 1. Mr. Watson, 4050, missing on Monday; it's a 2." He went through the remaining four passengers and their numbers.

"Now," Dunningham continued, "what's missing?"

"Six," the captain said.

"Precisely," Dunningham said. "And the sixth day of the week, according to a week where Sunday's the first day, is Friday. Now look back at the days of the week when passengers went missing. We have every day of the week except Friday, the sixth day."

"And?" the captain asked.

Professor Dunningham loved it when people asked the leading questions that he wanted them to ask. "Back to Moreau's theory and the cabin numbers; what number is logically next in that sequence?"

"Zero," Moreau answered. Once again he smiled. His theory was right after all.

"Exactly," Dunningham said. "We now have all the pieces of the puzzle. We just have to assemble the puzzle."

99

Thursday, July 25

8:40 PM

"Speaking of a puzzle, I'm still puzzled," the captain said. "I'm not a genius, especially in math, but I think something's still missing."

"That's okay," Dunningham said. "Watch this."

7+0+4+3   mod(7) = 0; 7043 mod(7) = 1

4+0+5+0   mod(4) = 1; 4050 mod(4) = 2

4+0+9+9   mod(4) = 2; 4099 mod(4) = 3

7+0+1+2   mod(7) = 3; 7012 mod(7) = 5

8+0+5+5   mod(8) = 2; 8055 mod(8) = 7

7+0+5+3   mod(7) = 1; 7053 mod(7) = 4

A+B+C+D   mod(A) = 0; ABCD mod(A) = 6

The professor continued. "We have one more port, and since we know that we need that zero to complete that first sequence, and we need that six to complete the second one, all we need is the cabin number that fits the pattern." Dunningham was pleased with his work. He felt like writing QED next to it as he did in school when he'd completed an assignment. (QED, Latin for *Quod Erat Demonstratum*, or that which was to be demonstrated)

"There must be dozens of cabin numbers that would fit pattern," the captain protested.

Moreau and Stewart looked dismayed. They thought they actually were getting somewhere, but maybe they weren't.

"Not really," Dunningham countered. "In order for a number to have the remainder of six, it means that the divisor, the number dividing the original number, must be seven or more. So all we have to do is to look for a cabin number on decks seven, eight, and nine that fits. And since the second digit of every cabin number is a zero, we really only have three hundred numbers to process." He opened the Excel program on his tablet and quickly typed in a recursive program to take all the four digit numbers starting with 7, 8, and 9, and that had zero as the second digit.

"Two," Dunningham said.

"Two what?" asked the captain.

"There are only two numbers that start with a seven, eight, or nine, and have zero as the second digit that would fit these two patterns." He paused to add to the suspense; it worked.

"Well, what are they?" all three men asked.

"The two cabins are 7034 and 8062," Dunningham answered. He went back to the board to show the calculations.

7+0+3+4 = 14; 14/7 =2 remainder (0)

7034/7 = 1004 remainder (6)

8+0+6+2 = 16; 16/8 =2 remainder (0)

8062/8 = 1007 remainder (6)

"Hum, 8062," Stewart mumbled. "Why is that cabin number familiar?"

The inspector had a thoughtful look on his face, and then said, "It seems familiar to me, too."

100

Thursday, July 25

8:50 PM

"Captain," Clive Stewart said, "would you please check to see who's in cabin 8062?"

"Certainly," the captain replied as he turned toward his computer. "Cabin 8062 is Olivia Cromwell's," he said.

"She's the hypnotist," Dunningham exclaimed. "This fits in with everything we've heard from those passengers and it might explain her bizarre behavior at that matinee showing."

"Right," Stewart added as he walked up to the board and pointed at the first name. "Mr. Jacobs said he was reading *Angels & Demons* when he just walked off the ship and took a train to the Vatican to explore all the theories proposed in that book. What if she placed him in a trance and told him to act on an impulse? That would sound innocent enough to anyone else hearing it.

"Mr. Watson said he was in Taormina and had two beers on a warm day. That wouldn't make him drunk. But then for no apparent reason, he goes into a bar and gets stupid drunk with a bunch of Sicilians. I don't know what she might have said to make him do that, but it's possible.

"Then our Mr. Brighton said he heard inner voices telling him to take pictures where he knew he wasn't supposed to. She could have put him in a trance and told him to do something that he knew he shouldn't do. Again, that could sound innocent to someone else." Stewart paused as he got to the last three names. They had no information on them except for one who was in a coma in the hospital. They could make up any set of circumstances for him and the other two, and they'd have no way to prove correctness or that it was wrong.

"We can't paint the scenario for the other three, but I think we agree that she's pretty suspect," Clive Stewart finished as he went back to his chair.

"So you're saying that she's going to make herself disappear tomorrow?" the captain asked. "She can just walk off the ship, so why disappear?"

"You're right, unless she has something else in mind," Dunningham replied.

"It sounds a little far-fetched to me, Professor," the captain said, "but your mathematics did solve those murders down in Sydney last year."

"Thank you, Captain," Dunningham replied. "We have to restrain her and not let her put anyone in a trance."

"How are we going to do that?" Moreau asked.

Dunningham answered quickly, "I've done a lot of work with the FBI and one of the areas that has intrigued me is the compounding of different chemicals. That knowledge came in quite handy last year on that case. I don't know what range of chemicals the doc has down in medical, but if we can go take a look, I bet there's something that will work."

"You want to give her a tranquilizer and knock her out?" Stewart asked.

"No," Dunningham replied. "While that would certainly restrain her, it wouldn't help us learn anything about those missing men. We need to know why they disappeared, and she's the only who can tell us."

"You think she'd just tell us?"

"Yes," the professor said as he smiled.

101
Thursday, July 25
9:20 PM
Deck Two – Medical Facility

"Blend in on the eighth deck near her cabin," Clive said to Moreau, aka, Dubois, as the three men left the captain's office. "You're the cruise line's CMO, so I'm sure you can find plenty to talk with the passengers about."

"I'll give it a try," Dubois said. "What are you two going to do and when should I be there?"

"It might take about three hours, but keep a watch on her cabin," Clive said.

"We'll let you know when we see you," Dunningham said as he and Stewart got in the elevator.

"The doc's going to meet us there," Stewart said as the door closed and they were the only two inside. Most of the passengers were either partying for the last night onboard or were in their cabins getting a good night's rest.

The elevator opened on the second deck and the head of security and the mathematics professor walked to the door with red plus sign on it. "I've never understood why they call it a red cross," Clive said.

"It's complicated," Alfred replied.

The door was unlocked and they went inside. Doctor Khalid was waiting for them and a nurse was there also.

"What is it you want to do?" the doctor asked Clive.

The professor answered, "We need shots so that we're immune to any effects of hypnosis that Olivia Cromwell might place on us. If you have the right chemicals, I know exactly what will work perfectly."

"What are you thinking of?" Doctor Khalid asked.

"Most people think that hypnosis is a matter of mind control," Dunningham stated. "It's actually just an altered state of consciousness. So doc, I'd like you to mix us a cocktail of cocaine and hydrophenylsulfate."

"Cocaine?" Clive asked. "Are you crazy? I'll be fired!"

"Not at all," Alfred replied. "The cocaine will ensure that we are at maximum alertness so we aren't affected by the trance she tries to put on us. Then the hydrophenylsulfate will do two things. It will allow our muscles to appear to be loose and limp even though we're in full control of them; then it will completely erase any traces of cocaine in our system within five hours. So this means that we've got to do this tonight."

"Is he right, doc?" Clive asked.

"He's absolutely right," Doctor Khalid responded. "I've used hydrophenylsulfate in other cocktails before, but I never thought of how it would work when mixed with cocaine. But you could come down here in five or six hours and pee into a cup and your urine will show nothing unusual. What he's proposed is genius. I'll be right back; there's some paperwork I have to fill out for the narcotic."

"Math professor, huh?" the doctor added as he headed toward his office. The nurse just smiled; she didn't know what was going on, which was a good thing.

"Sorry it took so long," Khalid said when he returned after twenty minutes. "I had to do some more research and calculations to determine the exact quantities to give to you. Roll up your sleeves and let's do this."

The shot stung as it was given, more from the cocaine than from the needle. The nurse put a bandage on each man's arm.

102

Thursday, July 25

11:20 PM

It didn't take long for the men to start feeling the effects of the cocaine. "I can see how people could get hooked on this stuff," Clive said as they walked up the stairs to begin looking for Olivia. The cocktail combination did have one side effect and that was perspiration. Reaching the third deck, they went over to Guest Relations.

"Are you okay," Clive?" the lady behind the counter asked.

"I'm fine," Clive said. "I was just showing him one of the boiler rooms and it's a bit hot down there. Say, have you seen Olivia Cromwell tonight?"

"Yes," she said. "She's up in Sky View giving quite a show. People have been coming by here saying that it's really lively up there. You ought to go check it out."

"I think we will," Clive said. He and Alfred walked to the forward elevators and took one up to the twelfth deck. They could hear the music as soon as the elevator door started to open. "What a combination; music and hypnosis," Clive said as they stepped out of the elevator.

"Let's go, handsome," Alfred said. "It's time to charm the charmer," he said with a devilish grin on his face.

Even though they couldn't see Olivia when they walked into Sky View Lounge, they knew where she was. There was a huge crowd on the right side and the people were laughing and obviously having a good time. A few people were in the center of the room listening and dancing to the party band music, but the real entertainment was near the window. "Let's get a drink first," Alfred said. "Everything's got to be just perfect."

"Right," Clive said, and so the two men walked over to the bar which was noticeably vacant. The bartender came over to them and put two cocktail napkins up on the bar. "Looks like she's putting on quite the show," Clive said.

"She's certainly a bigger draw than the band," the flair bartender said. "What'll it be, Clive?"

Clive looked around; no one was nearby except for Alfred. "I know it sounds crazy, but I'll explain later. And don't say anything to anyone. Make some noise like you're fixing us some really fancy drinks, but just make them with no alcohol. Drop a shaker or two as you toss them in the air. I want you to draw some attention to us, so maybe wait until the band stops." The band obliged and announced they were taking a short break.

"Okay," the bartender said as he banged two metal shakers together, tossed them in the air and let them drop on the deck. Then he clinked a couple of bottles together and tossed them around, but didn't let them drop. He finally ended up pouring the drinks into tall glasses and served them to the two gentlemen waiting patiently for them at the bar. He finished the routine by ringing the bell several times.

The act worked; everyone around Olivia looked toward the bar to see what all the noise was about. "That's our cue," Alfred said as the focus was now on them. They picked up their drinks from the bar, removed the toothpick and the fruit and left them on the napkins and sauntered over toward Olivia and the crowd. It was now show time, and Olivia wasn't the star of the show this time; she just thought she was.

"What are you drinking?" Olivia asked as Clive got closer.

"I don't know," Clive answered. "I just told him to make something strong and fancy, just like you, and he said he had just the thing." Clive was ad libbing very well.

"And what about you?" Olivia asked as he turned her attention to Alfred who was attempting to be casual.

"Same thing, I'm afraid," Alfred said. "I'm not terribly original, but I'm pretty good at following orders."

The crowd around Olivia began to disperse as they saw her attention was being directed at the newcomers. It was also getting late on the last night onboard, plus the band was taking a break. It was a good time for most of them to head to their cabins. A few of them got another drink at the bar and waited for the band to begin; Clive and Alfred were the only two by Olivia. So far, so good.

"I'm really sorry about the other afternoon," Clive said. "As head of security, I had to take you to my office; it was for your own good. And I heard that your 9 PM show was fantastic. So are we okay?" Clive was working it with Olivia who was playing right into the plan.

"Sure," Olivia said. "I've been around more than once and I know you did what you had to do." She paused, looked around the lounge, took a sip of her own drink and continued. "Besides having a strong and fancy drink, what are you two men doing tonight?"

Alfred decided to take over. Clive had done a great job of setting them up. Now it was his turn to seal the deal. "It's the last night," he said, "so maybe the three of us could do something. Do you want to hypnotize us and take us back to your cabin?" Alfred surprised himself with what he just said. The cocktail, not the drink, must be working pretty well.

Olivia looked at Alfred, then at Clive and smiled. "Sure, boys; why not?" she said in a sultry voice. "Set your drinks down and look straight into my eyes. Keep your eyes open and don't blink." The shot they'd received would allow them to keep their eyes open for an hour straight if they wanted.

Olivia then chanted something as she put three fingers on each man's forehead. "You are now under my control," she said and she took a deep breath and let it out slowly through her nose. "Shall we go down to my cabin and see what games we can play?" Olivia's eyes were as wide open as the men's eyes as she thought of the fun she was going to have.

No one noticed as the three of them got up and walked out of the lounge. They took the elevator down four decks, got off and walked aft to cabin 8062. As they went by the open library, Clive looked in. "Good evening, *Monsieur* Dubois," he said as he saw the third man sitting in a comfortable chair, holding a Sherlock Holmes book. Dubois nodded his head.

No one else was in the passageway as Olivia opened the cabin door and let the two men inside. Alfred once again took charge as he was the one who'd developed the plan. "I like what you've done with some of the men on the ship, making them disappear; I think it's rather brilliant. There are a few people I'd like to make go away; perhaps we could work together."

Olivia smiled as she leaned over on the bed, head in hand resting on the elbow. It was a come-on pose for sure. "It is brilliant, isn't it," she said as she just smiled. Olivia was being reeled in, but she didn't know it. She thought she was the one in control right now.

"Tell me more," Alfred said as he sat down on the bed next to her. It was a good that thing that Sylvia couldn't see what was going on in 8062 because that was not her Alfred acting the way he was and doing what he was doing. He wasn't even sure what he was doing; he was just winging it.

"Yes, I put those men in a trance and sent them off so they'd never come back. Clive, I'm sorry that having those men disappear has caused you so much extra work. But I had to do that so that my own disappearance would fit right into the pattern. It's a perfect plan, right? You see, once I disappear tomorrow, and it will look just like one of the many disappearances from this ship, then no one will hear from me again. Once that happens, my significant other can collect on the five million dollar life insurance policy and we can move to South America and live like queens."

"But why did you make only men disappear?" Clive asked.

"I've been jilted three times by men who said they wanted to spend their life with me," Olivia said. "Then they left me for another woman. I decided to use my powers to get back at men in general, plus it helped to set the stage for my own getaway. Pretty clever, don't you think?"

"Brilliant," a fawning Clive said.

103

Friday, July 26

12:15 AM

"You've thought of everything, haven't you?" Alfred asked as he intentionally slurred his speech.

Olivia smiled as she knew she'd thought out every detail of her plan to perfection.

"As I said," Alfred continued, "I'd like to do your little plan and I wouldn't mind faking my own death just like you, but I don't know what terms I should have in the life insurance policy." He was hoping that she would take the bait.

She did.

Olivia grabbed Alfred's arm and pulled herself up. She gave him a kiss on the cheek as she stood up and started to open her safe. "We're still going to play a little bit, aren't we?" Clive asked.

"Oh yes, dear. I have some fun games in store for you two," Olivia answered as she continued to turn the dial. The last number was under the arrow and she turned the handle. The door opened and she reached inside and pulled out an insurance policy and handed it to Alfred.

Alfred read through the insurance policy as he pretended to be under her spell. He gave a slight nod to Clive who quietly walked to the cabin door. Alfred stood up and said, "Brilliant job, Olivia," as he hugged her.

Clive opened the door and saw Moreau waiting outside. Clive nodded to him and the Inspector entered the cabin.

"What's this?" Olivia asked. "I thought it was just you two boys. You want to make it three against one?"

Moreau pulled out his handcuffs as Alfred held her with her back to the Interpol agent. As he put the handcuffs on her, he read her rights. "Olivia Cromwell, I'm from Interpol and you're under arrest for attempted fraud against an international insurance company. As far as these two men are concerned, they were never under your spell, but you'll have plenty of time to work on getting it right in prison."

Clive and Alfred shook hands and Clive looked directly into Olivia's eyes. "I saw evil the first time I looked into your eyes and I saw it again tonight up in the lounge. Say goodbye to your bed because this isn't where you're sleeping tonight."

Olivia started to yell something when Moreau stuck her with a syringe and injected her with a tranquilizer. "She'll be calm now," he said.

"Let's take her below," Clive said. "That cell hasn't been used in a long time; I hope the mattress is still there."

What's Next?

Professor Alfred Dunningham, PhD, had been called away from his recent Paris trip, cutting short the few extra days that he and his wife Sylvia were going to enjoy in that magical city. His absence from the City of Light was short-lived, however, as he was brought back to Paris months later to help the local officials uncover who was behind a string of thefts from the city's many art galleries and museums.

Which establishments, both fine art and otherwise, are most vulnerable during this rash of blatant and bizarre heists? Was the professor's discovery at the clock in the Musée d'Orsay instrumental in his innovative approach? What role did numbers and mathematics play in his ability to lead the local authorities to the culprits and the prized possessions? What did those symbols on the back of the recovered art mean? What was the significance of Père Lachaise Cemetery?

Were these things significant, or were they just coincidental to Professor Dunningham's discovery?

Get the answers to these and other intrigues, along with visiting some Parisian sights and delights, in Stuart Gustafson's next novel *Art Thefts in PARIS*.

About the Author

Stuart Gustafson learned the love of travel at a very young age when the Gustafson family moved often as his father was in the U.S. Navy. The frequent relocations also ensured that he was able to establish new friendships as well as integrate into established ones. He was born in Southern California, and while he moved many times as a youngster, Stuart ended up back in San Diego where he met and married Darlene Smith in 1974. They have one daughter, one son, and one rescue dog.

His formal education includes a B.A. in Mathematics from San Diego State University and an MBA from the University of San Diego. He spent twenty-nine years in high-technology endeavors, including a move from San Diego to Boise, Idaho, in 1993. He took early retirement in 2007 to devote more time to writing, traveling and spending more time with his mother, who lived to the wonderful age of 94. She also loved to travel and the collages on her walls showed some of her more enjoyable trips.

One way that Stuart enjoys traveling is speaking on cruise ships. This activity has allowed him to visit over one hundred cruise ports, thus ensuring the authenticity of many of his book's descriptions and locations. In addition to novels, he writes travel articles and posts pictures of great travel places he's visited. With his Million-Mile Flyer status on a major air carrier and his visits to over 50 countries, it's easy to see why he has the U.S. Registered Trademark *America's International Travel Expert*®. For more travel information, and to read about Stuart's other books and speaking opportunities, visit **www.stuartgustafson.com**.